2000andWhat?

Edited by
Karl Roeseler
and
David Gilbert

The names, characters and events portrayed in these stories are either the products of their authors' imaginations or are used fictitiously. Any resemblance to actual persons, living or dead, or to real events is entirely coincidental.

Printed on acid-free paper
Printed in the United States of America

A complete list of acknowledgments appears on pp. 239-240.

ISBN 0-9639192-2-9

First Edition. 1996

Cover and book design by Clare Rhinelander
Printed by McNaughton & Gunn

Trip Street Press books are distributed by
Small Press Distribution
1814 San Pablo Avenue, Berkeley, CA 94702
Telephone: (510) 549-3336

Trip Street Press • P. O. Box 190201 • San Francisco, CA 94102 USA

2000andWhat?

TABLE OF CONTENTS

2000andWhat?

INTRODUCTION

The turn of the millennium, if it will turn and not collapse under media assault, is, if nothing else, an excuse for an anthology of short stories. This anthology, then, is a collection of stories about the turn of the millennium.

We have come to consider the millennial "about" in two ways: stories that concern themselves with the event itself, and stories that reflect the realities of being alive during this particular era. Many of the stories concern themselves with similar themes — the definition of self, gender and sexuality; the negation of the individual; the compulsion to respond to celebrity; the impossibility of evading the vestiges of the past; and the problem of surviving the brutalities of our own time.

Our stories were either written specifically for this collection or found and solicited. Each story, in our opinion, is a fictive response to the question: **2000andWhat?**

—*The Editors*

MADAME REALISM'S 1999

by
Lynne Tillman

It's a weird custom, seeing in the new year carrying around a pig. Madame Realism wasn't sure where it originated. Some say in the south of England before the Saxons invaded. According to tradition, a young pig is placed on a round table in the center of a room. At midnight, a handkerchief or scarf is dropped over the pig's eyes, symbolic of the wish that fortune in the coming year, like justice, be blind. Then everyone sings *Auld Lang Syne*. Pranksters change the words to acknowledge the pig. "Should old acquaintance be forgot, in the days of old lang syne, should old acquaintance be forgot, in the days when swine were swine. We'll drink a cup of kindness, dear, in the days of auld lang syne."

When swine were swine, swine were swine, swine in 1999, swine in 999, swine throughout time. Madame Realism walked into the bar and pushed through the dancing crowd to a table not far from the one on which the young pig lay. Did everyone identify with the pig? Madame Realism was never certain what to expect.

"Expect the unexpected," her friend Ameena had advised months before, "and remember what Nostradamus prophesied: 'The year 1999, seven months, from the sky will come/a great

King of Terror: To bring back to life the great King of the Mongols,/Before and after Mars to reign by good luck.'" Expect the Unexpected, Madame Realism repeated, laughing. And even though Madame Realism didn't believe in prophesy, she went to the library and looked up Nostradamus. That night she telephoned Ameena and asked, "How can he have predicted that and also that the world would end in 1996?" Ameena said, "You depend on reason." Madame Realism pondered that and replied, "I believe that Tertullian was right: 'It is certain because it is impossible.' But," she added, "I also believe the reverse is true: It is uncertain because it is possible." Madame Realism hoped Ameena would be at the party.

From across the room, the party's host, Kai, waved excitedly to her. He was the son of an African-American man, a soldier, and a Vietnamese woman, a bargirl, as she was called then. Kai had been born in Saigon during the war in Vietnam, which hardly anyone remembered except as movies about the loss of masculinity and national pride, shown on TV especially on Veteran's Day. It was like Kai to have chosen a neighborhood bar, which was known for its "territorial defensiveness," as Kai's friend, Eiko, put it, its emphasis on "small group identity." Kai loved the poignancy and irony of this quaint place, with its horseshoe-shaped bar, wooden tables, and Art Deco light fixtures. His guests had been invited to wear costumes, as if it were Hallowe'en. Kai and Eiko wore masks and were made up defensively, something like camouflage or obstacles.

Madame Realism had vacillated between dressing as a vestige or a ruin. Miming partial poses and ruinous expressions, she had rehearsed the unrehearsable. Perplexed, she even placed a chunk of concrete on her shoulder and secured it to her neck with rope. A ball and chain. That's the way history is, she reflected. But did she want to spend this coming New Year's Eve so burdened? As if one weren't burdened enough by attempting to distinguish the true new from the old new. After all, at the beginning of the 20th century, the Futurists had named and colonized the new, and nothing could be new that wasn't modern, and we weren't modern anymore, were we?

Instead Madame Realism outfitted herself as a Gypsy, her idea of one. Long ago Gypsies were supposed to have migrated from India. To Madame Realism the modern was inexorably connected to the nation state, but Gypsies, as far as she knew, had never agitated for their own. And now that the nation state was simultaneously on the rise and in collapse, the history of the Gypsies, in a sense, suggested past and future, before and after. Madame Realism knew she couldn't ever adequately explain this.

Prince's song *1999* was playing on the laser box. Whatever happened to him? she wondered as she watched Kai pat the pig. *1999* was popular when? 1984, 1985? "Tonight I'm going to party like it's 1999." 1999 had been like *1999*. Would 2001 be like **2001**? Madame Realism remembered that way back in the sixties preparation had begun for the new millennium with **Space Odyssey: 2001**. And even in the middle of a noisy party, Madame Realism could recall the voice of **2001**'s computer, Hal. It was similar to an echo or an aural aura, something usually associated with epileptic seizures or migraines.

Memory was a game Madame Realism enjoyed. She was indifferent to virtual reality and surrogate travel. When she watched television, she didn't want to interact; she wanted to disappear into the screen. When Madame Realism traveled, she didn't want to project herself there before she left the room. She hoped to get lost, to lose herself. The uncharted pleasures — mystery, oblivion, abandon — could never be mapped. Or could they?

"Absurd," Dorothy shouted to Madame Realism, "we are bordering on the absurd, irrelevance. Borders invite transgression, and religion's a border, don't you think?" She was a globe festooned with hot spots and religious symbols. It was awkward for Dorothy to move. Hard to think, Madame Realism thought. The two women studied the partygoers. John stood out — he was simulating extinction. "Look at Uncle Desmond," Dorothy urged, "in a thirties outfit."

Uncle Desmond was resplendent in a threadbare tuxedo. Everyone called him uncle, though he was no one's uncle that Madame Realism knew. Uncle suited him; he was amiable and insistently old-fashioned, which was a ruse, Madame Realism was sure. He was not a traditionalist yet he followed the pig ritual to the letter. In fact he had brought the pig. Madame Realism gazed at Uncle Desmond, now stroking the pig fondly. What would happen to the pig later? Imagine, she caught herself, worrying about a pig's future at the start of the year 2000.

Madame Realism tugged at her Gypsy costume, concerned that she or it would be misunderstood. She had once attempted to dress as a man and in that outfit hadn't recognized herself. Stymied, she came to realize that the greatest source of misrecognition and misapprehension resided in oneself. The sardonic pianist and wit, Oscar Levant, she read, once quipped when asked about playing himself in a movie: "I was miscast." It was probably Levant upon whom Uncle Desmond had modeled himself.

There was scarcely the right word to characterize Desmond, not one in her limited repertoire. Parodic, Roberto offered — he was dressed as a fan. Desmond was enigmatic, inaccessible. Remote, Madame Realism decided, and already removed. Desmond had never set out to change the world. To life his response had been — just get on with it. Roll the dice. Shuffle the deck. Play your hand. Grab a few laughs. That's all you can expect. He wasn't easy to talk to. But no one really tried to talk to him tonight.

No one could talk tonight, not tonight. The future was inarticulate, inarticulable, dumb. Unspeakable desire longed for a wanton night. It demanded a wild, long night, a night to erase all other nights, an urgent night to end it all — the century, the millennium. A night to remember, and one to forget. You wanted to have been there and not to have been, just for the experience. "Like the sinking of the Titanic," Madame Realism whispered to Uncle Desmond, who grinned historically. It was almost midnight.

"Now, now," he murmured to himself or to the pig, "now, now." And very gently he dropped the handkerchief over the eyes of the trembling animal. "Now it's time. It's over."

Madame Realism knew Uncle Desmond would not be remembered. His greatest inventions were practical jokes, a lost art. Practical jokers concocted elaborate plans to fool friends. During the forties, Desmond and his crowd lived in cheap hotels; the desk clerk was often the inadvertent bearer of the joke. Once a Mr. Jello telephoned Mr. Riley every afternoon for a month and left a message: "Mr. Jello called." Every evening Riley complained — at this very bar — "Jello phoned again." No one ever let on. At the end of the month, Riley returned to his hotel. There was no message, which he'd come to expect. But when he got to his room, he discovered that his bathtub was filled with Jello. Who could record that?

Auld Lang Syne was sung. People kissed and hugged and worried about catching something. Madame Realism wondered if this was Uncle Desmond's long good-bye, his swan song. Or, she brightened, his swine song.

January 10, 2000: Can't decide whether to say two thousand or twenty hundred. Kai told me that in the fifties Jell-O company was advised that its ads showing complicated molded shapes made consumers feel inferior. Tacked Dorothy's photograph of Desmond, pig, me, on wall. Might mean anything.

Could suspect D. of bestiality or imagine he was about to kill pig. New photoelectronics computer process supposed to reveal thoughts at moment photo shot. Called image busting. Don't believe D. would be revealed. Can past (or future) be seen through present lens? Can present? My costume, no doubt, a dismal failure.

CRACK

by
Lewis Warsh

He handed me his card as we stood in the hallway. We were waiting for the elevator, side by side, our shoulders touching, and he reached into his pocket for his wallet and fished out his card. It had his name on it, in gold letters, his address and phone number. If I ever needed help, he said, I shouldn't hesitate to call. I assumed he thought I needed help (if not now, then someday), though I didn't know how he could tell. I had been alert and restless all day but after the encounter with the stranger in the hallway I began looking forward to going home, getting into bed with a long novel, and falling asleep for twelve hours. The elevator was crowded; I stepped in and turned a full circle so I was facing the door. For a moment the smell of perfume, the physical contact with people I knew only by sight, the swift plunge from the fortieth to the twentieth floor, made me feel like I was going to faint. One woman, who I saw almost every day as I passed through the marble lobby, was pressing against me from behind, her hand on my thigh. But when I turned to say something she didn't even smile.

The phone rang that night and Irina answered it and said it was for me. The curtains were billowing at the open window and the radio was playing a song by Nat King Cole, Irina's favorite singer. The song matched my mood (sullen, restless: why couldn't I sleep?), and the temperature outside had dropped ten degrees in the last hour. I was wearing the same pin-striped shirt I had worn that afternoon when I met the man in the hallway, the man with the card (which was in my jacket pocket), but I had removed my tie. I stared through the window, parting the curtains with one hand and lifting the phone to my ear. The woman who lived in the apartment above us was walking her dog at the edge of the curb. I tried to visualize the face of the man in the hallway but all I could remember was the bandaid on his chin where he had cut himself shaving.

"It's for me" I said to Irina when the phone rang again. She folded the newspaper she was reading and left the room. By now, there was another song on the radio and the voice on the phone said "Remember me? I gave you my card." I wanted to ask him how he got my number since it was he who had given me his, not the other way around. I don't have a card and even if I did I'm not one for giving my number away to strangers, even those who attract me. I knew that Irina was listening to the conversation at the door of the living room. Or beyond the door where I couldn't see her, but only a shadow. The voice on the phone apologized for calling once and hanging up. "A bad connection," he said, but I knew there was some other reason. I knew that when I got off the phone I would have to tell Irina who called and what had been said. It was our habit, after five years of marriage, to report back to one another about everything that happened when we were apart. And since we're apart most of the time there's always a lot to say.

She was standing in the hallway, in the vestibule near the mailboxes, when I returned home from work. I had loosened my tie on the subway ride home and I was carrying my jacket over my arm. The day was late spring and evening had slipped by without the usual drop in temperature. As I tried to brush by her, I had never seen her before, she put her hand on my arm and asked me if I would give her ten dollars. Not loan, give. Even when she asked me for the money, I noticed, she didn't look at me directly. Didn't make eye contact the way people do when they meet for the first time. When you want something from someone you look them in the eye (that's what I do). I knew I had a twenty in my wallet, a five and some ones. It was a warm evening in late spring and I had stayed at work longer than usual. I had no idea how long she was waiting in the lobby, or if she was waiting for me.

I asked the man on the phone where he got my number and he said "Bob" and I said "Bob who?" but it was just a technicality like running outside the baseline. I knew a lot of Bobs, from childhood on: Bobby Kennedy, Bobby McGee. I was glad that he had called but I didn't say that. Some music, the ideal form of communication (no words), filled my head, but I didn't say that either. I knew, if I said anything, Irina (who was listening) would ask: "What did you mean?" Later that night, lying in bed, she would question me about what he wanted and I would say: I don't even know him, I never saw him until this afternoon when I was leaving work. Then Irina would roll on top of me and let her nightgown slip over her shoulders. She has a closet filled with nightgowns, some of which she's never worn, at least not for me. This one was yellow, my favorite color, with doves embroidered on the sleeves.

That night, as I was going through the pockets of my jacket, I found the card which the stranger had given me. Irina was already in bed reading a volume of Proust. Before getting into bed she usually puts on lipstick: *mango, blushing tulip, panic pink*. Then she reads to me or we listen to music before going to sleep. She was lying in bed reading with the book balanced on her knees. Her knees (raised) made a tent of the sheets and blankets. Soon, I thought, we would no longer need the covers which had kept us warm that winter. We could sleep in the nude, with the window open, like we did last summer, and the summer before.

The woman in the hallway told me she could get me anything I wanted. "Anything" (I felt sleepy). She held the bill I had given her in her hand, not anxious to leave, no longer desperate for whatever she had needed that had inspired her to ask me for money. Now that she had the money she could get what she needed whenever she wanted. She had stringy brown shoulder-length hair and wore an old winter coat with wooden buttons. Possibly she didn't want to feel that she was just taking from me without giving, without at least offering me something in return. The word "anything" hung in the air between us like a falling leaf buffeted by the wind.

The next day at work a woman named Sara asked me if I would join her for lunch. We sat at a table near a window in a French restaurant and she touched my knee. She put her hand on my upper thigh under the table and told me she knew I was married but... "I can't help myself," she said. She was biting her lips and crying and I asked the waiter to bring her an aspirin but she shook her head and dabbed at her eyes, the eyeliner running down her cheeks. People at nearby tables began poking one another and staring at me angrily as if I were the cause of her suffering. I looked through the window of the restaurant and noticed that the people on the street were wearing less clothing than the day before. The light on the street was golden and the buds were soaking up the sun.

I felt like I was part of everyone I knew. I felt I was divided into parts and that I wasn't a person who could say "I did this" and really mean that it was "me." The "me" seemed like someone else, or everyone else, and not only that: not only did I have to keep the faces of everyone I knew suspended in my mind at all times, but I also had to keep track of the lights of the city, the cars, and even the music floating out at me from an open window. I felt I was a composite of all these things; the absence of any one thing was the source of my sadness, my regret. If you asked about "me" I would say: look at the light on the side of this building. Look at this tree.

When I arrived home Irina said "He called again" and I thought of Sara. That night, lying in bed with Irina, I had to admit that I was thinking about Sara, how she had wept in the restaurant. It was a hopeless feeling to make love to one person and think of another. The man with the card asked (when I told him about this): "Does it happen often?" The next day when I saw Sara at work I blushed but she averted her eyes (too painful). The man with the card said he had his office down the hall from mine and when I stepped inside he locked the door behind him and loosened his tie.

The advantage of friendship is that there's no jealousy involved. Plato said that, I think, in the **Phaedrus**, which I read in college. "To be curious about that which is not my concern, while I am still in ignorance of my own self, would be ridiculous" (Plato said). He said: "In the friendship of the lover there is no real kindness" (of course not). The man with the card said, we were in his office, "Why don't you make yourself comfortable?" I thought of the time my mother, who left me with a babysitter when I was a child so she could go back to work, came home early one day, dropped her raccoon coat onto the living room rug, and announced: I'm quitting.

She was wearing the same coat and dress she had been wearing the week before. And this time, when I gave her the money and she said "anything," I followed. Across the street, down an alley, into the basement of a tenement. This is it, I said to myself, this is what I want, always want. She reached behind her and took my hand and lead me into the darkness of rats scurrying and black plastic garbage bags and cans. It was the engine of the building down here, all the cables and meters. I couldn't imagine going any deeper but I still wasn't sinking. My head was above water and I knew a few nouns and adjectives so that describing it to myself was still an endeavor I could aspire to at a later date. I heard voices (do rats speak?) and someone asked: "Who's that?" Someone was standing guard, in the darkness, like a sentry. And then the woman said, simply: "It's me, I brought a friend."

We were on our knees on the floor of the basement amid the garbage cans and rats. The vial of white powder had fallen from her hands and I lit a match but we couldn't find it. The woman and the men behind us were cursing and someone was laughing. It was probably odd for them to see a man with a jacket and tie crawling around on his knees. Until this happened I have to admit I didn't know it was what I needed. I saw Irina, just a flash, but she wasn't in bed reading. I could see her body floating out the window above the city. Irina, in her red nightgown, an adjective, a clause, her arms outstretched above the rooftops. It was all I could do to prevent myself from following her, but I knew that the experience of flying would be different for me. I knew if I stepped off the ledge I would plunge like a rocket to the pavement.

When I came into work the next day there was a vase and a single red rose on my desk. Sara beamed at me from across the office and I realized it was her doing. I thought of what I could do to reciprocate, a rose for a rose, amazed that she didn't hate me after what had happened the day before. She leaned over my desk and pushed her breasts against my shoulder and I felt a twinge in my neck as if I'd slept under an open window. Later, I said to her, I have to go out for awhile: take a message if anyone calls. And she nodded, subservient, no questions asked: I'll do what you want.

I put my hand through the broken window but I didn't feel anything. "It's like having an orgasm, isn't it?" the woman said, wiping away the blood. She had taken off her blouse but I didn't notice as she gave herself a sponge bath with the water from a basement tap. I no longer knew what "feeling" meant, only "intensity" seemed to convey the sensations I had previously described as "love" or "anger." The excitement was no longer prearranged but seemed to blur my sense of what was most familiar. It was like my first night in Paris, after taking the boat-train from London. Or Venice, getting lost in the maze of alleyways, canals and streets. So when I came to a new feeling I had to stop for a moment, like a tourist, and say: this is it.

I sat at my desk at work, in the large open area where everyone can spy on everyone else, and leafed through a book of photographs of Marilyn Monroe. I had a hard time focusing on words but I could still look at pictures and I kept going back to the one where she's running from the ocean in a white bathing suit holding an umbrella with red dots. "Obviously posed" I kept saying to myself, and then "larger than life." I was tempted (who knew who was watching me?) to press my lips to the different parts of her body when the phone rang and it was Sara to say she was feeling under the weather (her phrase) and wasn't coming in. There was a pause and she said "I'll be expecting you" and then "don't worry, you won't catch anything." Her assumption that I was planning to visit her caught me off guard and I started stuttering. "I'm b-b-backed up here," I said, which wasn't true. There's never enough work to do — I spend most of my day reading the newspaper — and she knew it.

The man who gave me the card locked the door of his office behind him. There was someone else in the room but he didn't introduce us. Instead, he addressed the stranger, a young man in a suit and tie. He said: "Ernie, I think our friend here needs a wake-up call. Don't you?" I was standing in the center of the room with my feet planted firmly on the carpet. Ernie walked out from around the desk, stood in front of me, and punched me in the stomach. I fell to my knees and he hit me in the back of the neck and kicked me in the ribs as if I were a dog. "That's enough," the man with the card said. He knelt beside me and turned me over onto my back and slapped my face lightly with his fingers. I felt his hands on me, loosening the knot of my tie and unbuttoning my pants, and I felt like reaching out and pushing him away but I didn't have the strength. "I told you to call me," he said. "This is something to remember me by." He snapped his fingers. Ernie disappeared for a minute and returned with a glass of water. He propped my head beneath his arm and tilted the glass to my lips but the water spilled out of the corners of my mouth and down my chin. I tried to stand up but he kept pushing me back against the carpet. The office was empty except for a desk and a chair. There were no diplomas on the wall to indicate that he was a doctor or a broker. "Now you know what it feels like when you hurt someone," he said. "Like a punch in the stomach."

That evening, when I told Irina I was going out, she retaliated by saying that her ex-husband Sid was in town and they were meeting for a drink. In the past, I always expressed anger when she told me she was meeting Sid. He came to New York maybe twice a year and called her up every time. But this time it meant nothing to me. I genuinely hoped they had fun together. I thought of all my old lovers and how happy I would feel if they called me up. Then Irina said: "A woman named Sara called" and I stopped what I was doing. She said: "You're going to meet her, aren't you?" and ran into the kitchen in tears. I guess she assumed I was being unfaithful to her with the woman from my office and I realized that if she thinks that she doesn't know me at all. I had never lied to her once in the five years we were together. If I was going to see Sara I wouldn't try to hide it. "Believe me," I said, putting my hands on her shoulders, "I'm just going for a walk," but she wasn't listening.

This time I went directly across the street to the basement. I lit matches to see my way through the dark. "I knew you were coming," the woman said when she saw me. Some of the faces of the people there were already familiar to me but none of them said hello. There were two people making love on a mattress in a corner with the woman on top. I took out my wallet and emptied it on the floor of the basement. "You must have robbed a bank," the woman said when she saw all the tens and twenties. "It's Cash McCall," one of the men in the background said, and everyone laughed. The woman scooped up the money and said "I'll be right back." I leaned back against a garbage can and lit a cigarette, trying to blend in.

My father was a dentist and encouraged me to follow in his profession but I dropped out of dental school in my first semester: it just wasn't for me. After that, I took some art courses, painting and sculpture, and for a few years I lived in a loft and attended parties and openings and even had a show, but nothing sold. I was going to have a second show but the gallery folded and I began doing office work, first as a temp, then as a fulltimer so I could get the benefits. For awhile I continued painting after work and then I met Irina and we moved to the apartment uptown and the past began to fade. All my old paintings are still in storage somewhere. Occasionally I get an invitation from an old friend who's having a show but I never attend. The office work involves pieces of paper (non-threatening) and voices on the phone. And then there are my co-workers, Sara and the others, with whom I try to get along, if only to make the job more interesting. It's hard to spend forty hours a week with the same people and not feel intimate in some way. I would have to be blind not to realize that Sara was falling in love with me, but I didn't want to admit it for fear I would do something to hurt her. I became the personification of indifference: who cares what you feel? She leaned over my desk and I felt myself slipping down the side of a well. I felt like I was lost in an endless sentence, a maze of words, where my only escape was to reach out and touch her breasts: what was being offered. We would go to lunch and she would ask me about my past and I would tell her: "My father was a dentist..." but I knew she wasn't listening. I could feel the tip of her shoe against my leg and her head would tilt to one side but I kept on talking if only to appease the guilt, the mixture of guilt and longing. At night, I would lie in bed and Irina would read to me from the volume of Proust which she was finishing, and I felt like I was sinking, clause after clause, into the maze of words, where the only escape was to roll over on top of her and lift her nightgown over her breasts, the pale blue nightgown or the silk one, the one she had worn with her ex-husband. I deluded myself into thinking that thoughts were a form of action and that it was permissible to think about Sara while I was making love to Irina. I couldn't understand why Irina, with whom I had lived for five years, was incapable of reading my mind. It made me self-conscious, as if someone were looking over my shoulder as I turned the pages of a magazine with pictures of naked women in poses that invited you to enter their bodies. I could even pretend for a moment that these women weren't being abused, fucked-over, that most of them hated men. By day, during the week, I would try to avoid Sara's advances, I would discourage her, I would literally push her away when she leaned over my desk, while at night I would pretend I was lifting her dress, right in the office, when everyone else had gone home. We would go to lunch together, maybe twice a week, at a small French restaurant near Eighth Avenue which we thought of as "our place." The same waiter lead us to the same table and chatted with Sara in French. I let her pretend that I was available, that something was happening between us, I even let her hold my hand as we waited for the food to arrive. But most of all I never stopped talking.

The woman in the basement said I could spend the night there if I wanted or I could go with her to an abandoned building on the Lower East Side where she sometimes slept. I unlaced my shoes and sat on the edge of the mattress and I could sense that she was dozing off, that she was going to sleep in her clothing. I pulled at her hair and said "wake up" and she started cursing at me so I stopped. By now I was used to the sound of the rats and the hum of machines. At that moment I felt I could make love to anyone, woman or man.

Everyone who lived in the basement had a name: Aloha, Conrad, Vitamin G, Washout, Bedtime Story. "You can call me Sylvie," the woman said, after we spent our first night together. She apologized for falling asleep when I was most awake and promised that she would make it up to me somehow. She leaned over and bit me on the side of my neck and told me that she had been living in the basement for almost a year. And before that? I asked. There was a child, a husband, a house in the suburbs. There was a station wagon, with which she drove her son to school, trips to Europe every summer. As she told me her life story, she began licking a callous on the side of her thumb. She took my hand and placed it between her legs. I tried not to think what the man with the card had told me about what it felt like to experience pain, that it was worse than a punch in the stomach or a broken jaw. Is that what he said?

After a week in the basement I decided to return to my apartment, what I thought of as my "old apartment," and visit with Irina. I had lost my keys in the basement, the buzzer system wasn't working, so I waited in the vestibule until someone let me in. It was the woman who lived above us, walking her dog. I hadn't shaved in a week and I don't think she recognized me at first. Her dog was black with a white spot on the top of its head and began pawing the cuffs of my trousers, as if I had something he wanted. The woman, who was in her early forties, tugged at the leash and began climbing the stairs. Once, when I returned home from work, about a year ago, she had been sitting on the living room sofa next to Irina, who was showing her photographs from our album. She had stood up to leave almost immediately and lowered her eyes as she brushed by me. Her hair was almost down to her waist and as I followed her up the stairs I had to stop myself from touching it. At the third landing I paused to catch my breath but she continued on, without saying goodbye.

At first, when I knocked on the door of the apartment, no one answered. Then a man's voice said "Who is it?" and I shouted out my name. It was Sid, Irina's ex-husband. I could hear Irina's voice in the background: "Who is it?" All the furniture was gone and there was a stack of cartons against one wall and an open suitcase on the floor filled with Irina's clothing. "I don't think she wants to see you," Sid said. "She's moving out." Then Irina appeared and began pounding at my chest with her fists. "I think you better leave," Sid said. He took my arm and tried to steer me out the door but I pushed him away. "Five years," Irina shouted. "Five fucking years." I wanted to explain that I accepted the blame for what had gone wrong, that she shouldn't punish herself, that it had all been my fault. The apartment looked tiny with no furniture and I couldn't imagine how we had ever lived there for so long without killing one another. The fact that we had survived five years together in such a close space was a kind of triumph. I wondered what she had done with all my possessions, all the things we had bought together and which, in a sense, were half mine. Out on the landing, Sid pressed a fifty dollar bill into my palm. "If you're going to kill yourself," he said, "do it in style."

Sylvie disappeared for a few hours every afternoon. She had a friend who worked in a hotel in midtown who let her use a room. The rest of the time we sat on the mattress in the basement listening to the radio or playing cards. If the weather was especially warm, we went to Tompkins Square Park and sat on a bench. My money had run out and we lived on the money Sylvie made at the hotel. As soon as she arrived at the hotel she called a woman named Dora and Dora told her the day's schedule and what each of the customers said they wanted. One afternoon, when Sylvie was at work, I dozed off on the mattress in the basement and when I woke up Aloha was kneeling over me. She was an Egyptian woman, with graying hair, who always wore a long striped ankle-length gown. "I wanted to surprise you," she said. "Sylvie won't mind." She unbuckled my pants, lifted her dress, and climbed on top of me. She leaned forward so that her mouth was against my ear and began humming a song that sounded like *Some Enchanted Evening*, but more uptempo, in the old bossa nova style Irina and I danced to when we first met. Afterwards, she fell asleep in my arms, which is how Sylvie found us when she returned from the hotel. I sat up, quickly, as if one of the overhead pipes had exploded in my head, thinking Sylvie would be angry at me, but she just laughed, as if to say: We all need our privacy, don't we? Then she took off her clothing and joined us, with Aloha in the middle. I remember, hours later, leaning back against the basement wall smoking a cigarette, watching them make love, something I'd never seen before except in pornographic movies. *Two women*. My head began aching with the thought of all the time I'd wasted in my life, all the possibilities I'd backed away from, fearful of the risk, that I might go crazy if I acted one way and not another, deluding myself into thinking that happiness was a function of order, that security was like a tunnel where you never look back. Even when I was painting pictures I was never *inside* the painting (an experience which the painters I admired most had described) but thinking of the final result, wanting it to be over with so I could play the role of spectator (which I preferred), admiring my work from a distance as if someone else had done it. All my old paintings, locked away somewhere, resembled coffins, dead objects, and the last thing I wanted was to create something for others to admire, as if they were speaking a eulogy over my grave. What I wanted was to be like one of the stripes on Aloha's gown, not a line on a map between two points but something that was somehow bent out of shape and restored to life at the same time, so that the act of healing would go on as long as the body kept moving, but with no contours. I was sitting on the edge of the mattress, leaning back against the wall having these thoughts, when Sylvie looked up from between Aloha's legs and said, reaching out and taking my hand: "Don't be sad, honey, we haven't forgotten you," and we all laughed.

DOOMSDAY BELLY

by
Susan Smith Nash

I. In my idea of a perfect world, I would be a model son, and you would be my model parents. You would do what I wanted.

But, this is no perfect world.

You're not my dad. He's dead. At least, that's what they told me when I got out of the hospital after my last suicide attempt — the one where I tried to enema myself to death with hot buttered rum while reading Baudrillard's **Fatal Strategies**. But, that's another story. For this one, I promised I wouldn't mix postmodernist intellectual icons with the gritty, sweaty, ass-clenchings of an ugly kid from an ugly, cheap, suburban wanna-be place.

They tell me Dad's dead. Too bad. While he was alive, he was the original maverick over-the-top, semi-suicidal, semi-Parnassian, bolt-of-lightning-to-the-head, awe-inspiring entrepreneur worth $1 million bucks this week, not worth a kick in the scrotum-sac the next. Local newspapers and business 'zines loved to put his smarmy, toothy, grifter grin on their covers. They would interview him & he'd talk about his work, his life, his new cabin in Montana. He never mentioned me.

But, why should he?

I should know it all by now — especially now I've become my own Dad — only in a matter of speaking, of course. I think, therefore I heave. Bitter tears while dark sky inverting under black plastic cups held under bathroom spigots and mouth drooling with the nausea of **Phaedrus** realizing transcendence is only another form of rejection. I'm telling you, the voice never got any nicer — "You're FAT! You're SOFT! You spend too much time in front of that DAMN TV! Don't eat so many GREASY TACOS!"

Not likely.

"Good God, you make me sick. Look at you. So fat I can't tell if you're a boy or a girl!"

I started wearing t-shirts that hung down to my knees. What could I do to not be me? My shadow on the sidewalk was like an ink tide on the white granite shoreline during a full moon in Maine.

My shame made me sweat. I would have kissed a ragged sock if it had come from the foot of someone who cared.

It was my body, of course. My forearms were cotton seizing up with every baptism of steamy, salty sobs. I tried to bleach the stains, but my sins could never know redemption. I only called them sins because I had no other vocabulary. If I had more time and more energy, I would rename "Sin" and call it by its functional name — something like "STAPLE GUN" or "AIRLINE BAGGAGE HANDLING SYSTEM" — anything to communicate the mangling, mutilating, immobilizing power of that single word.

For me, SIN began and ended with the body. My sin and my body were synonymous. Bad joke, but true enough.

I should never have been born in this impossible body — my father could see through to the dark black echo where my heart should have pounded rebellion and a long, fat smear of toothpaste over the mirror.

Sartre would have been proud. I had disconnected identity with image. My face in the mirror was not my heart on my sleeve. What fogged up my windows on a cold, gray morning was a nothingness that imitated the existential anxieties of men and women facing certain death by plague.

What will be the new psychobabble word for "denial"? Tweezer? It fits, doesn't it. Tweezer. Something you use to pluck and shape and sculpt, but it's not radical enough to get rid of the thing. The eyebrows will always grow back. But still you pluck. And still you deny. You're in a state of "Tweezer," Baby, now hand me a fresh razor.

If I could construct a utopian society, no one would be a zit on someone else's ass. Every person would have a place, and everyone would be appreciated for her or his unique beauty.

This is not what happened to me. The story of my life is simple. I reached puberty. I went to college. My voice faded like a silk screen put through too many washings. What I wanted was a gold-plated falsetto when I wept alone, driving home. What I got was a hoarse, snuffling gurgling that sounded like I had just inhaled the foam from a fresh decaf latté at the Jamaica-Side Coffee House.

I could only cry decently after a box of amaretto biscuits, a vacuum-packed tin of beef jerky, and a round of Sir Thomas More's **Utopia**, followed by Wilhelm Reich's early essays on the origins and implications of sexual repression.

The last book I read said I could blame everything on alien abduction and repressed memories. But, that won't work. They've got it backwards. Aliens did not abduct me — I'm an alien who was abducted by humans — not all humans, but one. I still dream in my native tongue — I hear and speak in the low whistles, whines, and vowelless spackle of my original alien language.

The worst summer was the summer I ended up in the Carson City, Nevada Community Hospital Nut Ward. They called it Generalized Anxiety. I called it "Life With Dad-the-Nuts-out-Nevada-Necrophile." It was the summer he hired me to drill for gold. It wasn't pretty to be out there, if you ask me. The Earth-Rape he called "Exploratory Drilling" left a scar in the desert that would take about 2,000 years of dust storms, flash floods, and mustang trampling to erase.

Can you imagine the hell it was for me? He divorced my mom while she was in the middle of chemotherapy because he said that women in wigs just didn't turn him on. That didn't make sense, though. The women I saw him with in Nevada had Big BIG Hair.

I was willing to try. I went to FloraLee's Wig Shop and bought the biggest, blondest, Dolly Partonesque wig you could imagine. Then I bought some silver strappy high heels and a fuschia lycra mini skirt and tube top. It's what I wore to work one morning I was sure old Big Hair Dad would show up. Sure enough, there he came, in a cloud of playa lake-bed dust kicked up by his decade-old Range Rover.

That old fuck. I wanted him to love me, even though I hated him.

The first time I dressed up in women's clothes for Dad's benefit was when I was 13. I won't call it drag because I was not the least bit camp about it — I believed in what I was doing — I thought I wanted to win against my mother once and for all. But, of course, it was a vicious parody of all those Apple-Pie-&-Pass-the-Prunes values. Imagine, those coat-hanger eyes.

Dad came home from the airport, and there I was in full lycra regalia. I was fat. The lycra was wet with armpit sweat and greasy, tomato-y stains from the lasagna I had dripped on it.

I wanted him to look at me & realize that Mom was no different. Women are ugly, I said. Women sweat under their arms and they spill sauce on their clothes. They will embarrass you.

Hate her. Love me. It was that simple.

Dad didn't see it that way. Or, if he did, he mixed it up.

Hate me. Love her. It was easier like that. He'd lose a son, but gain a few contracts from confidants he bitched to about me.

Love is never saying you are spit and grease in the morning. My love is like a red, red rose-shaped blob of vomit or hairball on the carpet. Love and a hairball. They're the same thing — disgusting, even though natural processes.

He said, "Never — I mean NEVER — let me catch you wearing ANYTHING like this." But, I had already changed back to my Dress-for-Success suit and tie, so I didn't know what he was talking about.

He must have been confused.

Bite the weak. Maim the sick. Gouge the eyes from the artists, shove pointed sticks in the ears of the musicians, break the fingers of the poets and sappy utopians. I love the smell of memory.

II. They told me I was a male child. They called me their son.

Why didn't they ever tell me the truth? Being part of the great circus called MALE GENDER meant having a penis. I didn't have one. They told me that since I was a premature baby, some parts of me hadn't grown in yet. I guess that included my penis, and, if they expected me to believe them (which I did), part of my BRAIN.

The man with no penis and half a brain.

No wonder Dad was ashamed of me. No wonder my mom left. No wonder I began compulsively overeating to fill the gnawing void in the pit of my belly — the place I pointed to as my heart.

I saved the little metal keys on the Spam cans and tied them to the laces in my boots. I threw the razor-sharp Spam cans into the backyards of people who had dogs that had tried to bite me. I drank the clear, pulpy, gelatinous goo from the bottom of the Vienna Sausage cans and thought of pigs getting their throats slit.

It was a pig-eat-pig world & I was queen/king of the swine. String me up by my cloven hooves, baby. Water the unsprouted penis bud that was somewhere within me. Spray weedkiller on my brain.

And still, there was Dad, Range-Rovering around the Nevada desert, hoping to find gold or have some excuse to dig a kick-ass pit the size of the one at Yerington that would fill up with the bluest, most toxic water you've ever seen in your life.

But, Dad's dead. The Dad I'm talking about could never have been my real dad, anyway. What I'm talking about is more like a Patriarchal Composite Dad-head of Psycho-mythological world. It's no closer to painting the picture of a real individual than are Karen Horney's sketches of feminine neurotic personalities.

Dad was a desert rat. He couldn't see his ratness. He didn't know he was wandering the desert like a guy split off from the tribes of Israel and the Promised Land.

And I was his son, he said. But I was split off from my gender and I had no hope of entering into the Kingdom of Sexual Certainty.

Would it help if I didn't hate Dad? Would it help if I didn't hate myself? You can guess the answer to those questions — I only remember the time I tried to cut all the carbohydrates and fat out of my diet so I'd be complete muscle & sinew over bone. I wanted to see what kind of shape I'd have. Would I still have big, sloppy, soft pectorals? Would I still have a wide, flat ass? Would I still have jowls?

I never found out.

The pressure of having no carbohydrates or sweets made me eat six tins of Argentinean corned beef and Hormel tinned meat product at a sitting. I hate meat. Why did I eat it? Ask a cannibal. It was an act of appropriation. Could I simply eat the attributes I wanted for myself? I revered the slaughter — the way the animals faced death. I wanted to taste their death hormones. I wanted to swallow their fear. I wanted to get ready for my own end. Tin me up in my coffin, but what will you put on my label? I have a name, but that doesn't begin to say who I am.

Dad's a modern-day Lost Man. He's no Victorian, but I can see him going from encampment to encampment, pretending to be mapping, but really simply running from the limited self they had back home. In the desert they can be as expansive and grandiose as they want. They can also be invisible. No one can find them. No one can get them.

When the moon is full, all the craters are visible.

Had he seen the desert as a place where you dig for food and you sniff out sex where you can get it?

"It's like drilling," I told Dad the last afternoon we were together. We were in Nevada, driving near American Barrick's Goldstrike operation. "Pure sex — no hope of pleasure. If it's beautiful it's because it's violent."

He looked out the window without blinking. "I feel sorry for your mother. And for me. But I don't know why. And I don't know why I don't know. I just don't know anything."

Maybe those weren't his exact words. Does it matter?

Dad's dead & I'm not going back to the hospital, no matter what happens.

The sunset was caustic but meaningless that night, like ammonia fumes on diamond chips. The sun set on iron. The moon rose slippery on a large, blank bowl of oil.

III. One night I woke myself up at 3 a.m. screaming. "The Bunch! The Bunch!" I had dreamed I was the entire Brady Bunch all balled up in one body. I had pigtails, bellbottoms, a Father-Knows-Best voice, an eggbeater in my hand, and I couldn't decide whether I wanted to be a junior high cheerleader, a budding entrepreneur, or an incestuous touchy-feely stepmom figure. At least I wore sensible shoes.

When I got up, I discovered my toenails had been painted a light, pearlescent shade of pink.

I wasn't the scrappy little hockey player Dad was. I wasn't from Brunswick, Vermont, and I didn't join Merchant Marines the minute I got out of high school. Dad said he thrived on hazings, initiations, and rites of passage. He said he liked eating shit when crossing the equator.

The truth was, Dad got off easy because the ship happened to have passengers each time he crossed the equator. Passengers meant potential witnesses. So, Dad just heard the stories. Perhaps stories of hazings were simply a part of a utopian theory — an experiment never carried out.

The Marquis de Sade was just another loony guy scribbling page after page after page of language that comes straight from the brain — no sanitizing middle loop to go through — it's just a straight download from right-brain, left-brain, half-brain.

Aren't they the same thing? Religious mania and sexual mania?

It's a linguistic convention that we have that makes them differentiated at all. In the end, all the commandments are the same.

THOU SHALT pluck out the weird, the weak, the faint of heart. If that wasn't on the **Dead Sea Scrolls** or in the early Nicene writings, it should have been.

My own flesh is as pallid as lust. It glimmers like polished ivory in the pale streetlight illumination that streams in my bedroom window. My flesh's high fat content makes me alabaster. I can be carved like soap with a wet saw. My sadness makes me glow.

Roman bronze masks from the second century A.D. reflect the pain of being a man. Gender will hurt you when the myths catch up to the fiber covering your eyes.

Dad told me the same stories over and over. I hated hearing them, and I think Dad knew it, but he wouldn't stop, and I couldn't seem to get up the courage to tell him to shut up — I already knew too much about man's inhumanity to men &

women, and how people like to masquerade as gods in the face of the weak, the sad, the lonely, the self-reproaching.

I have never been touched in love or in any other expression of tenderness. Love is a check. Love is cash. Love is a tax dodge.

Mine arrived like clockwork every month in the mail. I treated the computer generated check like a love note or a birthday card. It wasn't. I was Dad's little write-off. Still, I liked that Christmas, birthday, bar-mitzvah, christening, graduation, and shower present all rolled up together and sent to me every month by Big Daddy — the Great Tooth & Cavity Fairy in the Sky.

I was a write-off in every sense of the word.

I should never have been born into this puffy, soft body — my mother's only legacy to me. Its refusal to harden into defined muscle taunted me with a mother I couldn't really remember. When a face appeared in my memory, I knew it was wrong — it was some sort of composite I had constructed from catalogues, fashion magazines and religious icons. I have no idea what kind of relation it bore to reality. My own sense of self was the same kind of composite — something I had either constructed myself or had been delivered to me by Dad.

Dad told me I was his son.

What happens when you find you're not? What do I do now that I don't think I'm a member of that gender at all?

IV. My mother left when I was 14 months old. Most of my

life, I had no idea she was alive. I thought she had died.

For a while, I thought I'd become an architect, and I'd design the perfect house and the buildings for a perfect community. The houses were solar-heated, there were gardens, parks, and fountains. Murals were everywhere — between houses, on walls, on fences. I designed it after Tommaso Campanella's *La Cittá del Sole* — the murals were illustrations from a book of knowledge. Like Campanella, I wanted to illustrate science — the science of identity and forgiveness. But, I couldn't think of how to do it, so each wall was a blank.

It didn't mean anything to me any more.

Tearing down the model city was as creative as the original act. Couldn't complete annihilation of a corrupt world be as utopian an impulse as building a world of total control, where the oldest and most stubborn fathers called the shots? A water well drilled into brass and brocade twisted the fabric of Reason until it curled in on itself like two actors kissing on-screen. My hands were cavalcades of sadness and sleet. My windows would not open except in the collisions of night and decay. My father's smile was a spotlight on a catacomb wall. All he illuminated was death. My lips were nothing but highways that doomed you to travel around and around the words that spewed forth from a yawning, opened grave. My dawns were funereal and weak. I could no longer even begin to construct a model of a perfect world. It was no longer within me.

Finally, I tore it all down.

V. For the next year, I tried to teach myself Mayan hieroglyphics and art techniques. I made a plaster of paris human skull, painted it black, and inlaid it with turquoise, black onyx, and garnet. In the eye sockets I placed two green neon tornados. For teeth, I glued in dead rosebuds.

When I was 20, I found out — in the worst possible way, that my mother was alive. She called me up, told me she was down on her luck, and asked if I could loan her some money and put her up for awhile. I didn't have any money, but I didn't want her to suspect — I would use any pretext.

At that point, I would say anything to get her to take me back.

Didn't she know I just wanted to talk to her — to get to know her? The light of maternity is neon and quick and pink like a hangover. The antidote is a jalapeño sucked dry. The remedy is prayer sobbed into a steamy, soapy shower. Why did she throw me away?

She said she'd meet me at the Denny's near I-10 and El Centro Blvd., so I went there as fast as I could. I waited in front next to the dessert case with merengues, Boston cream pies, brownies, apple crisp, and peach cobbler, but no one showed up.

To ease the tension, I read the labels of the desserts aloud, and tried to recite the ingredients, and the recipes by heart. I kept my voice soft, and — I thought — discreet, but after about twenty minutes, people were beginning to stare. One girl in particular — a pimply, oily-faced blonde wearing a sweatshirt that read "PASSENGER SIDE AIRBAG" — kept curling her lip, snickering, and nudging her friend.

I looked at her face rather pointedly and raised my voice so she wouldn't fail to hear me. "CLEARASIL WORKS! TRY SOME!" I shouted. She huddled with her friend, who looked up. I grabbed my crotch, even though I knew there was nothing there. That made the joke even better. "OXY-CUTE THEM!" I said, this time a little louder. They didn't know there were no little bags of pus or otherwise gooey, sticky liquid to get rid of. She flinched and ducked, as if I had two big zits in my hand, squeezing them so that the puss would hit her full in the face.

The assistant manager I knew as "Hello, My name is WAUKITA JO" watched part of this piece of performance art, and came rushing up to either seat me or swish me out the door. I tried to look studious and analytical. I pretended to have been debating the relative merits of Denny's preservative-laden pies, shipped frozen from the wholesaler.

"Can I help you?" asked Waukita Jo.

"French Silk," I said. The way I said it made it sound like a cheap porno film title or the brand name of a line of Made-In-Haiti lingerie. Believe it or not, it was the name of a pie.

"What?" She looked suspicious, but then her face changed. She had decided I was drunk.

"One piece. With coffee. For here," I said. "But, maybe you should seat me first. Then I'll give you my order." "Oh, yes, of course." She looked at me a little uncertainly, then added an anarchistic little "sir."

On the TV above the take-out counter, a couple of preachers were describing the evils of legalizing brothels. They had films, and they interviewed a haggard, drug-addicted whore. Her body screamed for redemption. I said a prayer for her. Not for her sins, but for her humiliation. What were they paying her to tell her story? They acted like they were listening. Wasn't that the cruelest kind of lie?

The waitress brought me what I had ordered. It looked clean. A thin woman, who held her vestiges of beauty around her like a ragged version of the Bayeux tapestry draped over a castle wall, walked into Denny's. If she was my mother, she wasn't letting me know.

Raising myself up out of my aqua vinyl booth seat, I got a better look at her. I decided she might be the one. I'd keep my eye on her.

I ate my French Silk pie and drank the WE MAKE IT FRESH FOR YOU AT DENNY'S coffee. It occurred to me that maybe my mother was too ashamed to meet. Perhaps she didn't want to have to deal with the enormity of her guilt. Perhaps she, too, was suffering from a state beyond redemption. Perhaps she should never have been born into her impossible body, because female was not the gender she was cut out to deal with.

Talk about a sad situation.

There were too many ambiguities, and being female meant there were consequences for every action — being a woman involved dire consequences much beyond the imaginings of any male.

Pregnancy, for one. It's different for a woman than for a man. A man can see pregnancy, touch the belly, and fall down in awe in the spectacle of sprouting life, but can he really feel what it means to be pregnant? Once, I talked to a pregnant woman at the pool who had just finished swimming laps. She looked like hell. Big varicose veins, and stretch marks. Poor woman, I thought. Her husband is probably lusting after other women while she carries his child.

She seemed happy enough, though.

Swimming kept her from getting elephant ankles, she said.

How about backaches? I asked. Well, yes, it helped with that, too. How about with heartache, betrayal, rejection, denial? How about with being kicked in the gut? Getting thrown away? I didn't ask her those last questions. With her standing there bulging, I could feel an uncomfortable warmth in my swimsuit. I ducked into the men's locker room.

Just thinking about it was making my face flush. The waitress who was warming up my coffee looked at me oddly. "You okay? Need anything else, hon?"

I mopped my forehead with a napkin. Across the crowded dining room, the pimply-faced girl, who was now paying her check, glared at me with open hostility. I looked up at the waitress. "My name is not HON," I said. "It's SWEETIE-PIE. But you can call me ALDOUS, or MR. HUXLEY."

"Geez. Don't have a cow," she said. I decided to give her a better than decent tip. She lacked a sense of humor, but she had a nice little belly.

I returned to my daydreaming. After I had talked to the pregnant woman at the pool, I strapped to my stomach an inflatable camping pillow which I had filled with water. I wanted to see what it would feel like to walk around with a big pregnant weight on my gut. Within two hours, I had a backache. The breasts swell, too, I remembered. So, I strapped on two 5-pound water balloons. The experience left me with a pulled shoulder muscle and a lower back pain that would make a grown man squeal like a pig. War is hell.

The haggard woman I had observed coming into Denny's was handing the cashier some money. As she exited the restaurant for the parking lot, I bolted out of my seat to catch her before she drove off into the cold, dark neverland of abandonment. The way she never even looked back into Denny's convinced me that she was indeed my mother.

It was cold in the parking lot. My veins were as rigid and intractable as diesel exhaust compressed into a bicycle tire. My eyes were thick with hope.

"Mom! Mom!" She didn't turn around. I thought I'd try a new approach, a new form of address. "Mother!"

The sound of engines backfiring made a melted liquid memory of my brain. The act of going away was a gunshot into the sunset. She wasn't going to stop.

"Mother! I'm here. I got your call. You can stay with me. I've got money."

Up close, she wasn't as ragged and down on her luck as she had seemed when I first saw her in Denny's. Her sweater was one of those hand-knitted novelty sweaters festooned with hearts, doves, and satin ribbons. Her earrings were long, dangly ropes of baroque pearls. Her perfume was Marcella Borghese's *Il Bacio*. She was driving a gold Lexus. She didn't need money, that was for sure. Something must have been bothering her, though, to call me.

"Mom, are you pregnant again?"

The woman, who had previously not even looked at me, spun on her little pointy-toed Italian tasseled loafers.

"Are you talking to me? You get back from me or I'll shoot you with pepper spray! I've really got some."

"Mom, please don't be mean to me. You called me and I'm here. I'm your son, Kristian. I'll help you."

The Denny's sign made a halo around her head. Her face had that same scouring searchlight look Joseph in search of a clean, well-lighted bale of hay he could shred so his wife could calve. Did the madonna know the implications of being a madonna right away, or did she have to wait until her son was dead?

"Are you out of your mind? I'm not your mother! How could I be? Take a look at yourself. You're no son of mine! You're a white boy!"

That was something I hadn't considered. She had a point. It didn't make me feel any less bitter, or any less abandoned.

"I'm sorry, ma'am." I shuffled back to Denny's, where my waitress was running toward me brandishing the check in her hand.

The woman got out her pepper spray and squirted some in my

direction. "Now, don't you come following me!"

I watched the taillights of her Lexus disappear in the direction of I-10, and then I trudged back into the restaurant. I had lost my appetite, but I still had a restless, gnawing sensation inside my gut — not hunger, exactly, but something I couldn't push out of myself.

"Was that the person you were waiting for?" asked the waitress. Perhaps she felt sorry for me. I hated the fact that she was only pretending to listen — that she was just working me over for a good tip. While I pretended to sip on coffee, I slipped my hand beneath the table and pretended to jerk off into a paper napkin. Then I placed the napkin on the table, and stuck a $5 bill on top. That was her tip. One was worth something, the other was worth very little. She would spend the wrong one.

VI. In my own utopian world, mothers stay with their sons. If they leave, they take their sons with them. They don't leave them with a father whose best years were in the Merchant Marines, who does nothing but repeat the same anecdote until your memorized version of it is clearer and more lucid than his pathetic retellings of it.

You and I know his story is a lie.

Dad's not even my dad. Dad is a cultural composite.

This is the litany: Torture & terrorize the weak (forgetting that everyone is in fact weak). Make the act of denying your own mortality a moment of teeth-grinding fun. Cross entire oceans while ignoring your own need for the oceanic. Re-enlist in the Merchant Marines. Find a lover and write every day that you crave closeness. Sail away while you make your professions of love. Hurt people when the paradox is catching up to you. Tell no one your secret — that you encourage their bodies to get into you, but you don't know how to say NO. Don't let anyone see you cry. Live your life numb. Avoid them when you think they're becoming angry with you. Live in hopes of the next sleazy port. Maybe things will be different there. Maybe not. Maybe that cruel streak is something that can't be avoided, and you know it. You want to be hurt the next time you cross the equator. You pray there will be no passengers. Then you're afraid you'll fall in love. You pray for passengers.

After awhile I began believing that I had once been in the Merchant Marines. Me, on a beautiful little Ship of Fools memorialized by Hieronymous Bosch. Is this how I could start? Back up. Make it an anatomy lesson. A cold, sterile anatomy lesson where no one comes away with anything except confusion.

VII. The waters of the River Styx are blue, not black. Its depths team with air pockets and denial. I can't breathe when I think this way. I'll find my mother. I know I will. It will just take time. My eyes reflect the sky and that final journey from flesh to earth.

My mother paid for my sin — my sin of existence. I exist. That is my sin. Is this something I know, or is it something I see in the walls of my city which contain the illustrations of an age? I'll find my mother, and I'll ask her. Will she know the answers? In a perfect world, we would have perfect knowledge, and we would understand even the most flawed and broken mind. I'll find my mother.

People hurt me. People who don't even know me sense that I'm confused about my gender. That makes them hate me, but I don't know why.

It has happened so often that it's like clockwork — my body knows before my mind perceives it that it's going to happen again. I tell myself that I don't even mind it any more. Still, I understand that primitive urge to hurt the weak — but, since I am invariably the weak one, I don't know if it means I've internalized the urge and I won't be able to resist hurting myself.

If you don't want to be left out in the dark, you have to get ready to be hurt. That's just the way it is. Get ready. It's one more preparation for the death hormones. Eat meat. Don't eat meat. Swallow your own blood. Don't let your tears escape, but suck them back inside and swallow them, too.

Maybe they'll make you pregnant.

POPE-MOBILE

by
David Gilbert

The mob closed ranks behind the Pope-mobile as it bounced over those who had fallen. The most devout among the Swiss Guard drove Teddy's Oldsmobile, the lead car in the procession. They drove it recklessly, with abandon and disregard for life. Lots had been drawn and those who came up short ran beside the Pope-mobile gasping for breath. The guards who had drunk in excess eventually fell and disappeared into the mob.

The Pope waved, acknowledging the throngs who were there out of a necessity that was final, yet unending, and absolving those who fell under the Pope-mobile. Teddy watched in horror. He knew the motorcade needed to go faster, but there was little he could do driving the Pope and Mary in the Pope-mobile. The road to the bridge was almost impassable with the dead and no-longer-human who remained standing in the press of bodies. The disappeared reappeared on what had become a vast planet of tombs.

The pond below the bridge was chaotic with obsolescent creation, awaiting the divine and final account. Teddy's agony fell short of the moment, oppressive in its banality. He was entombed in the Pope-mobile with less than a six-pack; he was damned as a witness to the final hour and the need to explain his failure to the world on the night he left a party in the Pope-mobile.

When the road was cleared of bodies the Oldsmobile lurched forward again on the way to the narrow bridge. The living hurled themselves at the tires, in a doggish hunger for death. As the Pope-mobile approached the bridge demons began to appear as U.N. Officials, Teddy's aides, handlers, journalists, hangers-on, then, just as demons in demiurgic irony among those who'd made their pilgrimage.

Time had unwrapped its failures. Demons took to the air only to swoop down and wound, to mock grace and gravity. When they saw a severed arm stuck to the Pope-mobile they pelted the bullet-proof glass snapping their rubbery necks. As a matter of honor the guards used their weapons to recover their comrade's arm. It was put on ice in the cooler.

The guards worked to clear the bridge. Those who had come early, to enter eternity from the front of the line, did not move easily. The pious could not stomach perdition in its infancy. They would be happy to drown in the pond where the Pope and Mary would enact the historic hour.

Overcome by the spectacle, Teddy, fevered and drenched in sweat, reached for his last beer. Not even at the Morristown regatta on a lifeless sea waiting for the sails to lift had he been so thirsty.

The Pope-mobile was covered with blood. Teddy could not see the bridge. The armless guard cleaned the glass with a squeegee. His Holiness turned toward Mary, overcome with doubt. Was the blood a saving blood? Was history nothing more than a grainy snuff film?

Teddy floored the Pope-mobile. Its torque was only enough to spin tires on the dead and come to rest on the bridge. The surviving guards kept at bay those who were hoping for a better deal or had found new life in the imminent judgment.

A silence moved from the scene at the bridge across the island and shifting land masses. It was time for the Pope-mobile to go over into the drink. Light hesitated. The guards sought instruction. They screamed into the ventholes, but the Holy Father was in a final reverie with Mary.

The water below was choppy with the would-be drowned. Teddy, arms outstretched, palms up, had the presence of mind to wave for the guards to push. At first they would not step forward. They were afraid of beginning an anti-eternity by disposing of the Pope at the wrong moment. Assured by Teddy's frantic gestures — his Holiness had given the word! — they stepped forward and pushed. They put their shoulders to the Pope-mobile as demons taunted. With the help of exhausted believers they pushed again, but without movement.

The moment was irreconcilable. Teddy despaired; he would be blamed. He knew that if the Pope-mobile did not go into the water he would end with the world as a failure. If only they'd taken the Oldsmobile like he'd said and cut a deal with the demons to clear the Dike road. They could have hit the bridge at the speed limit.

The door to the Pope-mobile was sealed against assassins. Teddy wrenched the handle to throw his divine passengers into the water. When he realized he could not get the door open, he stepped back, then threw himself against it. The impact of his body eased the Pope-mobile over the edge in a slow but certain fall.

Those among the Swiss Guard who made it to the bridge and saw the Pope-mobile in its downward orbit danced and fired their weapons into the air in a revolutionary excess. The trunk of the Oldsmobile had been torn open and Teddy's beer was passed around. Teddy saw them drinking as the Pope-mobile slowly sank into the radiant and bloody water. As he went under he saw guards waving cold bottles from the bridge.

The dead were quickly at the glass, bloated, bleached, fatty, but slowly dissolving. The Pope-mobile righted itself on the bottom of the pond. Teddy stood ankle deep in brine, his loafers ruined. The Pope knelt in front of Mary and would not turn again as they waited in the final tableau. Teddy asked for confession in the wet murmur. The hour was late, too late for confession. There would be no sacraments diminishing in his blood stream with the passage of time.

Teddy waited for the sign to leave, to swim heroically, then make his way to the Shiretown Inn where he would dress and wait for the best and the brightest to finish his final statement. As he waited breathlessly, a demon dove from the bridge and swam around and around the Pope-mobile With a small snout and a child's voice, the demon, at the door, announced that heresy, all of it, was true.

The hour had come and the Pope told Teddy to go. As the smelly water trickled into the Pope-mobile, Teddy, sickened, managed to say good-bye to the Holy Father and Mary. With help from the outside the door opened and Teddy was taken quickly into the water.

The demon followed him ranting on about heresy. When the demon finished, it dissolved, organs floating out of its soft belly. The water was full of those who had come apart and those who could not make it to the end.

In confusion, Teddy tried to return to the Pope-mobile in the missing center of a bad dream where the water, almost ice, had risen with the displacing ballast of the dead. In his hallucinations he believed that if he swam harder he would eventually awaken and see wondrous things.

The hour was late. The chief of police, Jim Arena, jumped from the bridge and found Teddy. The chief took him by the arm and they swam to shore. Teddy, delirious, clothes clinging, lay in the human mulch and wept. The chief told him that he must get up and make his final statement.

"I'll wait for you, Senator, at the station in Edgartown, God willing."

The crowds shouted Teddy's name as he moved blindly from heap to heap, encouraged, his spirit light. He shook hands and talked with those who lined the road back to Edgartown and made an effort to keep up appearances, to carry on as if nothing had happened. Teddy promised them a final statement.

As his sight returned the world passed for itself again, but the road ahead was blocked. Teddy came upon a uniformed policeman, Officer Look, who was waving flares. He informed Teddy that a contingent of sexologists, pedophile priests, abortionists and liberation theologians were gathered in scandal and dishabille. Teddy ignored Look when he saw a bevy of Vaticanisti drinking beer by alter boys in a queue awaiting their instruction. At the risk of having to explain himself, Teddy asked for a beer. The Vaticanisti would treat him better than the American press.

Demons also had beer. They were drinking with attorneys who were billing for time while they could. Teddy asked if his attorney was among them. In the commotion he found a boiling can of beer which he could not drink. He pitifully called for his attorney, declining offers of representation, even on contingency.

There would be cold beer at the Shiretown Inn. Teddy staggered down the road until he came upon drunken revelers from the party he'd attended earlier after the regatta. The revelers were standing in the road without their clothes, singing the songs of society bands.

Teddy knew he was getting closer, although he could no longer be sure of where to walk as the earth liquefied and ran toward the pond. He saw lights, so many lights. He saw a city the color of stars rising slowly out of the earth in an aesthetic triumph, the other moment before the end.

The Shiretown Inn and the compound were floating like ferries on an inland sea. Teddy waded through the mud to reach a small boat. The boat slid easily on the slick surface, brightening into a vast horizonless whiteness. Teddy bound his eyes to save his sight and rowed on toward the compound. The oars stuck and went under. The boat slid on in silence.

Aground, Teddy staggered up the beach, hands outstretched to find what was familiar, a barbecue pit, a railing, a stair case. He made it to the stairs and climbed quickly, opened a door and slammed it shut behind him. He unbound his eyes to find his aides.

The compound was full. People had come for refuge and to help with the statement. Teddy found a cold beer in the kitchen and when his thirst was quenched, he thought, to hell with everybody.

A maid entered the kitchen.

"Prepare a bath," he said.

Upstairs Teddy chose his clothes carefully. The room filled with the smell of soapy water and a woman singing in the tub. Teddy walked down the hall and found Marilyn washing herself, her back arched, head upturned and her tongue bleeding. Teddy kissed her on the cheek.

"Is there anything I can do?" he asked.

"Help us. Go and prepare your statement."

There were too many voices inside the compound. Teddy heard the wrong laughter, the wrong voices. He did not know everyone. He made a move to clear the compound. They can party on the beach, he said. He didn't pursue it, but instead returned to the bathroom.

Lee Harvey Oswald sat on the toilet, done up as Patsy Cline. At the mirror Cardinal Cushing applied pancake to his face, improvising a death mask. He opened his mouth and hissed, then pursed his improbable lips. He brushed his robe with a clothes brush, acknowledged Teddy's arrival, then left stiffly.

"Just be a minute, Ted," said Oswald.

"Don't worry about it, Lee."

Marilyn moaned, shuddered and slowly slid down into the tub. Jack joined Teddy at the door.

"We've been looking all over for you."

"Had to drive the Pope-mobile."

"How could I forget? By the way, have you seen my medications?"

"No. Jack. I'll help you look for them if you want."

"Maybe Frank has them. You've got enough to do, Teddy."

Oswald finished and stepped between the brothers to leave. Teddy slipped by Jack and relieved himself. Marilyn, standing by the tub, helped Teddy out of his clothes. When he was in the tub, she began washing him. Teddy loved the warm water. Marilyn wrapped her tongue around Teddy's neck and began choking him. As he was about to pass out, Sam Giancana stepped into the bathroom and stuck Marilyn with his cigar. She recoiled and Teddy gasped for air.

"Don't do that in front of me."

Sam sat on the toilet, sniffed at the burnt-flesh smell and relit his cigar.

"Teddy, when you get through fucking around you should make your statement so we can get this fucking business over with. It gives me the fucking creeps."

Teddy's face was purple.

"I was thinking that the differences between people don't matter any more," said Sam. "If I knew what I know now I'd sell heroin in good neighborhoods too."

Teddy stepped into a large cotton robe. Marilyn crawled back into the tub looking bad for the hour.

"Shouldn't let yourself go like that, honey," said Sam.

"We want to talk," said Oswald, standing in the doorway.

"Who's we?" asked Teddy, drying himself.

"Sirhan, Ruby and Mahmet what's his name."

"I'm kind of busy, Lee."

"Make time."

"OK. Where will you be?"

"In the library."

Lee did not walk well in his boots.

"If you want some protection," said Sam, "I got guys all over the place. They're probably with Frank. Just let me know. I can't stand these fucking creeps."

"Thanks, Sam."

Teddy had chosen a blue blazer and tan slacks.

In the library, Teddy fixed himself a rum and Coke and helped himself to a large plate of canapés.

"Did you make these, Lee?"

"Ruby did."

Oswald sat with one boot in his hand. He was washing Cardinal Cushing's feet in high liturgical camp. Cushing, ticklish, revealed himself as Jack Ruby.

"Where are my aides?"

"Fucking off."

Two men entered the library in costume.

"You're Gandhi," said Teddy to one of the two men.

"Yes," said Sirhan. "You guessed right away. That's no fun."

"Looking good. Who have we here?"

The second man stepped forward.

"Do I know you? Let me see if I can get your name right — Mahmet Ali Agca."

"Yes, but who am I?"

"You're Frank Sinatra."

"No. No."

Everyone laughed and hooted.

"Christ," said Teddy. "I'm in the middle of a crisis. Has anyone seen a draft of my statement?"

"Who am I?"

"The crew cut should help... Jimmy Hoffa?"

"Yes."

"Bobby should see you. Where's Bobby?"

"He was around," said Ruby, slowly releasing one of Oswald's toes from his mouth. "Isn't the moon landing soon?"

"Let's watch TV," said Oswald.

The set was shelved between rows of books. Teddy loved rooms with books.

"I've got to practice reading my statement. I just can't deliver it cold."

On television the lunar landing module touched down on a area of the moon's surface known as the Sea of Tranquillity.

"Where the hell are they?"

"In the living room."

"Of course."

A coterie of Teddy's aides was at work, too busy to notice him standing with his drink at the end of the hallway. They'd pushed a table up to a bank of open windows. The aides were trying to get Frank, standing alone on the porch with a drink and cigarette, to come back inside for his own safety.

An aide handed Teddy several pages.

Frank burst into flames. The aides jumped away from the window as Frank shriveled, crackled; fat sputtered and ran and a skeleton emerged from flesh, white, then black.

Cardinal Cushing brushed against Teddy as he went to give Frank last rites. As he prayed, his flaming robes lifted and swirled out into space, and, in one great swoop, he disappeared. Ruby howled and ran back toward the library.

"What a mess," said an aide mixing drinks in a shaker.

"I need to be by myself," said Teddy, thinking the best and

the brightest were ultimately worthless. Teddy returned to the library. He sat at the desk where he felt most comfortable.

"Do something with Ruby, would you," he said. "Pack him in ice."

Oswald helped Ruby — singed hairless — out of the library. Ahmet was smoking one of Sam Giancana's cigars. The room stunk of burnt flesh, cigars, soap and the earth as it had not been known to smell.

Teddy drew the curtains. The musty smell promised a familiar death, the intoxicants of an afterlife. Suddenly, he jumped back against the desk. The astronauts were outside floating in a gritty indeterminacy. If they were trying to land they were making a mistake. Teddy waved them away then closed the curtain and went for another beer.

Sirhan and Ahmet were arguing in English and Arabic. Ahmet resented the Pope's visiting him in prison and offering forgiveness. He spat. Sirhan regretted that the jihad against Salman Rushdie had never been completed.

"Gentlemen," said Teddy, with his statement in hand, "I have my own problems."

"How's the statement?" asked an aide.

Sirhan jumped up and began pistol whipping the aide. He whipped the aide down the hall. Teddy sat again at the desk, squared himself to speak in front of a camera. How does one finally take responsibility, he wondered, without looking at the text.

Glass shattered against the curtains. Teddy threw the curtains aside and opened the windows. His aides were floating outside with bloody faces.

"Tell Sirhan that if he can't be civil he can leave."

"I'll tell him."

"Have you read the statement?"

"Not yet. I haven't had a minute's peace since I returned."

There were many bodies floating outside the Hyannis Port compound. Frank, in a heavenly body, was crooning for his goons and the astronauts. Chief Jim Arena was waving frantically and pointing at his wrist watch.

Teddy stuck his head out the window to yell, but had a sudden attack of vertigo as he looked down into deep space. There is no use talking to people now, he said to himself.

"What's going on?" asked Ruby, looking ghoulish in one of Teddy's robes. Ruby stepped to the window.

"These can't be the blessed?" said Teddy.

"I doubt it," said Ruby. "Where's the creep?"

A body count was a waste of precious time. Teddy sat in the leather chair by the fireplace. He found a coat on a clothes tree. It was getting cold. A fire would be nice.

The assassins came in with rifles. Ruby had a pistol. They pushed the desk across the floor against the window sill. Oswald used the butt of his rifle to knock out the panes of glass. They took turns shooting. Ruby let Sirhan use his pistol, but complained when he emptied it without aiming.

"Don't be a putz, Sirhan."

"What is putz?" asked Ahmet.

"How can a guy concentrate?" asked Teddy, drinking out of a glass he found that was leaving a ring on an end table.

"Take a shot," said Ruby.

"Why not? Might was well learn how to use one of these things."

Ruby handed Teddy a reloaded pistol. To his surprise Jack, Bobby and Sam floated by. Jack was thumping his chest like a target. Teddy aimed, but missed, all six shots. Jack yelled from a distance.

"Where's Marilyn?"

"Is she still in the tub?" asked Teddy, putting on his glasses. He was trying to work on his statement.

Sirhan was the first to shoot at Teddy. Then Ahmet ran up to Teddy and stuck the pistol in his gut and emptied it. He turned and smiled at Ruby.

"I find this annoying," said Teddy.

"Give me the gun," said Ruby. "When you've been paid to do a job professionalism goes with the territory. A fanatic is worthless over the long haul. You just kill indiscriminately. You can't shoot straight when you hate. Watch this. Stand up, Senator."

"I'm really busy, if you don't mind."

Ruby stepped up to him and shot him point blank.

"Damn. That ain't right. When I plugged you, Lee, you were a goner."

"It's very weird," said Oswald.

"I want you people gone when I get back," said Teddy.

Teddy walked down the corridor to the bathroom. Marilyn was washing herself in the tub.

"How you feeling baby?"

"I'm depressed," said Teddy. "The assassins are in the library. They're using their last moments to ply their trade."

"Don't let them get you down. Get in the tub with me."

"Let me finish my statement. I'll read it to you."

"Goodnight Teddy. Goodnight sweet Teddy, goodnight, goodnight."

Teddy returned to the library.

They were waiting for him, but did not open fire immediately. They gave him a chance to sit and compose himself, adjust his glasses and stare blankly at the first page of his statement. Then they opened fire.

In the statement the aides apologized for themselves, as if appealing to history. Teddy tore the opening page in pieces and wrote on the back of the second page. He believed that if he had time he could succeed in making his statement. But he was not a writer, like the hacks, who were floating away from the compound. "I'm disappointed," said Teddy. "If there was ever a time to stop shooting it's now."

"This is a Zionist conspiracy," said Sirhan.

The noisy assassins made work impossible. Teddy stood and struggled through the bursts of gunfire. Oswald had a rifle with a scope on a tripod and he was beginning to get close. The rush of gunfire was exciting, but Teddy began to disarm the assassins. He tossed the guns out the window. Sirhan jumped after his gun and disappeared. Ahmet, screaming, jumped for Paradise. Ruby collared Oswald and with his bulk dumped him over the window sill. He screamed after them, "Schmucks."

Teddy, with Ruby in front of him, watched the assassins tumble head over heals.

"Do narcissists recognize deep space?" asked Teddy.

"You talking to me?" asked Ruby.

"I want you to leave."

"Jump," said Marilyn walking into the library in a beach outfit. She approached Ruby.

"How about a quick one on the desk like Jack got?"

"You're not Jack."

"No. I revenged Jack's death. That should be worth a quick one. A hand-job."

Marilyn closed in on Ruby. She pressed up against him as he backed up to the window.

"Can't get your skirts up, Cardinal?"

"I tried," said Ruby as he turned and jumped.

"He's got the right idea," said Marilyn, "the house is falling apart."

"I'm cold," said Teddy.

They crumpled newspaper and stacked kindling. Teddy made a fire. They sat together on the love seat. The bookcases tore away from the walls and books began floating out the windows.

"Hold me," said Marilyn.

MY FRIEND KATE

by
Etel Adnan

When I first saw her there was a black halo around her and that could have been scary but there was also an elegant look about her that endeared her to me and it turned out that we became friends pretty soon after.

As I was then much foreign to America everything she said or did presented great interest: through her I was initiated to all the little and apparently insignificant things that make a new world and learned many idiomatic expressions which ran back to the nineteenth century. We were in the Bay Area but she had just arrived from Ohio when we met, and that entrenched her solidly in the heart of the land and I was thrilled to know somebody so rooted in the country.

One day she introduced me to her friend Dean, a good-looking fellow who was her childhood neighbor and knew her whole family from those distant days. Little by little I discovered that she was quite in love with him, in a different way, for it didn't take much time for her to let me know that Dean was gay and living in San Francisco with a young man who was originally from Oklahoma. Tony was his name, and Tony was known for his passion for trains.

In those days — at the beginning of the sixties — I had a degree from an art institute in Paris, and was working for a design firm. Kate (that's her name) was the librarian of a small public library in Marin County. She had a beautiful car and was happy to be in California although, I learned later, she had come to San Francisco on a sudden urge prompted by one of Dean's phone calls. She secured a retirement place for her mother and drove West only to be met by Dean who told her he was on his way to New York... That's about the time that I met her, when she had something tragic about her and she told me over a few drinks in the shine and sounds of the Jazz Workshop that when Dean had gone, she drove to the Golden Gate with the purpose of jumping off the bridge. "I didn't," she said, "it was too awful."

For years, I could say for decades, Kate remained my best friend. At its start my friendship for her had a lot to do with the fact that I was much younger and that she represented a kind of archetypal American in my eyes. One has to know that for some foreigners their encounter with America is an phenomenon of major proportion. She was extremely thin, a very determined person, the movie image of a Yankee. We did many things together, trips to the Monterey Jazz Festival, weekends on the Mendocino Coast. Little by little our conversations were opening up my mind to an America I didn't know.

She was born in Warren, Ohio, to a father who was a Pennsylvania Dutch, a businessman who lost it all in the Great Depression. "He lost his mind too," she used to add to her story. On her mother's side, Kate was English, although her own mother's grandma was French. Kate's grandmother was a DAR and it was explained what the "D," "A" and "R" stood for. "Of course," added Kate, repeating the story many times, "I could prove that she was also Mayflower. But I never took the time. What's the use of it?"

The photographs that she used to show me were brownish and I knew that she was the only child of her family with no cousins on either side. To be so American and so alone! I could not easily accept such an idea.

After the Depression, when Kate in her early twenties had lost half a million shares in copper mines, besides what her mother had lost, and the father having died within a few years, something had to be done to keep the mother and the mother's unmarried sister alive: Kate worked on an itinerant library which toured a series of small towns all around Warren. That's how she became an on-the-job trained librarian and the bread-winner of the three of the them. Dean was her younger neighbor, and she became one night, and only for that night, his first and only woman. Neither forgot that experience and they remained attached to each other for the rest of their lives.

I loved all the stories related to Kate's early life. They used to take place in my imagination's field, in some round and deep landscape with blurred trees, in fact blurred seasons, in a time which was itself imprecise, a midwestern "somewhere," a mythical time, to be honest, a wonderful construct of our two minds.

There was magic to these days that were unfolding in front of me. From Warren we used to move to Columbus, the capital of the state, I thought, and to Cleveland, and sometimes I didn't know exactly where we were, but it was Ohio, for sure, and then I learned the names of the best pitchers, one of them having lived on Euclid Avenue when Kate had moved to Cleveland too.

Cleveland itself was a magic name, for Kate had two loves, Dean, and Margaret.

Margaret was also a childhood friend of hers, a recurrent name in our conversations. She was related to the Clevelands, the founders of the city, and her grandfather's farm carried the prestige of having been the land on which, later, the Cleveland Museum of Modern Art was built. As that museum has one of the most beautiful Monets that I ever saw, Margaret acquired in my eyes an endearing aura. That was not reciprocated, though; I remained for her an intruder who could have as well come from another planet. When she came to visit in California, and when I was also invited to lunch, I would follow, without interfering, recollections of which they were both particularly fond: how, for example, John D. Rockefeller went to the same Baptist church as Kate's father, and how the father would come home at the end of the service and tell that the price of oil must have gone up because John D. had added a dime to the Sunday collection. They also talked about the Packard boys, the ones who built the cars I used to see in movies, boys that made a lot of noise cruising the main street of Warren! That's what Kate used to repeat quite often, oh yes, she was also mentioning the Tafts, and Margaret's only child grew to go to college with one of the Tafts' boys, and as he was Kate's godchild I saw him quite often, when he was visiting her on his way to the ski slopes of Tahoe.

But Margaret lived in Danbury, somewhere in Connecticut, and that gave Kate many occasions to declare that she wasn't an Easterner anymore, but a Californian, which was true enough, given that she wasn't drinking vodka anymore but California Chenin Blanc and Mayacamas reds.

One day when I asked if Ohio was Eastern or part of the Midwest, they both said simultaneously that it was both things and they added, together again, that it was once a western frontier and, of course, Margaret's great grandfathers were the heroes of that migration... That's also when I heard about Angie, Kate's maternal grandma: Angie was 'quite a character,' not an Ohian by birth, and a person of fame as she was a charter member of the Prohibition Party. Angie even took her family to live in Prohibition Park, near Boston. I think that I even heard that she was on speaking terms with both angels and demons, knowing very well what they were up to: she knew demons helped some otherwise good citizens fill their bathtubs with homemade alcohols. No, Kate assured me, that did not happen in Prohibition Park; and there were all these summers in Maine when Margaret used to come, all this when everybody was still young and happy.

I also discovered that there was something religious in Kate even if she represented the most perfect agnostic that I ever met. A French woman living in Tiburon had told me that Kate reminded her of some French XVIIIth century marquis, of Voltaire and Diderot, by her elegance and skepticism, by the generosity of her spirit in spite of her total lack of illusions. But, nonetheless, there was something utterly religious about the absolute value that she put on her own dignity, in a way that for her resolved the question of God.

There was a bond between Dean, Margaret, and Kate, which appeared to be unbreakable, almost ancient, something that could go back to the Greeks. But Dean, during one of his stays in New York, used Kate's credit with a fashionable store and bought for himself two pairs of pants... Kate mentioned it to Margaret who became furious: how can anyone take advantage of a woman with as little salary as the one Kate was earning! That year Dean did not get a Christmas card from Margaret, and never after.

Kate was sorry. Deeply so. The more so that Dean was, according to her own expression, 'deteriorating': he was losing his friends, having borrowed money from almost every one of them, and was losing his jobs: during World War II he had been an intelligence officer in the British Army (yes!), and had met Durrell somewhere in Egypt, for a brief time, and after that it was 'downhill.' He ended up teaching high school in San Francisco, and couldn't stand it, he dreamed of writing a novel, of sending a story to **The New Yorker**, his favorite magazine; in the late sixties he was a gardener around the Haight-Ashbury, but by then he had become an alcoholic and Kate had to count so many empty bottles under his bed. It's true that Tony had left, like that, suddenly, without leaving a trace behind him. Kate was worried because Dean was also a diabetic and one evening, at Marin Joe's, we were eating, she and I, hamburgers, and I was pouring a lot of ketchup on my plate and she looked worried and told me: "You know, Margaret, Dean and I, back in Ohio, just after the Depression, we swore one day — a winter day and in front of the fireplace — that we were going to be together at the end of the century, at the beginning of the new millennium. I want to see that millennium start, that January the First of the year 2000, and I know we will make it." She looked calm, and there were so many repressed dreams in her eyes that I was sure that this one was going to be fulfilled. She reminded me of the surface of some rivers, forever calm, forever flowing.

Dean was fired from gardening job and went on unemployment. His phone calls were becoming lengthy and his stories repetitive. Kate would say: "He isn't fun anymore." There was more to it than that casual remark. She herself became edgy, visiting him more often, while dreading these visits. One late evening, when California was drenched in one of its usual apocalyptic storms, she insisted on going to the city. That night I was awakened by her physician who told me over the phone that Kate had been found in her car, off the highway, in Marin, just after the tunnel. Nobody found out what really happened. Kate didn't remember a thing, only that she found herself on a hospital bed. The car was squeezed like an accordion and her slender frame was covered with bruises. Her face was swollen and her eyes barely visible. When I went to visit her the first thing she said was: "You see. I told you I'm going to live to be 94, at least!"

The ebullient sixties were over. Life was settling down and people were counting their blessings and their losses. At the public libraries, the readers were gradually asking for new kinds of books. Something had turned sour. I was getting restless, again, as I do every ten years or so, and I left the Bay Area and went to Europe.

When I returned to Marin County it was, at least for me, a new America. Some spirit of seriousness had taken hold of the minds of those whom I knew. There were more pleasure boats all over the Bay but the winds, somehow, were tame.

Kate was close to retirement and, eventually, she did retire. Margaret, from Connecticut, was complaining of the cold, and her Christmas presents, I had to admit, were getting unimaginative. At least her phone conversations were getting longer and Kate was enjoying the news about the grandchildren. All the Ohio memories were being repeated regularly, down to the dogs and cats.

Kate wasn't driving to the city much anymore. Her bridge club and some new friends she made were taking all her time and attention. Whenever I asked about Dean the answer would be: "How do you want him to be? He brought it all down on himself." Yes, Dean was hospitalized in the middle of February, he had pneumonia and other complications, and his nurse asked Kate to come and see him, and she refused, and he died a few days after his final request. Kate was pale and determined to not utter a single word about the event. And ever since she wouldn't say much about him.

I settled in San Francisco happy to have found both a new job and a new apartment, this one with a view of the water. The city lifted my spirit. I wanted to recapture something of my early days in California, wanted to feel at the edge of the world, with my back turned to the past, its joys and failures included. In fact I was looking for a feeling of daring transiency and I found it.

Kate was barely managing with her very small income. Ever since the Depression she had to learn to live with very little without having to admit poverty. She watched baseball games, even double-headers. She got excited about golf and her nightly glass of white wine. She gave up smoking and sold her two-door BMW. She even found a studio in a complex for senior citizens: she hated the word and even the place, in the beginning, but she managed to endear herself to the gardener and she repeated to him regularly a few stories about her parents' garden in Warren (it had begonias and squirrels) and the trains she rode on the lap of her maternal uncle Holloway. The gardener wanted to teach her some special flower names but she rebelled: besides Jazz, she loved only Gertrude's books and Shakespeare.

Everything seemed fine and she appeared to be cruising pretty well the tedious waves of the passing years until very recently: her friend Margaret, the only witness to the eighty-nine years of her life, on a hot afternoon by Chesapeake Bay, where her son had moved her, her friend Margaret passed away. Her son, John, had to give Kate the terrible news by telephone. He didn't know how to go about it and just said: "Mother has died. This morning mother has died." As she could hardly hear, and sensing trouble, she asked: "Whose mother, what mother?" and he answered: "Margaret. Our Margaret. She is no more."

I said to wait a minute, that I was coming, and I did hurry and found her sitting in her armchair in front of a silent TV, her door as usual unlocked. Her studio was grey and beige and the clock was ticking. "How are you?" I said, and she said: "All right." She did not repeat the news to me. She looked awfully frail and was wobbly when she tried to stand and bring me something from the kitchen. "Oh! Please sit," I begged, and her honey-colored eyes, which had kept their look of longingness for a lifetime, gazed at my face, and beyond, and I said that I was sorry, but she remained silent. She saw my tears coming down my cheeks and I saw her shake and she tried to reassure me: "Don't cry," she spoke softly, "we'll make it. I don't understand why Margaret quit. There are only four years left. I guess that for the sake of the two of them as much as for my own, I will face the turn of the millennium all by myself... unless you join me there, too."

WHO IS KEVIN KILLIAN?

by

Kevin Killian

. . . I'm always reading the **Chronicle**, every morning, at work, and I saw how the guy died, the guy who invented sodium pentathol. And you know, I felt bad for him. Didn't realize he was still alive.

Did you know him?

No, as a matter of fact I didn't. I mean, sodium pentathol's been around so long — part of my consciousness, you might say — I never realized any one person actually must have invented it. Like last year when the obit columns said the man who invented the Tequila Sunrise died. Same thing. And two years ago this old Swiss nut who had thought up Velcro. But with this sodium pentathol guy — maybe he was in Chicago, maybe it was some kind of offshoot of the Manhattan Project — I really felt bad, not because of anything pertinent to my life — I just got swept away with thinking how pathetic life is, that you could do something and nobody would know it, and how eventually you die and eventually everyone alive who remembers you will die — then you really don't exist any more. I remember Jerry Ackerman telling me he had written the life of Gerôme, the French painter, and he found one ancient old woman who had actually met him — and she was, like, three-and-a-half and she'd sat on his lap for 15 minutes.

I found that so pathetic. After she goes — and, who knows, she's probably dead now, because this was some time ago Ackerman met her.

Well, but his work remains — although I don't know it myself.

Yeah, I guess so. That's a nice tie you have on. No, I mean it. One doesn't often see fabric like that, is it naugahyde? But anyway that's when you said you had some pentathol I said, Hell, why not, let's do it in memory of this *guy*. Shitty thing is I don't even remember his name. But I'm almost sure he worked in Chicago.

I don't know Gerôme either. He's one of those big, blowsy French romantic painters, Ackerman's the expert on him. I guess they all have one expert on each of them. It's funny that here in the City there's this painter, Jerome Caja, they just call him "Jerome," — just like the French guy! He's got this show now at Southern Exposure. Jerome does all his pictures from makeup — he's into drag and shit. Anyhow — oh, and all the pictures are real little, like a few inches square, because I guess, because of the price of cosmetics. So at Southern Exposure he had this show with this other man, Charles Sexton — and Sexton died — and he said to Jerome to have him cremated and give the ashes to Jerome, and make pictures out of them. And one of the pieces there is this ashtray — like that — filled with Charles' ashes and Jerome painted this little tiny picture of Charles at the tip of one of the cigarette butts in the ashtray. Isn't that gross? I don't know why, it gave me the creeps.

I really like that tie. It's very sensuous. My dad had a chair like that. Who gave it to you?

It's silk.

Did somebody give it to you who loved you, must have been, it has that feeling coming through it. I like the blue and the yellow. Steve Abbott had a few of Jerome's pictures, and Bruce and I were talking about, well! — about what will happen when Steve dies — because we have to sell his stuff for Alysia; and gee, I guess all he really had are books — *and* these two Jerome pictures. So we were so depressed thinking about the day coming wow, Steve will actually die. And you know how when you're down in the dumps, brooding, sometimes one of you says something absolutely tacky and you both crack up. Well, we said we would charge the estate the rental of a helicopter — because we'd have to fly the books to Berkeley — and then each take one of the Jerome pictures, and we'd tell Alysia, *gee, I guess those books weren't worth all that much but here's ten dollars*. Oh, it was awful, but we were cracking up. Don't tell Alysia.

I don't know her. Otherwise I would.

Oh, she's really sweet. I guess I always say that, about people. Doesn't give you much sense of her character, does it? I'm a jerk. No, not a jerk, but sometimes I feel very inarticulate. The people I admire speak well: speak rapidly, firmly. They use intellectual precepts. But isn't kindness the important thing? You know what Cat Stevens said, we're only here for a short while. You don't get love without you give love back.

So in your heart of hearts you're kind of a drip?

Well, I'm sentimental, "drip" is in dispute. I cry a lot, these tears well up constantly, especially when I see **West Side Story**. When Natalie's on the fire escape and says, "*Te amo*, Tony," that's when I start to spout, like a geyser or a — I don't know — widower or something. There's always this displacement between the characters of my fantasy and the sentence I'm stomping around in, wild, big-footed, like Lucy and that Italian woman turning grapes to wine.

There's not much I want to know about you.

There is something I want to get out of my system, as long

as I'm feeling this pink-way . . . I remember Lynne Tillman has this analyst for so many years she was totally transferred — I mean this woman was like her mother. And one evening after she got home Lynne did this double-take, her key in the latch — remembering the funny look on this old analyst's face right when they said goodbye. It was the same look Lynne's father had had one night when he went to bed and he had this tremendous stroke. So Lynne rushed to the phone and all night long started calling her analyst, no answer, finally she took a cab all the way uptown or wherever and there was the ambulance, pulling away, and sure enough, she had had a stroke and — you could predict it from an expression? . . . It's not only your tie, it's your whole ensemble, the finish of your package. Henry James could have invented you — no, Abel Gance; but your gilding, the embonpoint, those Henry James might have supplied.

Thanks. In your stories there's a recurring figure — a drugged or otherwise helpless male, married off, without his consent. Does this have anything to do with your own marriage, to Dodie Bellamy?

Hey, I — gee, I wonder . . . never thought of it like that. Maybe. I guess. You know, that's the writer's unconsciousness bubbling up, like goat's head soup, right? But hey, I'm forty years old, I've been on drugs all my life. Every day I remember less, it's like dissolving. So life is like a drug, my consciousness has always been impaired, but also magnified I suppose. What happened is I fell in love with her, I know it's odd and everyone said it wouldn't last, not to my face of course.

Although people say such mean things to one's face I'm surprised that wasn't one of them. It's just that I'm gay, why get married?

Maybe you're afraid of AIDS.

Yeah well sure. I was really frightened, for myself, then after those tests less frightened for me, more frightened for the

— whole fabric of society. You know. I felt this funny twinge of fear when Anthony Perkins died. I saw myself as one of those pathetic figures in the **Midnight Tattler** who say Richard Simmons paid them money to spank him. Or Merv Griffin had them dress in cellophane on Easter Sunday and pelt him with painted eggs. When he died I got the cold shivers. I met him on an elevator, in a hotel in midtown Manhattan. A winter afternoon, not too cold. I was all agog, fairly bursting with excitement. Of course I thought of him as Norman Bates. He was taller than most people in the crowded elevator. This was during the MLA Convention, of course. That's where all of us sexual deviants went every year during the 70's. It was like — the Mineshaft and the MLA.

It was one of those cases where one thing led to another, but it was definitely my chasing that did it. Now when I see him on television, which is like always, I really get cold. Not that he was so good-looking to begin with. He kind of looked like a tortoise face, like the happy turtle who played a guitar they used to have on cartoons when I was a boy, I can't remember the name — like "Touché Turtle" or someone. And he always plays this weirdo, like Jim Piersall or whoever, I mean Norman Bates was the least of his problems. He was a busy man, there to see his old friend Ingrid Bergman. Who I also got to meet. She was raddled with cancer, but still luminous — a Mexican lantern you plant in the sand.

Why do you love the stars so much?

. . . . I can't really answer that. I don't know. That's a side issue. I guess the worst thing I did was this one star, I wanted his autograph terrible, and nothing seemed to help — I mean I wrote letter after letter, pleading for this autograph, and then I caved in on myself and said I had the HIV virus, and right away, snap, he sent me this long letter, saying to me, don't give up, a cure's right around the corner. I felt so guilty. Also it seemed like such bad karma, know what I mean? I had to take another test right away. It just seems like a miracle. I remember telling Nayland about this incident, and how bad I felt, and he was saying, "Oh that wasn't such a heinous," you know, "thing to do, Kevin," but his eyes were just shocked and all the color drained out of his face no matter what his mouth was saying. I mean I remember being on top of that bar, so drunk I couldn't see, with the bartender straddling the bar . . . Couldn't remember if he'd had his dick in me or not but I assume he did, I assume he came. I remember him jamming this thing up my ass, this crazy thing you squirt different mixes with, ginger ale, Coke, etc., this long wily thing lives at the end of a metallic kind of telephone cord, and it was like — whoosh! Ginger ale, whoosh! Lemon-lime or whatever — water I guess — and him saying, can you tell what this is? when he'd press each button. And drunk as I was three times out of four I could guess right.

Like those Russian ESP experiments when they hold spades and hearts behind their hands up to their heads real hard like they're concentrating — anyway, you can see why I was nervous, especially because within six months this man was dead, dead of AIDS, and I was trying to stay sedate, not to panic.

Or that Argento picture that opens with the psychic, seated in front of an audience in one of those grand European halls that looks like an opera house. Suddenly she calls out, "There's someone in this room with 'danger' attached to him!" She starts mumbling about this child with a knife, a Christmas tree, this terrible danger and blood — the crowd goes wild. Oh I know, it's *Deep Red — Profondo Rosso* in Italian. It figures with Argento it's a gay guy who does it in this one, no it's not, it's his mother, that's right, well, what's worse? Me and Dodie were at Just Thai with Kathy Acker, who was telling us all about Argento and how marvelous and sick he is, this led us to watch oh, all his shows, they're so disturbed and sick and luscious.

Do you have sex with a lot of men?

It's like, she thinks of it as being faithful. I don't, but I do it anyhow, because I don't want to hurt her. That's the only reason. She says, you're in love with that boy, or that man, and I say, like, no. I'm not. Why aren't you? she says. You're gay! I say I don't know, I'm in love with you. She says, it's not natural, how can I satisfy you, you're gay! So I'm gay, doesn't mean I'm a cheater.

That makes it sound like I think I'm better than cheaters, I'm not. I used to depend on cheaters. I liked nothing more than playing *back street girl* to some married man. They're safe. They don't want to rock the boat, yet they're torn by these tremendous longings. And now I'm one of them myself but I learned from their example. I guess you could say I'm the new improved model. Oh and Kathy's new book has this huge incredible section that re-tells the plot of **Suspiria**, the weirdest of all the Argento films, only she calls it **Clit City**. Am I talking too fast?

No — I'm getting it all down. Did you really see those pictures by Jerome Caja?

No — but Rex Ray and Glen Helfand told me 'bout them. Isn't that the same thing? I mean, Southern Exposure's not on my *route*.

And then Dodie and Bob went, with this visiting priest from Italy. The jet set priest who told Dodie she looked like the young Iris Murdoch.

This sent her to the bookshelves and she read **Nuns and Soldiers** and **The Italian Girl** — gobbled them down like candy.

And this priest is so charming. We were sitting around this white garden table at lunch, him sitting there with this urbane smile as if to say, "I know everyone who's anyone, try me," but I couldn't think of anyone Italian, off hand, and I said, "Do you know Dario?" — Argento — and what d'you think, he says, "Yes, he was one of my students," like in high school, "and so was Cicciolina." Can you top that?

But why do you lie?

It's not lying, it's a — an attempt . . . to do something about my life. Before Steve's death we would go to the movies, or rather he would come by in a cab, just this one fleet that took those voucher tickets — his eyes were so bad he could only watch movies not TV. He said he was having this one dream, over and over, took place in London, where Mama Cass Elliott died, and he was this flake of ham lodged in her throat. And we were watching **Encino Man**? And he was too tired to get up after the picture was over, and so we just sat there, and I saw this big bucket of popcorn that these people left — they had hardly touched a bite — so we sat there and he told me about this one time, he had gone to New York, there was one person he wanted to meet, to make a pilgrimage to, and this was Helen Adam, the poet. And she was about eighty-five at the time — but still spry — it must have been ten years ago. And Steve says, "Kevin I thought I'd tell my grandchildren about meeting Helen Adam and now it looks like just the opposite," and I said, "Well, I'll tell your grandchildren if you can't. Or she can tell them about meeting you, Steve. Because she'll outlive us all if she's such a diva."

You eat food other people leave behind?

It just doesn't seem as important as the show. *I* have this one recurring dream that my fingernails keep growing — they grow all around the world, and stab me in the back. What's that about? In another I'm walking across this rickety bridge of life, and knives are flying everywhere, and some people are stabbed by them, some get to live. It was Halloween, I think, and David Rattray came to town. I had never met him but Eileen gave him my phone number, well, he was awfully nice, and he came to town and read at the store, he was like this weird spaced-out cross between Dario Argento and Anne Bancroft — I wonder if he was Italian. Afterwards me and Avery went to have a drink with him, he was telling us about all these drugs he spent the sixties doing — oh first he said he'd written this story about this very chic 20s lesbian in Paris, like Natalie Barney, killing her girlfriend, did I think it would upset the lesbian community, here, in San Francisco! His head was large, and his eyes were these — pools of darkness, though he spoke very sweetly. He was from Long Island like me. Then Dennis came around a month ago and said Rattray fell down in front of his house and he has this brain tumor, and what can be done?

And then Kush over there called up and said, "I have sad news to report, David Rattray is dead." You know, he was courteous. Michael Palmer said he visited Rattray in the early sixties, and he scared Michael, but by now all the fierce wild horror stuff had burned out of him except inside his brain I guess. I'm glad I got him to sign my autograph book, but that sounds so shallow, doesn't it?

I'm not here to pass judgment, though tradition says I should.

When I was young I had this friend, who was very powerful in my life. He made me do these things I wouldn't want anyone to know about. Things I hated myself for doing. But when I did them I got sexually stimulated.

Should I stay or should I go?

Oh that's okay, you go and sit down, but I want you to come back, you hear? I need you to imitate this powerful friend of mine later. "Now you take Philip Mandel," said my powerful friend. "The kid's a clown, but he's not all bad. Lives in the Bronx, right, he's got nothing going for him. Lives with his Mom or some shit, she's an immigrant I guess, she's fucking got garlic and cabbage on the stove all day. Works at the Museum which is no job for a man. Sometimes he shows up in the office smothered in some fairy Chanel perfume, and you know why? and you know why? To try to hide the immigrant cooking smells, but like covering up shit with sugar, some things a man can't hide! Christ, no wonder the kid's a mess. Envy eating him up. Just like it's eating you, Kevin.

"Why," he continued, "why don't you go up there and schmooze with him. He's just asking for it and although he's not my type, I wouldn't mind watching the two of you, you know?"

"Fuck *you*."

"No honestly Kevin!"

I'm a friend of Philip's, I told the woman who came to the door. Bits of vegetables clung to her damp pale forearms, I guess vegetables just kind of cling to one. Face to face we stood there for a long moment, before she recollected herself.

"I'm his ma," she explained. "Fixing dinner." In the humid air, just as my friend had foretold, hung garlic and cabbage, and another odor, too, tangy and bitter. Herring perhaps. Goldie Mandel seemed overwhelmed by my car, a 68 Mustang with nothing to live for. As I came into the house, I had the chance to study her further, a chance I welcomed, since my policy was "Know the opposition." In profile her face seemed doughy, irregular, in that her chin was slung back under her jaw like a bridle, and her rough, orange-tinged skin had some of the hard sheen of a ripening pumpkin, but her sharp velvety eyes missed nothing: she should have been a reconnaissance gunner instead of a mother. "Phil's taking a nap. I see to it he gets his rest."

So saying, she ushered me into a parlor which shared some of the traits of the waiting room of a doctor's office: low ceiling, subdued lighting, three or four glossy, but out-of-date magazines spread across a black, square table in front of two straightback chairs — Frank Gehry kind of chairs. "Philly works good and hard you know."

I remembered his languid impassivity at the museum office and marvelled once again at how easily the young seem to be able to deceive their parents. "Indeed he does," I hastened to agree.

Soothed, Mrs. M. favored me with a slight smile. "Sit, Mister? I fetch the boy."

"Thank you," I said, and busied myself with an old copy of "Modern Romance." *I Gave Myself to my Doctor,* I read. *I Needed "Crack" to Keep my Husband Free from Pain.*

"Mother, please, you *know* about my beauty sleep."

Philip's mother, her marrowlike face flushed with excitement, burst into his bedroom breathing hard. Her hands poked into his side under the blanket. Shaking him, she took inventory of the dark room. What had to be straightened up before I could be allowed to see it? She didn't want me to think she kept a sloppy house — that would never do. While Philip rose from his dreams, she began systematically to pick up the clothes that lay strewn across the bookcases and the armchair, meanwhile humming a popular song.

"Sit down to dinner, it's hot and ready. Look, Phil, look at the flowers your friend bought for me."

"They're beautiful," Philip allowed.

"My mother always told me, don't come to visit with empty arms."

"That's a Hungarian expression, was your mother a woman of Hungary?"

"No," I said. "She was an Irish colleen."

"Like Maureen O'Hara," said Mrs. Mandel.

"Or Sinead O'Connor," I said. Dinner was tasty as anything you'd ever eaten at the UN Embassy or somewhere. Who knows what it was, some kind of Eastern European airlift vine mush —

I'm not too good with food if it isn't what I'm used to. People laugh at me for drinking Tab, that's okay, at first I started doing it for an affectation, because it was a girl type drink.

Over and over again these affectations and not much sense of a real personality underneath them.

Well anyway — Philip's mom kept shaking her head with happiness watching me eat and I got a queer kind of loser feeling in my stomach. For I'm just this phony nut boy and you'd think she was serving the Duchess of Windsor. I wanted to be noticed, I think; to feel *different* somehow, so I did a lot of stupid things, I remember in graduate school all us grad students had these offices in the English Department and the other students put up posters in theirs, oh, these dull things, D H Lawrence or Virginia Woolf, and I had my posters of Farrah and Raquel Welch, and this one guy comes into my office and says, "God, how jejune!" After dinner I remark on how dark it's getting outside. "Can I stay over?" I asked Philip, all bright-eyed and bushy-tailed, this phony garbage.

"Sure, if you want. It's no palace, but — sure."

Goldie Mandel dried her hands on her apron and joined in the fun of digging out the old cot from the basement storage room. The cot they used when relatives came to visit. Must have been rats in it all summer though. No, this is no good. The three of us stared sadly at the discolored chewed cot like relatives at a funeral.

"You'll have to sleep in Phil's bed," she said. "Philly can sleep with me."

"I don't mind sharing," I said demurely. "Philip and I can sleep together."

"Goodnight, Philly, good night, Mr. Killian, thanks ever so for the mums."

"They're not mums," Phil said.

"Listen to Mr. Luther Burbank with his wide flower experience," I heard her snort in the darkness.

"Do you *have* wide flower experience?" I asked him, and when I saw him blush I knew he was thinking of me.

In bed he was careful to turn away as I stripped to the skin. "There's some extra pajamas," he ventured, "in the dresser."

"I want to be your friend," I said, ingenuous as a china doll. Naked I approached the bed and stood beside it, my elbows close in to my sides, my hands outstretched. "There's this gap between us I want to close over. That's why I came. Hey, this looks plenty big enough for two," I added, lifting myself by the cock into the bed. "Shove over, Philip, don't be a hog."

How old were you when this happened?

Oh real young, like twenty something, or yes. Philip was older than I, but he seemed like a boy to me. His long smooth body like a field of new snow, in his immaculate blue pajamas, striped with thin lines of black, buttoned up to the very top of the neck. "Aren't you warm in those?" I asked.

"Why are you here?" he kept asking me, just like an ignorant tourist or something. "You and all the rest of you treat me like dirt under your feet."

"I want to make it up to you," I told him, honestly. Then I lied, "You and me just got off on the wrong foot, that's all."

"What do you mean, wrong foot? What are you implying?" Like I wasn't supposed to know he was queer as Cole Porter.

"Listen!" I cried out. I shoved my pillow and face near to his, and lowered my lashes. Demure. Oh, I thought of this story about what I'm afraid of, I mean besides AIDS, and also being homeless and so forth. But Dodie and I went to lunch or something with Leslie Dick and Peter Wollen and for some reason, maybe a dog passed by, and he said he's afraid of large dogs, ever since he was a child in his native country, which I'm pretty sure is England. Then it turned out that Leslie is afraid of rats. I forget why, it was something about she had a rat in her cradle or something. But anyway she was working at Cal Arts, and had to inspect the art projects of the students, and this one girl disliked her and she had to go into this girl's room, this big warehouse type dorm like a cave, and this girl had put all kinds of wood up to make a fort, and vegetation, I mean like barrels of rotting food in this awful warren of spores and —

And rats.

It was like this installation like Joseph fucking Beuys she was making, this awful girl. And this was at night, too. In what little light there was she wore this malicious grin — it was as though she somehow knew ahead of time that Leslie hated rats. Well anyway there I was and I was saying to Philip, "I — feel funny saying this, but — ever since we met I've been fighting this strange attraction, to you, Philip. . . No, wait, don't get up, I just have to get this out of my system," and I told him of all the lonely nights I fought my strange attraction to him, and how I went to analysts for help, but how it was just too strong to deny any longer, and believe me, Phil was lapping this up. His eyes widened, narrowed, did every trick thing under the sun. His breath grew short, then he made himself hold still. "You'll think I'm crazy but hell, so do I, I just had to let you know, I don't know why."

"I don't know what to say," he brought forth finally.

"I know. I'm a pervert."

"No, it's not that. I understand."

"You do?"

His dark eyes closed and opened again. "I have some of the same — feelings, I guess," he told me. Gosh, scoop of the fucking century, but I put surprise and joy all over my face and gulped at him. Then I waited, then I whispered.

"You want to do anything? Philip? I'm right here." So saying, I reached out in the dark and put my hand to his smooth face, feeling the blush in his cheek, in the dark, unable to see his expression except for the fright in his tired, confused eyes. Something within me weakened my resolve, a variation on the feeling you get watching **60 Minutes** show Canadian trappers crushing minks in steel traps. "Relax now, this won't hurt a bit, and Philip? No one will know."

"Kevin," he said slowly, in little chunks, so I could barely make out my own name. Under my hand his mouth moved, jittery, alive.

"Don't worry," I told him, as though he'd been in a terrible car crash and help was on its way. "No one will ever know. Kiss me," I said. "I want you to, it's okay."

His whole head was shaking on the embroidered pillowcase, as he faced me. I slid closer to his body, and waited until he got his breath. I continued to probe his face, his ear, his nose, his moving mouth that trembled but made no sound. In the night a succulent tenderness dislodged itself from my brain to take an eerie shape between us, like a third person we had both loved very much. But there was no such person, as far as I knew. Philip finally spoke. But only to say he couldn't breathe. "I used to have asthma," he said, downcast. "As a *child*. Maybe it's coming back."

"I don't think so. You're just surprised."

"No, seriously, I can't swallow." He pointed to his throat and his nose with the exaggerated fright of Harpo Marx, a dumbshow to convince me.

"I won't make you swallow," I promised, and I lowered my hand to find the hole in the front of his pajamas, and I found it, while Philip protested his asthma, in weak lost syllables. I clutched part of his dick in my hand, felt it warm and hard, its slick surface dry and smooth, like slate warmed in the sun. Gave him a squeeze, he liked it. He tried to say no, with his voice, and my finger slid down the length of his cock to his balls, poking them a bit as if to say, anyone home, and out of nowhere Philip stopped demurring and laughed a laugh of pure pleasure, his head thrown back and his mouth open to the big world.

"Quiet, now, you'll wake your mother."

"I can't fucking believe this," Philip yelled, a little less loudly. He seized my head and made me face him, and face to face we cracked up, in the blackness of the night his face was alight with joy. In a minute I had him naked and adoring below me as I pressed his shoulders down with my weight, his mouth smiling into the mattress, I tugged on his ears and brought his neck and head up high, riding his back like a jockey, his thin strong waist my saddle. "Now you'll get that wide flower experience." His pajamas lay crumpled on the rug like a blue and black candy wrapper after a fair.

And then careful to face him, I lowered myself onto Philip's face, felt him suck all the rich juices out, while his hands crept up along my legs like cunning cloths. I saw the whites of his eyes gleam in the dark, his head thrown back in excitement, his lips wrapped around the shaft of my cock. I guess I was trying to give him something back . . . He swallowed me up, I felt the walls of the room come in close for a minute like anxious spectators — then they retreated to their proper place, made corners again, yanking the books and furniture back to themselves, realigned.

In the morning when I awoke he was awake already. Biting his nails and so forth. He was very nervous. I wasn't really thinking about him that much, no, just more about my friend and what next. You know, we were kids. Thom Gunn told me — you know I'm writing this book with Lew, this book about Jack Spicer's life — anyway Duncan and Spicer and all these gay Berkeley guys were living in this one house, and somehow so was Philip K. Dick. And Thom Gunn once asked Duncan what it was like to be a roommate of Philip K. Dick. And one night

Duncan thought he was all alone, reading and writing in his room, and he looked up and there in the open doorway Philip K. Dick is just standing there you know, jerking off, or getting ready to come. And he made this one, you know, motion of his hips, like Nijinsky in *The Spectre of the Rose*, and came onto the floor, and Duncan was too astonished to say a word. And Philip K. Dick just turned around and went back to his room and they never talked about it, or nothing.

But why did he do that?

I don't know — Duncan said, years later, that it was just the pressure cooker atmosphere, this steam heat . . .

So Philip was biting his nails — my Philip, nervous, you know. "Everything's going good," I said, stroking the soft length of his prick. Skittish at first, Philip began smiling halfway through, like a kid at the circus. In daylight his skin shone as though the sun was trapped into it. "Yeah everything's working," I said. "But the thing is, I have this friend and I was wondering, could he come over sometime — he's real nice." Now here's where I want you to be my powerful friend.

Okay.

At his look instantly I realized I'd outsmarted myself. In a violent motion, as if stung by bees, Philip slid his hips further down the mattress. "What *friend*?"

"Just this guy."

"What his name?"

"He's sharp, real sharp."

"Real sharp, eh? Name wouldn't happen to be George Dorset, would it, Kevin?"

"Yeah, so what about it? Do you want to?"

"Is that why you came here? To be his pimp?"

Philip vaulted up out of bed, pulled the bedspread round his waist. He wouldn't look at me. "The fabulous George Dorset who gets under everyone's skin like *cocaine*!"

I wondered if his mother had knitted the spread, large splashy patches of green, blue, orange and zebra, like a Mondrian crossed with a traffic signal. "Your mother knit that quilt, Phil?"

Furiously he struggled into a pair of pants, under the blanket, with the usual success.

"Is she *Amish*?" I persisted. "They do wonderful work down in Pennsylvania Dutch country."

I arose from the bed and, made an invisible camera with my hands and thumbs, held it to my eyes, and pressed the invisible shutter. Phil flinched and held the blanket tighter, cowering by his closet door. I took the blanket and whipped it off his waist, and brought my mouth close to his ear so I could whisper, "You're *still* hard, Philly boy. Look at it, wriggling like an animal. Don't hide it with your hands, look for a change!"

He was weakening, well, who wouldn't? I didn't hold it against him. My hand tightened around his balls, pleasurably, so he couldn't help but gasp a little, in a goony way that recalled the heroines of my favorite romance comic books. I traced the line of his lips with one finger, hushing him. Then I traced a circle around his nipple, my arm over his shoulder, and circled again, tighter and closer, feeling him relax against my hip, backing into me weakly, as though overpowered by a super-serum or chloroform. I pinched the nipple between two knuckles and bit the side of his taut neck, till he caved in completely, fallen apart, his hard-on a tool for operating like the gearshift of a car I could swerve in and out of first and second. "My boy," I said to him.

So I got on the phone. "George? This is Kevin. Guess where I am."

I don't know where you are, how should I know, am I supposed to be like Kreskin to you, where are you, at home?

"No, I'm at the Mandel residence. Philip's here too. His mother's out at the market."

And where is Philip, tell me Kevin.

"Phil? He's down on the floor, sucking my cock. Want to watch?"

Uh-huh, uh-huh.

"My big hairy red hard dick."

Yes, Kevin, yes, Kevin.

"Want to watch?"

THE ONLY LIVING BOY IN NEW YORK

by
Ameena Meer

Adam is in an Indian restaurant in Queens, little red plastic tables with yellow tumeric stains on them, Styrofoam bowls of dal and chicken curry, slippery with orange oil.

Adam's fingers tear a chapati and dip it into the dal. He gulps it down, the smoothness of the dal mixing with the wheaty taste of the chapati. He eats some chicken, carefully licking all the masala from his fingers, almost tasting each spice alone, the sweet cinnamon and cardamom, the bitter cumin and coriander, the sting of the chilies. The smell makes him so homesick his eyes start watering. He thinks of his grandmother's chicken curry.

"Food all right, sir? Not too spicy?"

Adam swallows. The chicken is so sweet. He looks up at the waiter. "It's perfect," he says.

The waiter looks worried. "You want some yogurt, sir? To make it less spicy. Some raita. That is yogurt with cucumber in it. You know, cucumber."

"No, thank you," says Adam, smiling. "I know what raita is."

"Oh yes, a lot of Europeans eat Indian food now. It's very popular in England as well. Yes, I can see you know how to eat like an Indian," leaning on the table now, he hangs the wet cloth over the back of the chair. "Me, I like American food. I never eat here. I eat at McDonalds or Kentucky Chicken. It's so funny, isn't it? Indians like American food and Americans like Indian food."

Adam laughs, "What's even funnier is that I'm Indian."

The waiter's face is incredulous. "You're Indian? How can it be? You look English." He scratches the baby hairs sprouting on his chin. "You are from where in India?"

"From Bombay."

"Oh, Bombay. Even I have an uncle who is living in Bombay. Bombay is a very exciting place. Like New York. Me, I come from Julunder. Do you know where that is? It's Punjab."

"No," says Adam, taking a bite. "No," he says through the dal, "I've never been there." He swallows and stuffs more chicken into his mouth. "Actually, I've been away from India for some time," he wipes the grease from his lips and gulps his Coke.

The waiter sits down in the chair. "Good food," he nods approvingly. "I also like chicken. What is your name please?"

"Adam." He doesn't want to look up again from his food. The waiter smells of old sweat. His face is brown and spotted with red pimples. He pushes his stained sleeves up to his elbows and taps his dirty fingernails on the laminate.

"I am Talvinder — but everyone calls me Tom. You can call me Tom. It's easier to say for Americans." He holds out his hand for Adam to shake.

"Mm," protests Adam, trying to keep as much of the food in his mouth as he can. "My hands are dirty. I don't want to get chicken curry all over you. But it's nice to meet you. As soon as I finish I'll wash my hands."

"No, no problem," laughs Talvinder. "You are eating. Eat. You want some tea also?"

"Yes, thanks, I'd love some. It's the perfect way to end this. The food, I mean."

"Yes, first, you finish your food," Talvinder nods. "Where do you stay in New York? You have some relatives here?"

"No, I'm staying with a friend in the East Village. I have an uncle in America and his daughter, my cousin, her name is Sabah, comes to New York quite often, but I don't know where she is."

"Is she Indian? Then she must come to Jackson Heights. But why are you staying in Greenwich Village? It's very dangerous. There are all the strange people walking around there and taking drugs and all that." Talvinder looks concerned, then his face widens in a grin. "But you're there for the girls, aren't you? That's a good place for girls. They're all over there, the fast ones, wearing short frocks and all."

"It's actually the other side of Greenwich Village. There are all these Indian restaurants near there. On East Sixth Street."

"What? Those? Those restaurants are all owned by Bengalis. That food is terrible. Horrible. They should stay at home and eat the fish heads their wives make for them. You should only eat here in Jackson Heights. Only here. You just bring those girls with you. That's the way to catch them. This is the best Indian restaurant in New York. Really. Just read that newspaper there, the **New York Times**, that is an article all about this restaurant, just written last year."

"I promise I'll read it before I go," says Adam, taking the last bites of his food. "Could I have some tea?"

"Tea? Of course." Talvinder looks around the restaurant to make sure no one is in earshot. He leans forward. "Listen," he whispers, "you know a lot of American girls? I know some here, in Queens. They're not like our girls, yaar. They completely crazy — *puglee* — you know. You come out with me and you'll meet some wild girls. Really wild. And they'll love you. I promise you. *Masala chai*." He gives Adam a quick pat on the shoulder and gets up to bring the tea.

Adam sighs and piles all the little Styrofoam cups into a little tower. He swings and slaps it with his hand. It topples down, orange oil splattering all over the tray, globs of yellow dal flying out, dripping down the sides of the cups and soaking into the paper napkins.

Talvinder plops a cup of thick milky tea on the tray.

"Thank you." Adam lifts the cup slowly to his mouth, inhaling the smell of cardamom. "Ow!" He jerks the cup back, splashing tea on his shirt and jeans, and squirming in his chair as the boiling liquid burns his skin. The tea is searing. His tongue is numb.

"Too hot, yaar," laughs Talvinder. "Hot, hot tea. Don't worry, I'll give you a shirt to wear tonight. I'm finished with work at seven o'clock. Then you come by my house. It's just here. Ok? No problem." He winks at Adam and picks up the tray. Adam watches Talvinder walk away, his eyes watering and his tongue still smarting. He touches his tongue with his fingers. It feels like it's covered with stinging sores. He sticks his tongue out farther, like an eel curling out of his mouth. He thinks about his tongue tracing the ridges of Marc's ears or moving around the corners of Marc's pink lips like a paintbrush on a piece of porcelain. His tongue burns.

"New York is great, really great," laughs Talvinder. "Here I am working in a restaurant and I meet the son of a movie star! It's great. You like this music? The best radio station in New York — hey, hold on — red light!" The car screeches to a stop, Adam flies forward, the seat belt slapping his chest, and then falls back, hard, into the seat, the springs creaking and poking into his legs. "Sorry, Adam, sorry. There's too many policemen in New York, you know?" Talvinder rolls down his window and turns up the radio. He puts his arm out the window and thumps the side of the car in time to the music. "My house is just here. Everyone will love to meet you." He pulls into the driveway of a split-level brick house. "Come on!" He jumps out of the car and runs up the cement steps three at a time.

A young girl opens the front door. She looks hopefully at them. "Hi Talvinder bhai, will you take me to a movie tonight?" She's wearing a pair of skintight stretch jeans and a t-shirt, a long black braid hanging down her thin back. Adam compares her pointy face to Alia's soft one.

"Sorry, Chotu, I have my friend Adam here. Adam, this is Chotu, my niece. She's real American, aren't you, Chotu? Chotu, who is Jimmy Al-Hussain?"

"I don't care," snaps the girl, crossing her scrawny brown arms over her chest. "Some Indian nobody." She flounces up the stairs.

"Hey," Talvinder shouts after her. "Get me something to drink."

Adam follows Talvinder down the green carpeted stairs. He can hear the sound of a Hindi filmtrack, a dance number. A girl is giggling and a man is singing *Que Sera, Sera* in Hindi. Suddenly, Adam hears a whole chorus of off-key voices. "*Jubh meh choti larkhi thee*... when I was just a little girl..." Talvinder walks into the darkness.

The television flashes colored lights around the room. Adam can make out people sitting on sofas along both walls, their faces alternately red, green and orange. "Sit, sit," says Talvinder, handing Adam the glass of brown liquid his niece brought and pointing at a crowded sofa. Adam takes a step into the room, tripping over something and half-falling onto a body on the floor. "Watch out! Behave yourself," says Talvinder as the small body lunges for Adam's leg, teeth flashing. Talvinder gives the head a cuff, sending the child rolling into the others who begin shouting. "Stop it! Leave me!" Adam realizes that there are three or four children on the floor.

"*Chup*! Quiet!" warns a woman from one of the sofas. Adam leans against the door frame. "*Vilayet-ke-bacche*!" she growls. "Go and do your homework!" The children are instantly silent.

"I'll be right back," reassures Talvinder. "This is my family."

"Oh," says Adam, "they're very nice." He holds the glass in his hand, trying to guess what it is. He thinks it's Coke. The whole room smells of cold rice and dal and cumin and harsh drugstore perfume. With the curtains drawn and the door shut, the battling scents make Adam's eyes water. He leans against the door frame, trying to get fresh air from the hallway. He thinks of Marc's parents and their clean, drafty house in Paris.

"Talvinder!" shouts the woman as Talvinder leaves. "Oh Talvinder! You don't even see your mother anymore? Come here! Where are you going?" She sighs and the person beside her pats her on the back. "What a son I have." She notices Adam in the doorway. "Come here, *behta*. You are Talvinder's friend? Come, come," she gestures for Adam to approach. "What a nice boy," she reaches out and grabs Adam's face as he steps over a child, squeezing his cheeks as he loses his balance. "Good boy. You are American?"

"No," mumbles Adam through his mangled mouth. "Fren... Indian."

"Indian?" She is incredulous.

"Indian?" says the woman sitting next to her. "No, never."

"What is your good name?" asks Talvinder's mother. "Where are your parents?"

"He looks *ex-dum* foreign," says a man on the sofa, putting his running shoes up on the table and crossing his legs. "Are you Kashmiri?"

"Adam," says Adam. "I just met Talvinder tonight, at the restaurant. I'm from Bombay, but I live in Paris. I haven't..."

"Oh-ho," laughs the man, "*Bumbai-wallah*! Are you a film star?"

"He's so white, he must be an actor," says another voice.

Adam can make out three Indian men in salwar kameezes and sweatshirts lolling on one of the sofas. "Hey, Sandy!" one laughs.

"I haven't been in Bombay in a long time."

"Oh, you live in New York?"

"What is your family name?"

"Al-Hussain. No, I live in France."

"You are a Muslim?"

"Yes."

"We also have some Muslim friends," says Talvinder's mother. "They live just here," she waves her hand off into the darkness. "They're from Up, their name is Bothelwallah. Do you know them?"

"No, sorry. But I haven't been here very long."

"Muslims make the best halwah," she says. "Do you like halwah?"

"Yes, yes," adds the other woman, "remember they sent some halwah last month? It was so lovely. They're very nice. It must have been Eid. Was it Eid?"

"Muslim? Muslim?" says a quivering voice. Adam makes out a withered old woman on the edge of the sofa. As the idea sinks in, she starts coughing violently, her tiny body shaking beneath the swaths of white cloth. "Do you know what the Muslims did to us during partition?" she shrieks. "Get out! Get out!"

"Shh, shh, *Bari-ma*," soothes Talvinder's mother. "That was not all Muslims... this is Talvinder's friend. He's very nice."

"You know, not all Muslims are dirty, like in India," reassures one of the men. "In America, they are very good. Just like us. At Quaker Oats, at the factory, I work with a lot of Muslims. I am forklift operator."

"They burned down our house in Lahore! Burned it down, everything was burned! I had nothing when I got on the train. Nothing! Get out!"

"But in Punjab, the Muslims are so bad," explains another man, shaking his head. "So dirty and they are stealing and doing all bad things, not like in America. In America, Sikh, Hindu, Muslim, we're all the same. My job also, I make pizza, and we are all ***bhai-bhai***." He leans over and slaps Adam's arm.

"You stole everything! Everything my mother gave me! Get out!" shrieks the old woman. "Go!"

Talvinder walks back in and grabs Adam's arm. He starts shouting in Punjabi. "You don't have any *izzat*? This is my friend! His father is Jimmy! And look how you treat him! Come on, Adam," he says, in English. He takes the glass of Coke and puts it in the young girl's hand. "Let's go."

"Jimmy? The film star?"

"Get out!"

Adam hears the glass smash as he walks up the stairs.

MASON'S ISLAND

by
Niels Nielsen

In these wind conditions, Richard thought, a good sailor should be able to get out of the cove in three tacks. He took his first tack on the line that ran between the dock and the flagpole outside the old admiral's cottage. The flag, a white naval ensign with a red cross, floated lightly on the early afternoon breeze. Richard waited until he heard the reeds brushing the keel of the boat before pushing the tiller to leeward and releasing the jib sheet. Not too bad, he thought, as the boat smoothly turned onto her new course. Now he picked up speed running on his second tack between the flagpole and the remains of the ruined logging bridge. Another quick push of the tiller and he faced the open bay with only the guardian rock between him and deep water. The boat ran for the opening of the narrow cove and Richard suddenly knew that it would be a very near thing whether he'd make the open water or hit the rock. The boat charged toward the rock and Richard was caught in a moment of indecision: the moment stretched into two and suddenly the decision was taken from him. The marker buoy, a plastic bleach jug on a yellow line, sped toward him and thumped the hull; Richard glimpsed the rock for a second and then the boat surged untouched into deeper waters.

These trips had begun five years before when he had started going off alone once each year for a week at a time. His first trip had been a camping trip into the woods, but he hadn't really liked being in the woods all that much — too many bugs and too many people. The islands idea had been a substitute for the woods, one where the insects were minimized and where people could be met on his own terms. After all, when sailing on the sea or camping on an island, one could see a person coming for a long distance. With a quick change of course, or a short walk to the other side of the island, intruders could be easily avoided. As the years had passed, Richard had grown to think of the solitary trips as a way to cleanse and rejuvenate himself after a year's contact with the modern world. Some people went to a resort, some went on car trips, and Richard went alone to Mahone Bay.

The bow wave made a gurgling ripple as the boat swam through the sparkling waves. Houses and cottages were everywhere on the shore, some worth millions of dollars and some looking as if they were worth only hundreds. To the Northeast a passage opened up and led to the town of Chester, while behind him the southwest passage wound past Indian Point to the summer tourist town of Mahone Bay. Neither town was visible as the indented land hid both. Looking forward Richard could see down one of the main passages through the islands to the outer bay and the open ocean beyond.

A minor shift of the tiller pointed the bow of the boat towards the passage between the islands. Its name was Ernst Gut and Richard had often wondered where the name had come from. He knew most of the earliest settlers to the area had been German, so it seemed likely that one named Ernst had frequently used the narrow passageway to either go fishing or pursue some other commercial pursuit. Regardless of the logical explanation, the name still seemed whimsical to say the least. The Germans from that earlier time were still here, and recently a new wave of German citizens had come to join them. There was a difference, however, as the early immigrants had come to stay, while the new ones were only summer visitors who had bought land because the price was almost as attractive as the scenery. The island Richard was going to today was called Mason's Island and was owned by one of the summer visitors; by all accounts he was a man who regarded visitors to the island with suspicion. He did not welcome visitors, although he could not forbid them access to the beach as the law gave ownership of the land only to the extreme high tide mark (an uncertain boundary). Much of his vacation time on Mason's Island was spent shooting at skeet targets with a shotgun. The roar of his gun as he fired at the flying targets was sufficiently unnerving that most people avoided the island when he was in residence.

But Richard knew he would not be on the island this night. Each year he came for the month of July and returned to Germany in the last week of the month. Richard had spoken to a friend who had sailed past Mason's Island on Friday last and had seen the boats gone from the dock, no German flag flying from the mast, and the windows shuttered. The island was left behind, a dream, to the gulls and the beach goers — both would return without the booming of the shotgun to disturb them.

Islands covered the bay in all directions as far as one could see; islands covered in fir trees, bald islands with only grass on them, and the occasional island with a long deserted farm crumbling into the earth. The water lay shallow in its basin with large rocks reaching upwards towards the surface in many places. The chains of islands were the predominant feature of this body of water and they contained hundreds of islands. The locals claimed 365 islands, one for every day of the year including Christmas — and Halloween. From his knowledge of local history, Richard suspected more than one could lay claim to that grim date of the calendar. It was that connection that attracted him to Mason's Island.

He had explained it to his friends Jon and Anna earlier in the summer when they had met in the Trident Café. Jon was in his early thirties but his curly brown hair and cheerful disposition made him seem younger. His buoyant personality contrasted with Anna's quieter, often more serious mood. Slim with high cheekbones and large eyes, Anna was attractive and spoke intelligently. She often seemed reserved in nature, but once you knew how to read her the message was 'clear — but not en clair' as Richard thought. Open, but only to those with the key. The three of them sat at the back of the café, in the section where the wallpaper was hunter green and the chairs were of mahogany. Richard sat where he could see the front of the café, and the afternoon sun was reflected in a dazzling glare off the storefronts on the opposite side of the street through the café's windows.

"So what is the point of going there for a whole week by yourself?" Jon asked.

Richard didn't answer right away but looked towards the door as he considered what to say. The bell on the door tinkled as a woman shepherded a little girl out into the bright street. They paused, silhouetted in the doorway, and Richard saw the resemblance to his former wife. For a moment he felt the familiar pain and then they walked away. He brought his attention back to Jon.

"There doesn't have to be a point, you know," Richard replied. "The trips just give me something I need. After all, you know what I'm like. The year after I broke up with Cathy (Anna nodded, having known Richard's former wife) I just wanted to get away from people. However, after that, after I began to go to Mahone Bay, I became more interested in the social and folk history of the islands. When I began to do research on them the richness of the material impressed me and I found some very interesting things."

Anna paused after lighting up a cigarette, held it in her hand in one of her characteristic poses, and asked, "Such as?"

"Well, recently I've become more interested in the ghost stories from the bay. They seem to reflect not only the history of the area but also the culture of the people who tell them."

"You're starting to talk like a professor now." Anna leaned forward and smiled while teasing Richard.

"Yes, you're right. Sorry. I guess, what I really mean to say is, when I first began this, the stories gave me something to focus on, a purpose to my trips. Now I'm interested in the stories themselves. For me they've become more than just stories or history because I see the similarities to things that happen today." Richard, reluctant to talk at first about this topic, began to warm to it. "One of the really hot issues in North America today is native peoples. In the 1740's and 50's when the English began to settle the area around Mahone Bay, the local natives, the Micmacs, didn't take too kindly to the newcomers. The issues were the same then as they are today — who could use the land and for what."

"It was a little more sinister than that wasn't it?" Jon asked.

"Much more sinister, actually. When the English founded Halifax, they tried to enter into a treaty with the Micmacs. The Micmac response was to perform the war dance at the negotiations with the English and, for several years afterward, a state of war existed between the two. It was ugly on both sides while it lasted, and the Micmacs eventually gave in to greater pressure, but not before some bloody fights took place. Events in Mahone Bay were particularly cruel because the settlers there were largely Germans who were either retired solders or hunters. It must have been vicious because some of the islands seem to be still populated by the ghosts of both sides."

"It sounds more like Bosnia last week than Mahone Bay two hundred and fifty years ago," Anna said.

"I agree," said Richard, "but it is easy to see the similarities. A surprise raid on an outlying farm, a dead child, and the local settlers took matters into their own hands. I know of two occasions when groups of Micmacs including women and children were massacred."

"So tell me how ghosts are made," Anna said. She stubbed her cigarette out in the ashtray and picked up her coffee cup to take a drink. Richard noticed that unlike Jon and himself, Anna rarely touched her cup if she was not drinking from it. Both of the men had played with their cups or spoons intermittently since they had sat down.

"I think ghosts are made in moments of great emotion. I'm not sure if duration of the emotion is a factor or not, but it seems to me that all the stories lay great stress on the intensity of the emotion surrounding the making of a ghost. The reason I'm not sure about duration is that there are stories about the ghosts of insane people who linger still in the attics where their families chained them."

"That was done in the nineteenth century, wasn't it?" Jon said, more a statement than a question.

"Well, yes," Richard replied, "and it must have led to some pretty intense emotions — to be chained and locked for ages in the attic while you could hear your family living normal lives on the floor below you. Yet there are stories of ghosts being made quickly — the woman murdered or the horseman beheaded. These people had only one brief, intense moment of terror before death. So it must be the intensity of the fear that creates a ghost," Richard concluded.

"Or a sense of betrayal," Jon added.

"I hadn't thought of that but it makes sense," Richard said. "You go to bed in domestic tranquillity and wake to fire and sword — the formula to make a ghost. Perhaps that's why ghosts are considered to be 'scary.' When they return, they bring that fear or sense of betrayal with them."

"So where do you plan to go this year?" Anna asked.

"This winter in the archives I found two sites which have ghost stories attached to them. The first is Sacrifice Island, said to be haunted by the ghost of a fair haired girl killed by the Micmacs. I rejected Sacrifice Island as the ghost only appears in the fall, which seems to be her anniversary."

"So where did you choose?" Anna asked.

"One of the larger islands in the center of the bay has a reputation as being haunted," Richard said. "The island is not much more than a hump of red earth left behind by the last glacier in this region. A geologist would call it a drumlin. It's a low lying island with two small hills, neither higher than seventy feet. Best of all, the island is shaped somewhat like a question mark, with the top of the mark to the north and the bottom due south."

"It sounds as if you've been there before," Anna said.

"Yes, three years ago I camped on it because it has a nice beach to swim from. I set my tent on the beach and had an eerie experience in the middle of the night when some sea birds, gulls or cormorants, I'm not sure which, flew up, crying, from their nests and came to the beach where they circled several times before flying off. In the morning I went to the point where they had their nests, but, until I did, I would have sworn that the cries I heard came from dead souls."

"That couldn't be the source of the ghost story could it?" Jon asked.

"I don't think so," Richard replied. "The haunting itself is described as a large fire suddenly flaring in the night, accompanied by screaming and loud shouts. Some people have heard guns being fired repeatedly. No one really knows how many died there, but estimates range from eight to fifteen, and what is worse, the number of children killed was anywhere from four to six."

Anna frowned and concern showed on her face. "Is this safe for you, Richard?"

"Of course," he said. "We're talking about ghosts, after all, and I believe that if something can harm me, I can harm it also." But even as he spoke, he knew he had not addressed her concerns and she had not been fooled by the answer.

Jon diverted her attention by asking, "So when is the trip this year?"

"The anniversary is August second, once the correction is made for the changing of the calendar in the eighteenth century, so that fits in quite well with my schedule. I think it's important to go to these sites on the anniversary of the event. Some writers envision the haunting as a sort of tearing of the cloth between their reality and ours, and I think this tearing happens more easily on the anniversary date," Richard replied.

"Well I hope you have fine weather for it," Jon said. "Although, if what you say is true, then we certainly haven't learned much in the last two hundred and fifty years. It's nearly the Millennium and we still have these types of massacres. If what you say is true we should have a world of ghosts, ghosts in Somalia, ghosts in Bosnia, ghosts everywhere! What's the name of your haunted island, by the way?"

"Mason's Island."

Mason's Island. There on the starboard bow he could just see its northerly tip in the distance. As he sailed toward the island he reflected on the café conversation because Jon's comments about the Millennium had touched a chord in Richard. When he was little he used to ask his mother how old he would be when the year 2000 came. "Forty-five," she answered, "and I'll be old then too." He knew now that forty-five wasn't old and that she had been gently teasing, but the turn of the century had always marked a boundary to him.

Anna's concern had not been for his physical safety. When he had been married to Cathy, she had lost a baby late in her first pregnancy. Richard had not responded well, becoming very depressed and unable to speak to anyone, least of all Cathy, about the situation. Eventually they had drifted apart and she had moved in with Ian, a man she had met soon after leaving Richard. Richard remembered going to their apartment to give Cathy some ornaments she had forgotten in their home. "Why, thank you, Dick," she said, knowing how much he hated the name and taking her chance to be cruel. As she turned and slowly walked away from him, a rage had gone through him for the first time in his life, and he had wanted to hit her, drive her forward to the floor and hurt her. He saw the look of alarm on Ian's face and then the hate left him as quickly as it had come.

Whatever he had believed he would be doing in the future, his plans had died when he and Cathy had parted, and he had not replaced them. The end of his marriage seemed to have been a turning point for Richard's life; one where the focus of his life was lost. The more he thought about it, the more it seemed likely that the new millennium would bring not the Antichrist, not revelation, but only more of the same uncertainty.

The boat slid into the outer bay with Bella Island on the left and Zwicker Island on the right. Ahead, Mason's Island was in sight from one end to the other. On three sides the island was surrounded by beaches of fine white sand. In the South, the side he couldn't see, the face of the hill fell into the bay in a cliff of red earth that was marked on charts for mariners as 'Conspic Red Bank.' Conspicuous red bank — a fine landmark for a dull day when being driven by poor weather for shelter in Mahone Bay. Fifteen minutes hard sailing and he would be there. Beyond the island the clouds were building in the East, and Richard knew the land wind would be growing in force under the clouds. He stared hard to his right, looking for a flag on the German's flagpole or any other signs of occupancy. No flag, no boats, and no sign of people on the island at all. With that concern gone, Richard set course for the north side of the island, the head of the question mark. As he approached the beach he began to look for a good place to land. Perhaps it would be more accurate to say he looked for the bad places not to land because the entire north end was a white sand beach with few rocks. On the shore, the wreck of a lobster fishing boat lay half covered by sand. It was the custom in the bay to take worn out boats to the islands, strip them of valuable equipment and then beach them.

He aimed his boat at the shoreline below the wreck and, twenty feet from the land, raised the centerboard and released the jib. He coasted into the beach and ground to a halt on the sand. Richard jumped into the water and hauled the boat up the sandy beach until he could reach the bags in the cockpit without getting wet above the knee. Take care of the boat first, he thought, then take care of yourself. He furled and stored the sails in the boat. Then he removed the rudder and the centerboard. "That should ensure they don't get beaten to death in the waves if the sea gets up," he said to himself. He emptied the cockpit of his gear and put it on the beach away from the reach of the waves. Once done, he tied a line to the bow and took it to the engine of the wreck. The wreck had shifted from its motor and had come to rest above it, but the engine still remained close to the water. Richard tied the line to the engine and then pushed the boat into the water. Tied to the land it would not float away and yet, pushed from the land by the south-west wind, it would not drift ashore and cause itself damage by banging up against rocks. It would lie peacefully offshore, bobbing in the waves.

Once done with the boat he turned his attention to setting

up his camp. First he gathered some small sticks to start a fire. From his gear he took a newspaper and crumpled three pages into a ball. He used the sticks to make a teepee structure over the paper and then lit the paper. When the fire had caught in the sticks, he went to the wreck and found several boards that had come loose in the last year. These he placed on the fire knowing their age and the paint still on them would ensure they would burn. In a few moments he felt secure enough with the fire to add a much larger piece of wood.

Leaving the fire, he took the tent and his sleeping bag up to the top of the beach to where the island meadow met the beach. There was a natural hollow here where he would be sheltered from wind and sight. "I'd be a fool not to use it," he thought. As he set up the tent he wondered if this was where the massacre had taken place. It was, after all, a natural shelter, and once in it he had a feeling of security. The hollow was big enough to hold three or four tents without being crowded and a short walk brought a person inside the hollow to a place where three sides of the island could be easily seen. Quickly he put up his tent and then unrolled his sleeping bag inside. The last time he had come to the island, he had laid the sleeping bag on the grass outside the tent and, as night fell, the dew had condensed onto the bag. The discomfort of the wet bag had reinforced the lesson learned, as he had laid sleepless most of that night.

Finished with the tent, Richard turned to go back to the fire on the beach. He stopped at the top of the hollow and looked to his right where the gulls had begun to return to their nesting places on Mason's Point. To his left, the sun was setting in a glory of color. He went down the beach to the fire and began to prepare his supper, a prepackaged stew with bread. By the time the food was hot, the sun had set and the stars were bright in the sky. Sitting there, eating his stew, the notion of looking for ghosts seemed a more serious business than it had in the Trident Café. Off shore there was a splash, probably a fish jumping. What would he do if he found what he had come to find? he wondered. What would be the consequences for him if there was a tear in the cloth between two realities? As he sat in the firelight, Richard remembered the old saying that 'there are more tears shed for prayers that are answered than for prayers which are not.'

As the night grew cooler around him, he was glad for the warmth of the fire. The night grew stiller also, disturbed only by the rumble of a boat motor in the distance. When he became sleepy, Richard decided to take a quick walk around the campsite and then go to bed. He walked away from the fire without putting it out. No need to do that, he told himself. He always built his fire between the tide marks. The rising tide would put the fire out more thoroughly than he could. Even now, as he stood at the edge of the hollow and looked back at the beach, the waves touched the edge of the fire. It was only a matter of time before it was extinguished.

Between the tide marks — that area had been considered sacred for centuries. That was where the burnt sacrifice had been made to the gods in **Njal's Saga**, Richard thought, dragging the fact from his memory of a long ago university lecture about Viking literature. The sacrifice had been made between the tide marks because that area was sacred to no god and thus sacred to all. Twice a day the ocean cleansed the shore, and twice a day the water became land. That, at least, was one place to go from a persistent ghost should the cloth rip. As he lay in his tent he started to drowse and the last sound he heard was the mewing of the sea birds in their nesting area.

When Richard woke the tent was on fire above him — an orange tiger lily of a flame seen from below. He scrambled through the hole made by the fire and shed his sleeping bag like a moth sheds its cocoon. He noticed another tent on fire and a small group of ragged figures fleeing inland. As he watched, men came from the night and a volley of gun fire cut down two of the fleeing people. The men ran after their prey; there would be no escape towards the interior of the island. Two children and a woman remained behind. The woman turned to flee and a musket was raised and fired. The shot took her in the back and pitched her to the ground. The children were brutally clubbed with the end of a musket — no reason to waste ammunition on them — and silently fell. All was deathly quiet as the smell of gunpowder reached Richard. The man who had just shot the woman reversed his musket, took two steps, and drove the butt into Richard's jaw.

Pain exploded in his head and he tasted the blood welling up in his mouth. Staggering backwards, he saw from the corner of his eye another man, dressed better than the rest, run toward him with a sword outstretched in his hand. Richard turned and ran for the beach, and the only sanctuary he knew of — the area between the high and low tide marks. He stumbled as he ran, and falling, rolled onto his back. That misfooting gave his pursuer time to catch up with him. The sword flashed down and Richard felt it cut, burning, into his hand. For a moment he saw the swordsman clearly, standing over him. The gleam of metal buttons was matched by the gleam in the eyes, and in the swordsman's face was a hatred to outlast the centuries. Then the sword came free and recoiled for a second blow. Before it could fall, Richard rolled to his left and slipped down the bank to the beach. Bleeding from face and hand, he stumbled to the water with pursuit thudding close behind. Richard fell headfirst into the ocean and in his panic swallowed some sea water as his head went under the surface. He lurched to his feet and, choking with fear and water, faced the shore. Two additional figures had joined the swordsman but Richard knew that he was now untouchable to them. The night was quiet as Richard stood knee deep in the rising tide and faced the shadowy still figures on the beach. The waves surged past him, tugging at his legs and making his footing uncertain as he stood waiting for the coming of the dawn. As his blood fell into the tide foam, the sea birds rose in a sudden rush from the beach grass at Mason's Point. With eerie cries they flew to him, and after circling, they all went west towards an horizon only dimly perceived.

SOCORRO

by
Frederick Barthelme

Socorro was a ratty little town that dangled off the highway the way a broken leg hangs off a dog that's been hit by a car. It was mostly dirt, sand, red grass, and squat cactus peppered with little brown houses that might as well have been ovens. Jen and I had planned a driving trip to see some places where there'd been UFO sightings in New Mexico, but we'd picked up her father, Mike, and a college friend named Penny along the way, so it wasn't quite the trip we'd planned. Mike was short and bristly and Penny was lanky, long-haired, and angry about men. Fortunately, both Mike and I were near fifty, him on the top side, me on the other, so we weren't quite men in Penny's sense of the word.

We'd been through Roswell and Corona, and the next place to see was Socorro, because of the alien craft that landed there in 1964. Jen was keeping a trip diary on her notebook computer, a tiny Compaq she used to link up to e-mail services when we stopped overnight, and she had been writing notes to herself about Socorro all afternoon.

"First we find the site," she said, "then we go after Lonnie Zamora and Sergeant Chavez. Everybody O.K. with that?"

"They sound like a couple of real dweebers," Penny said.

"What's their deal, anyway?"

"Zamora saw the spaceship and Chavez came in later and saw the traces — burning bushes and all that," Jen said. "It's a big deal because the Air Force didn't write it off."

"Typical," Penny said.

We found the spot out of town where the deputy had seen the UFO. That was pretty easy. The UFO had supposedly landed there in this gully, and these little men were standing around it, and then when Zamora got out of his car or something the men got back in the ship and blasted off. The town had the spot marked with a big sign. But when we tried to find Zamora himself, that wasn't so easy. Everybody we talked to had a different idea of where he lived. In fact, some people had different ideas of who he was, which made tracking him difficult. What we did was cruise up and down the dusty, chuck-hole filled roads, sliding in and out of stringy subdivisions. We knocked on a few doors and finally ran into some people having a chicken picnic in the dirty sand that was their front yard. They invited us to join them, but we declined, though it looked to me like Penny was interested.

"We're trying to find the guy who saw the UFO," Jen said to an older, skinny man with a rubber-like complexion and a bum leg that seemed to point toward the other leg whenever he tried to walk. The Charlton Heston thing.

"Everybody's seen them," the guy said. "They're all over the place. You only have to turn around and you see one."

"Have you seen any?" Jen said.

"Well, I haven't," he said. "Not me, personally. But everybody else I know has."

"I hear that," Penny said. "Lot of young bright men seeing UFOs every day."

"We're looking for Lonnie Zamora," Jen said. "Or Chavez, the state cop. You know them?"

"There's a cop lives around the corner there," the guy said waving off to one side. "But he's new, just got here in town last year. He's from Anchorage, I think. May be an Eskimo, or have some Eskimo blood. That's what I heard, anyway."

The guy was standing knock-kneed in his front yard holding a quarter chicken by the end of the drumstick. One bite of chicken about halfway down the leg was already gone. He was sort of shaking this chicken at us as a kind of invitation. His wife and their kids, all of whom seemed extraordinarily tiny, much tinier than they ought to have been, almost like circus tiny — the wife was maybe four and a half feet tall, the kids were smaller — were back by the folding table on top of which was a fat pitcher of blue Hawaiian Punch. I figured it had to be Hawaiian Punch or Kool-Aid because it was blue, but these folks look like the Hawaiin Punch crowd. The kids were slurping this stuff out of giant lock-top plastic glasses that had elaborate roller-coaster straws coming out of them.

On the card table there was a boombox that plugged into an orange extension cord that slid back across the dirt, up over the porch rail, and into the front door that was cocked open a little. They had old-fashioned ballroom music swinging out of the boombox, dance music, and both the elders — him tall and skinny and her small as a medium-size dog up on its hind legs — were swaying a little in time with the tunes, threatening to dance in the driveway. We waved as Mike dropped the car back into gear and let us roll away.

"That poor woman got stuck and stuck hard," Penny said, shaking her head.

Apparently the town council had tried to set up a tourist deal in Socorro like the one in Roswell, but it hadn't worked out. They had a Spaceship Cleaners, a Fourth Dimension Café, and, on the way out of town, a homemade fast food place called OutOfThisWorld, but that was about it for UFO-marketing.

O-O-T-W, as its neon said, looked like a Dairy Queen that'd been caught between a couple of giant pie plates and then rolled in car aerials and whip antennas covered with SuperStik. The parking lot was spray painted a remarkable golf-grass green. We stopped in the drive-though and Penny got their specialty, a Littlegreenmanburger. She told Jen she didn't know whether to eat it or smack it so hard it blistered.

It was turning chilly when we pulled out of the lot. Mike was ready to pack it in, find a local motel, but Jen wanted to visit the UFO Museum, so we drove two blocks and parked nose in at the storefront museum.

Inside a retired postal worker from Cleveland did his best to explain the Philadelphia Experiment — those cables wrapped around that ship, the space in the water where the ship had been, anti-matter machines, all of that. He had wiry hair and wore his jeans nipple-high, and he was eager to please — a volunteer, he explained, at the museum. He was reluctant to let us browse without instruction. The place was the size of a shoe shop, three rooms, the largest arranged around a long folding display board with photos, texts, crummy sketches of flying saucers pinned to it. In a side chamber there was a four-foot high wooden alien with teardrop eyes and several coats of Testor's Alien Lumina Silver. We listened to the retiree tell us about the rash of sightings in 1947 and about how the Army Air Corps had clammed up about the Roswell incident. He was quick to put the kibosh on the Air Force's new bonehead spy balloon explanation of the original coverup, too. There were snapshots of the Brazel ranch where the Corona UFO crashed, but the property looked like nothing special, just dirt, like the rest of New Mexico.

"You see," the guy said. "In 1947 there were sightings all over this country — way up in Washington and Oregon, all the way down here, over to Alabama, up toward Minnesota, in New

York state — they were everywhere. Strange lights, abductions, interactions, exchanges of fluids — I mean priests, nurses, even military officers reported stuff. For several weeks in the summer of 1947 this went on and then it suddenly stopped."

At that, the retiree did a deliberate pause, a long pause, nodding, watching us with a shrewd smile.

"It stopped," he repeated. "What does that tell you? What does that say? Think about it. It says they came for a reason. It says they got what they wanted and they left." He slapped his hands together for emphasis. "Bam!" he said. "You have to keep up with these deals, or you miss everything. You have to think back to what happened in 1947. Who was born that year? What world historical events were precipitated by incidents that occurred then? What was invented in the year 1947? These kinds of things are the kinds of things you have to think about when you're trying to keep an eye on the big picture. Where there's smoke, there's fire — that's all we are saying."

"Amen," Jen said. "But what about that magic aluminum foil, you know? And where are the tiny purple I-beams?"

"Oh, a TV watcher, huh?" he said, shaking his head. "Well, they weren't purple, they were magenta, and where do you think? Government's got all that. Maybe Groom Lake, Area 51 — you know Area 51?"

"Where some aliens were held captive, right?" she said. "But somebody discovered there really wasn't any Area 51, it was all a hoax."

He smiled and took a look at his black shoes. "Oh, there's an Area 51, all right. And a Hangar 9. There wasn't any Hangar 54, maybe that's what you're thinking about, that's more TV stuff, but there were Rainbow, Phoenix, and Montauk projects. And there's S4, MJ-12, Zeta-Reticula, and there are underground hangars at Kelly — there's a lot out here. If you're interested, check into Groom Lake, check out the Vegas airport sometime, the white jets without markings that go into the desert at night." He thumped his temple. "Don't let 'em confuse you."

Penny's eyebrows were doing Groucho moves. She pointed out toward the lobby and mouthed that she'd be waiting for us. Mike slipped off with her, leaving me and Jen to listen to the Socorro story, how the deputy had been driving along, minding his own business, kind of a pleasant evening, enjoying himself after work when he'd seen this craft in a ravine just outside of town — the full story. While he was talking I read the actual front page of the Roswell newspaper the day the Army put out the story that it had recovered a saucer. I knew the story, but seeing the paper, yellowed and brittle and hiding under glass, gave me a new sense of that time, made it seem as if the world was a toy world back then. The way the story sounded, the people it talked about and quoted, what they said, how they said it, even the people you could imagine reading the paper — they must've been like kids in adult bodies running things. That was a little eerie.

The museum was strange in the same way. It was childish, it looked like a sixth-grade science show. But there was something edgy and nagging about the pencil drawings and the snapshots with their rippled edges and the Xeroxes of typewritten accounts, something that made you uneasy — why was this enterprise still so ragtag after all these years? I stared at sketches supposedly done by the medical examiner during the autopsies of the Corona aliens, at a photo of the supposed Soccoro deputy pointing at the place where he'd seen the aliens — there was a dotted marker line showing the path of the departing spacecraft — and I began to think that in spite of, or maybe because of, the farfetched and unconvincing displays, the UFO Museum was entirely disturbing.

About then the retiree rubbed his hands together and looked around, as if scanning for something else to tell us. "I guess that gives you a start on it, huh?" he said. "Why not kind of meander around and get your own sense of the place now that I've introduced you? That be O.K.?"

"That's great, thanks," Jen said.

When he was gone I said, "I envy him — living here, volunteering here, explaining everything to the tourists."

"Yeah," she said. "Cool job."

"Like the details of Corona, or the Philadelphia Experiment, or Groom Lake. Wouldn't it be great to go home every night and read new stories, watch bad video copies, go through new evidence compiled and distributed by the Society for Recognition of the Adaptations of Alien Life Forms?"

"S-R-A-A-L-F," she said.

"Yeah," I said. "Or just sit out on a dusty porch in the middle of nowhere and stare at the saucer filled sky."

"You're a wonderful person, Del," Jen said.

"Well, he's like those guys who spend twenty years building railroads in their basements, who really don't do anything but play with their trains. They live perfect lives, devoted to love."

"Oh, baby," Jen said, doing a fifties deal. "Come to me, baby." She gave me a playful and sexy hug.

I watched as the little guy stood at the front window for a minute talking to another volunteer, then he cornered three new tourists — husband and wife with child. The retiree took them on, brought them into the main room and then to one of the side spaces where he'd originally taken us. I heard him start his speech about the anti-matter machine, how even he didn't quite understand it, but he would try to explain it to them if they could picture this massive World War II battleship wrapped in miles of thick steel cable — cable as thick as your arm! — the ship tossing in the stormy ocean waves on a bleak, wintry night, rain coming in visible sheets, and then, suddenly, without warning, in a wash of lightning the ship vanishes, leaving an indentation in the water, a footprint in the shape of its great hull.

"I can drive," Penny said. We'd finished the museum and were climbing back into the car. It was beginning to get dark.

"If we stay here we can try to find Zamora tomorrow," Mike said. "I mean, get the story first hand."

"He's another guy who ain't ready for us," Penny said.

"You figure he ought to be standing out here on the highway?" Mike said.

"That'd be a start," Penny said.

"Dad," Jen said. "We're hitting the road."

So Penny took the driver's seat and we headed back down Highway 25 to the place where we could catch a state road to Arizona. In the dusk we could still see the mountains on either side of us, tall solid hulks criss-crossing the road up ahead. There was a big stream running down one side of the highway, silver, reflecting lights from the little cabins alongside it. Pretty soon we were higher into the mountains, and the cutoffs were smaller and the stream was gone and there weren't any houses, just a big, black hump squeezing the highway. We hadn't done much night driving and I was thinking that was too bad, because things seemed more comfortable in the car at night. The inside seemed a lot bigger. There was territory there between the riders, and the car was cooler and quieter. The road wasn't making so much noise, and the noise it did make was more soothing in darkness than daytime. Watching out the front window at the white lines edging the road and the yellow lines in its center, I had a vivid sense of riding on a seam, an edge between two voids, a track pointed somewhere, coming from somewhere, lit only by headlights. The big Lincoln seemed to shoot itself forward into that night. The few lights in the hills were glittering on the windshield. Headlights jiggled as they came toward us, and the reflectors embedded in the highway threw our brights back in our eyes.

The road was two-lane blacktop interrupted now and then by brand new sections of divided highway. These sections didn't make any sense, there wasn't a pattern to their appearance or disappearance. We'd drive a while and then suddenly there'd be a mile of divided highway, then back to blacktop. We passed a hut on the side of the road renting trailers, and our lights caught the taillights of all the trailers at once, making them look like a herd of small animals cowering there in the ditch alongside the highway.

Jen pulled out the Compaq and said, "I'm going to read your tarot. I got this program off the Net."

"I'd rather watch TV," I said. We'd been carrying Jen's hand-held TV, a Casio the size of a Walkman with a two-and-a-half inch color LCD, but I hadn't seen it for a while. "Where is that TV, anyway? I want to check what's on."

"Maybe you could tune in some aliens," Penny said. "You know how those spaceships always gray out the screen?" She and Mike, in the front seat, giggled about that.

"It's in the trunk, probably," Jen said, cranking up the computer. "But wait'll you see this — Celtic cross, a couple other spreads, and it explains everything, so when you get the Death card, I can explain the hell out of it."

"Death is just another word for nothing left to lose," Penny said. "Death is never having to say you're sorry."

"Oh, Penny," Jen said. "You're always so negative." She ran the program and asked me to shuffle the cards by punching a couple of keys. "You can stop whenever you want to," she said.

"How do I know the cards are shuffling under there?" I said.

"You trust me," she said.

So I stopped and then she said, "O.K. Now you have to

pick out your cards." The notebook had a trackball, which made picking out the cards difficult, but I got it done.

"Are you ready?" She moved the cursor to a button that said "Reveal" and clicked. The first card in the center of the cross rolled over. Death. I shook my head.

"That's great," Jen said. "Death's a really great card to get in that position. It's all about starting a new part of your life, putting the things of your past behind you and going forward, reaching out to conquer new challenges, stepping out of old, bad habits, leaving your worn clothes behind. It's a wonderful sign, really. It's about the best card you could possibly ever get in that position."

"Short of a letter bomb," Penny said.

"O.K.," Jen said. "I won't kid you. There is a downside. But it could be a lot worse. See, position is important. If it were up in the fourth house that would be a problem. I'd tell you that, too, I'd just come right out and tell you, but here, at the center of everything, it's a very, very good sign." She clicked on a button to bring up the explanation of the Death card. "See here," she said, pointing at the screen. "It says right here that 'the Death card represents the clearing of the old to usher in the new and, therefore, should be welcomed as a positive, cleansing, transformative force in our lives.'"

"Let's do it again," I said.

"What do you mean, do it again? You can't just do it again," she said.

"Give him another chance," Penny said.

"Let's shuffle and do it again," I said.

"Are you sure?" she said. "We'll lose this whole spread."

"That's the ticket," Penny said. She was watching us in the rearview, bobbing her head around to see me, then to see Jen.

So Jen clicked on the "Shuffle" button, and we went through the whole process again, dealing another set of ten cards. This time when she clicked on "Reveal" the first card that came up was the Devil.

"What is it?" Penny said.

"Progress," I said. "Satan."

Jen clicked the "Interpret" button and read parts of it out loud. "'The Devil represents hidden forces of negativity that constrain us and deceive us into thinking we're imprisoned by external forces,'" she said. "'There's a devil in each of us. He's like an inner force. He's an embodiment of our fears, addictions, and harmful impulses.'" She pointed to the screen picture of the card. "It says these two people chained at The Devil's feet are 'entranced with the paralyzing fear of his illusory power and therefore stand there and look numb.'"

"Dumb?" Penny said.

"Hush," Jen said. "But see, the chains hang loosely so they can break free of their hypnotic attachment if they really want to, if they have the will. That means you can, too."

"This is worse than last time," I said.

"Well, maybe," she said. "But there's a way it's better — a cleaner beginning, a solid ground against which to work."

"Why don't you go ahead and turn over the next card?" Penny said. "Take it one card at a time."

Jen clicked on the button to turn over the second card and the second card was Death.

"One of the most fruitful and positive cards in the deck," I said.

"Death?" Penny said, looking over her shoulder into the back seat. "Sorry, Del. I was rooting for you. Honest."

"Watch the road, will you?" I said.

"This is not good," Jen said. "I think maybe we want to move away from this spread."

The third card was the Hierophant. Jen said, "Let's just take a peek at what's here, not really taking this one seriously any more, but just to see —" She clicked through the rest of the cards. I had the Emperor in the recent past, the Moon and the Crown, the Wheel of Fortune in the future, and the other four cards were the Chariot, the Hanged Man, Judgment, and the Magician. "Now, this isn't really so bad," Jen said. "It looked a little iffy there at the beginning, but as it plays out, it's not so bad. I've seen worse than this."

"Yeah, I did one for Gary Gilmore that was worse," Penny said.

"I'll save it and we can look again later, O.K.?" Jen said. "You don't believe in this stuff anyway."

"I believe in everything," I said. "A little bit in everything."

Jen shut the computer down and slipped it back into the bag she had in the footwell on her side of the car.

"Penny," she said. "Where are we?"

"Thirty-one miles from Pie Town," Penny said.

"Is that all?" Jen said. "What are you doing? Eighty?"

"Something like that," Penny said.

Mike stirred and I realized he'd been asleep with his head pressed against the window glass. Penny waved a hand to hush us and Jen turned sideways in the seat, resting against the door on her side and running her feet across my lap into the door on my side.

"We stop there, O.K.?" she said.

Penny waved again.

Jen said, "I want to wake up in Pie Town. Just the idea is great. Maybe the idea is greater than actually doing it even. But I want to do it. I'm beginning to like this traveling stuff, this touring around and seeing stuff." She gave me a little kick. "Don't you like it?"

"Yes, I like it. I told you I liked it," I said.

"Could you guys whisper?" Penny said from the front. "The oldster is napping."

"I think it's worthy," Jen whispered.

Up in the front Penny sneezed a couple times and then looked up into the rearview to see if we were watching her.

Mike sighed, his head still against the window. "Why is everybody making so much noise?" he said. "Maybe we should call ahead to Pie Town and see if we can get reservations," Jen said, tapping his shoulder.

"Why don't you?" Mike said. He slipped the cellular phone over the back of the seat.

"I guess we can't," Jen said. "We'd have to call information and get somebody and ask about motels — they're not having a Holiday Inn in Pie Town."

"So why are you asking me?" he said. He was still bent against the car door.

"Wake you up," Jen said.

"We'll just get something when we get there," Penny said. "It's not going to hurt if we don't call."

"Let me have the phone," I said. "I'm calling somebody."

"Here we go," Jen said.

"I don't have to if you don't want me to," I said.

"No, go ahead," she said.

"Go ahead," Mike said from the front seat.

"Maybe you should call that guy back at the museum," Penny said. "Maybe he's seen some spacecraft."

"Is that the nicest thing you could possibly think of to say?" Jen said.

"I'm sorry," Penny said.

Jen patted my arm. "Go ahead. Call anybody you want. It's a free country. I'll join our fellows up front, give you some privacy." Jen leaned forward over the back of the seat and put an arm around Penny and an arm around Mike. "So, what's up guys?" she said.

I dialed our number at home thinking I'd check for messages as a first step, but the radio waves got crossed up or something and I ended up connected to a guy on a Continental Airways flight from L.A. to New York who was trying to call his mother in Akron. I told him I'd never talked to anybody on an airplane telephone before and he said it was his first time using one, so we talked for a few minutes. I told him we'd been driving across New Mexico, that we'd been to Roswell and to the UFO Museum in Socorro, and that we were headed into a place called Pie Town. He told me he thought he'd seen a UFO once, down in Costa Rica, but he wasn't sure. He said that right then and there everything was clear as a bell at thirty thousand feet. He told me he always called his mom at odd times and that he had a sixth sense about how she was doing, and lots of times when he called it turned out to be precisely the right time, just when she needed him. It was the kind of thing that made him wonder, he said.

AS I WAS READING

by
Lydia Davis

I had been startled to discover, some time ago as I was reading a history of France (beginning, with a misguided zealousness, at the very beginning of this book, three inches thick, with the intention of reading it straight through) how very little happened in a thousand years, back in the last Ice Age.

I had been seeing how our present millennium was creeping and climbing and halting toward its end. Every hundred years of it had been so fought-over, so exceedingly complicated, filling history books. Not only eventful, but each event breeding so much interpretation. But back then, it seemed, in what I thought of as those Paleolithic times (I was not really sure what "Paleolithic" meant) very little happened in a millennium. It was a restful thing to contemplate.

What about this thing, a millennium? After I made that startling discovery on page 30 of this 679-page book, I decided to spend a little time investigating. I wanted to find out some things — what other millennia had been like, how long a millennium really was, whether it was longer at different times, how much happened during one, what happened. So I started looking here and there to see what I could find out.

I wanted to start with the word "millenary." But as I was

slightly fuddled and more familiar with the word "millinery," I immediately became distracted by it, and instead of reading about a period of a thousand years I began reading about hats. I already knew that hats used to be important in the USA, or more important than they are now. I did not know that the simplest form of head coverings, in antiquity, were the cap and the hood. Hats developed from these. The first known type of hat (Greek) was distinguished as such by having a brim. (This hat tied under the chin and was worn by travelers.) In the 19th century, women's hats increased in size with their coiffures. With the advent of the closed automobile, hats became smaller. I knew that Danbury, Connecticut, had been a center of hat-making. I thought about that every time I drove near it. I did not know its hat industry began in 1780. In the 1960's, the industry declined.

That was interesting, although I wanted to know when, exactly, the Greek hat was developed. What, exactly, did they mean by "antiquity"? Elsewhere it was defined as: "in ancient times." But when was "in ancient times"? Roughly, they said, before the Middle Ages.

Next, I discovered that "the millennium" can refer to the thousand years in which, according to **Revelations** 20, Christ will reign again gloriously on earth and holiness will prevail. A millennium can also be a period of great happiness or human perfection. The article referred me to "Judgment Day."

I thought I knew what Judgment Day was, but decided to refresh my memory. On Judgment Day, this world will come to an end, the dead will be raised up in the general resurrection, and Christ will come in glory to judge the living and the dead; then the sinners will be cast into hell, and the righteous will live in heaven forever. *Glory*, specifically, means the splendor and beatific happiness of heaven. It can also mean a ring or spot of light. I did not know which meaning applied to Christ coming in glory. There was apparently no generally accepted teaching among Christians as to when the Second Coming would take place, but many individuals had ventured to prophesy its date. Those who lay stress on the end of the world are called chiliasts, millenarians, or adventists.

I wanted to know what the word *chiliasm* meant. I thought I could remember this word by thinking of chili and chasm. But instead of *chiliasm*, I looked up *chiasma*, meaning "crossing over." Crossing over occurs in the first division of meiosis. Two chromosomes of a homologous pair exchange equal segments with each other. Crossing over results in recombination of genes found on the same chromosome. Under the microscope, a crossover has the appearance of an X and is called a chiasma. *Chiasma* is Greek for "crosspiece" and comes from the Greek *chiazein*, to mark with a *chi*, or "x."

Once I found *chiliasm*, I learned that it came from the Greek *chilioi* meaning "one thousand." Belief in the millennium is called *chiliasm* by historians of the ancient church. Looking back from *chiliasm* I saw *chiliad*, a period of a thousand years. Looking ahead from *chiliasm* I saw *chili con carne* and *chili sauce*. Before *chiasma* came *chiaroscuro* and before that *chiaroscurist*, before that *chiao*, a Chinese coin, *Chianti*, and *chi*. After *chiasma* came *chiasmatypy*, the spiral twisting of homologous chromosomes during zygotene that results in chiasma formation and provides the mechanism for crossing over; *chiaus*, a Turkish messenger; *Chibcha*, a Chibchan people of central Colombia; *chibouk*, a long-stemmed Turkish tobacco pipe with a clay bowl; *chic*; *Chicago*; and *chicalote*, a white-flowered prickly poppy of Mexico.

A few days before, I had heard from a Rumanian visitor how the history of his country had been affected by having such neighbors as Turkey and Russia. I also learned that Rumania was successively overrun, after the Romans left it in the 3rd century A.D., by the Goths, the Huns, the Avars, the Bulgars, and the

Magyars. I was eating in a Salvadorean restaurant. Our waitress was of Swedish descent. Our host was English. His wife, who was American, apologized because she had to leave in the middle of dinner to attend a class in Sanskrit. She explained that the students were taught not just the language but also the concepts behind certain of the words. How interesting, I thought. But what did I know about Sanskrit, really? I knew it was very old. The only other thing I knew was that in the latter half of the 19th century, the 60 or 70 royal children of the king of Siam were studying Sanskrit. I learned this from reading **Anna and the King of Siam**.

Sanskrit: Some of the oldest surviving Indo-European documents are written in Sanskrit, though Hittite is probably the earliest recorded Indo-European language, with at least one text dated c. 17th cent. B.C. I was surprised that Sanskrit was an Indo-European language. When I said the word I must have been thinking of "European" more than "Indo." In fact I couldn't remember just what "Indo-European" included. Now I learned that it included those languages spoken in most of Europe and in the parts of the world colonized by Europeans since 1500 and also in Persia, the sub-continent of India, and some other parts of Asia. 1500 was beginning to seem recent to me, by now. I had to marvel that it was only in the past half millennium or so that Portuguese had been spoken in Brazil, or, for that matter, English in America. Indo-European includes, for instance, Romany, Kashmiri, Kurdish, Ukrainian, Czech, Lithuanian, Haitian Creole, Scottish Gaelic, Welsh, and Frisian, but not, for instance, Finnish, Hungarian, Lapp, Estonian, Samoyed, Turkish, Mongolian, Kalmuck, or Cree (which belongs to the Algonquian branch of the Algonquian-Wakashan linguistic stock of American Indian languages). Indo-European is a family of languages that may have descended from an original parent language called Proto-Indo-European which is believed to have been spoken some time before 2,000 B.C. and before writing was known to its speakers.

"Before 2,000 B.C." was vague, I thought. It covered a very long stretch of time. I had already learned from the French history, which had started all this, that "modern man" had been in existence since 40,000 B.C.

If asked, I realized, I could not have said much about the Hittites. And yet I thought I should have known something about them, if theirs was the earliest recorded Indo-European language.

I learned that the name "Hittite" came from the Hebrew *Hitti*, which in turn came from the Hittite *Hatti*. The Hittite language is sometimes considered part of the Indo-European language family. It is known to us from hieroglyphic texts. The Hittites were a conquering people in Asia Minor and Syria with an empire in the 2nd millennium B.C. The aboriginal inhabitants of the land were apparently the Khatti, or Hatti. The capital of the Hittite Empire was Hattusas. Hattusas still exists, in Turkey, though now it is only a village. In it were found, in 1906 A.D., 10,000 tablets bearing Hittite inscriptions.

I would not have paid much attention to the fact that the Hittites' neighbors to the southeast, in the Upper Euphrates, were the Khurrites, were it not for the fact that on the page before the *Hittites* was an entry for an American orientalist scholar named *Philip Khuri Hitti* who taught Oriental languages and Semitic literature at Columbia and Princeton and wrote at least four books. I was struck by his middle and last names. I also noticed, looking at the birth date, that the Hittite tablets were discovered at about the time he turned 21. Did this discovery come at just the moment to determine his subsequent career?

I stopped and reflected that it has only been as the last centuries of our millennium have crept and halted along that we have even discovered the existence of such earlier civilizations as the Hittites. I remembered hearing it said that at a certain point in the past — a few centuries ago? in the Enlightenment? much earlier? — a single human being could know everything — about history? about science? — that was known. In other words, a great deal less was known then. But I'm not sure how far back that was.

Before *Sanskrit* came *San Sebástian*, a city in Northern Spain on the Bay of Biscay; and before that *sans-culottides*, the last five days of the year in the French Revolutionary Calendar. The *sans-culottides* were named in honor of the *sans-culottes* ("without knee breeches"), the lower classes in France during the French Revolution. After *Sanskrit literature* came *Andrea Sansovino*, a Florentine sculptor and architect of the High Renaissance whose real name was Contucci and who took the name of the place where he was born. After him came *Jacopo Sansovino*, an Italian sculptor and architect of the Renaissance whose real name was Tatti and who took the name of his master Andrea Sansovino.

I was talking to people about my investigation as it went along, about time, history and dates, and I discovered that not just I, and not just Christians, but most people seemed to take their bearings from the year 0, the birth of Christ. It seemed to me the reason for this was not just convenience, but a failure of imagination, or the illusion that because of the 0, something had begun then. I said to myself that people also thought of 0°F as some kind of absolute, even though it was not any particular point such as the point at which water freezes. If the year 0 had been the beginning, two thousand would be many years. But it was not the beginning at all, only a point along the way.

What about this? What about years computed from a fixed point (like the birth of Christ and the hegira)?

I learned that in chronology, an era was a period reckoned from a fixed point in time. I wanted to know what some other fixed points were. My encyclopedia is Western, so it is biased toward information about the West and therefore limited, but some fixed points in time were: the creation of the world (Jewish, equivalent to 3761 B.C.; Byzantine, 5508 B.C.); the founding of the city of Rome (753 B.C.; year marked A.U.C. for *ab urbe condita*, "from the founding of the city"); the hegira.

But I had to stop. Did I know what the hegira was? Hegira: The word comes from the Arabic *hijra*, meaning "breaking off of relations." The hegira was the flight of the prophet Muhammad from Mecca, driven out by angry businessmen, in September 622 A.D. The Muslim era is dated from the first day (July 16, 622) of the lunar year in which the hegira took place.

I went on: another era was reckoned from the founding of the Olympic games in ancient Greece (776 B.C.; time in Olympiads); another from the proclamation of the French Republic (Sept. 22, 1792). The French Revolutionary Calendar was divided into 12 months of 30 days each, named after: vintage, fog, sleet, snow, rain, wind, seed, blossom, pasture, harvest, heat, and fruit. The remaining five days, the *sans-culottides*, were feast days.

I knew what a calendar was, but I looked it up anyway. I discovered one thing, at least, that I had not known. The word "calendar" comes from a Latin word meaning "money-lender's account book."

Before *calendar* came *Robert Calef*, a 17th-century Boston cloth merchant known primarily as the author of **More Wonders of the Invisible World**. I thought this was funny until I read on and learned that his book attacked Cotton Mather, condemned the view of witchcraft then prevailing, and had a salutary effect throughout New England. After *calendar* came *calendaring,* a finishing process for paper, plastics, rubber, and textiles; followed by *calendula*, an annual with yellow to deep orange flower heads and a popular garden flower in

Shakespeare's time — his "marigold."

The term "epoch" was apparently often confused with "era" in writing. I did not know specifically what that meant, but I was to learn later.

Before *era* came *Er*, Judah's first son; before that, *Er*, the chemical symbol of the element Erbium. After *era* came *Eran*, Ephraim's grandson; then *era of good feelings*, a period in U.S. history after the War of 1812 when people were anxious to return to a normal life and forget political issues, and there was little open party feeling.

I noticed that in my pursuit of history, I kept coming up against religion, often the Christian religion but sometimes another religion: Judaism (the creation of the world), Muhammadanism (the departure of the prophet). My encyclopedia was full of names of characters from "our" Bible.

"Religion" was defined as not only the service and worship of God or the supernatural, or a personal set of religious attitudes, but also a system of beliefs held to with ardor and faith. A system of beliefs.

I thought: People needed their systems of beliefs in order to make sense of a world of facts? Or what? I was close to a thought but not there yet.

I found myself considering the turn of "our" millennium with some dread not because I was a believer in any particular religion or any particular calendar, but because I was afraid of people who believed, and who tended to do insane and violent things in the name of their beliefs.

I began to wonder why I was pursuing this investigation. Maybe I didn't really want to find out how long a millennium was. Wasn't that a little too silly? Maybe I did think the world was going to end at the end of this millennium, and these years would be my last chance to study the history of the world. I had never paid enough attention to history. In school, I had gotten poor grades in history. Was that it?

Or was the real goal of my investigation to retreat into the millennia of the past, so as to make the present millennium less present? Was I afraid of the present millennium?

I went back to my history of France, maybe for reassurance. There was a calm and friendly tone to the book. The author was just as amazed as I was by the vast stretches of time he was describing. He kept expressing them in different ways: Neanderthal man remained essentially unchanged for 60 millennia, or 600 centuries!

Sheep were first domesticated about 5,000 B.C. The first use of their fleece for wool is dated at about 4,000 B.C.

Could this really be true? That a thousand years went by — the same number of centuries as between the Norman Conquest and now — before people saw how to use sheep's fleece?

I made a short list for myself going up the millennia: The first signs of the transformation from hunters to farmers (in France): about 7,000 B.C.

The first villages and transhumance (in France): about 5,000 B.C. *Transhumance* was the movement of the sheep up into the mountain pastures for the summer and back down into the valley pastures in the fall.

The first use of the fleece of sheep for wool: about 4,000 B.C.

The beginning of Greece's long Neolithic period: about 4,000 B.C.

"Important cultures" had developed in Greece by about 3,000 B.C.

Unification of Egypt under one ruler: about 3,000 B.C.

Age of the great pyramids in Egypt: about 2,500 B.C.

In India, the Indus Valley civilization, one of the earliest, and highly sophisticated, flourished: about 2,500-1,000 B.C.

The Minoan civilization and the Mycenaean civilization had disappeared by about 2,000 B.C.

Was it pure coincidence that so many "great" civilizations began or flourished between 3,000 and 2,000 B.C.?

The Mayan civilization began about 1,500 B.C.

First dynasty (Shang) in documented Chinese history: about 1,500-1,000 B.C.

Confucius lived around 500 B.C.

The Incan empire began around 1200 A.D.

Apparently Greece's long pre-history, its Neolithic Age, began about 4,000 B.C. Where, in the course of a Neolithic age or after, would a hat be likely to develop? How would I make an educated guess about the development of that hat? Could I start by supposing that Greek civilization would have to be advanced enough to have "travelers" rather than nomads? But I was not even sure what "Neolithic" meant. At least I was now beyond confusing "Paleolithic" with "Ice Age," as I had done when I first started my reading.

I had vaguely thought "Paleolithic times" were the same as "the Ice Age." I had also thought there was only one Ice Age. I realized later that perhaps I was confusing "Paleolithic" and "Pleistocene," because the Ice Age most familiar to us is also called the Pleistocene Epoch. Now I understood that remark about "era" and "epoch" being incorrectly used in writing. "Epoch" was a term belonging to geological time. In geological time, an epoch was a smaller unit within an era.

Paleolithic, on the other hand, meant "ancient stone age" and referred to a stage of civilization, so that one people could be in their Paleolithic stage and another in their Neolithic stage. "Paleolithic" related to the second period of the Stone Age characterized by rough or chipped stone implements. "Neolithic" was the latest period of the Stone Age characterized by polished stone implements. Of course, a people could be in their

Paleolithic stage during the Pleistocene.

Neolithic was a stage of cultural evolution or technological development also characterized by the existence of settled villages largely dependent on domesticated plants and animals, and the presence of crafts like pottery and weaving. The termination of the Neolithic period was marked by such innovations as the rise of urban civilization or the introduction of metal tools or writing.

Then I imagined, rightly or wrongly, that the Greek hat was developed late in the Greeks' Neolithic period, with the rise of urbanization. I was perhaps wrong, but because I imagined the Greek "traveler" would be going from one urban center to another, I thought the development of cities and the development of "travel" and "travelers," and the hat, would all have come at the same time.

The earliest known development of Neolithic culture was in Southwest Asia between 8,000 B.C. and 6,000 B.C.

I was confused. Did this mean the most advanced early culture was in Southwest Asia? Or the earliest known advanced culture? Maybe this would become clear to me with more reading.

Was this earliest known development of Neolithic culture connected to the melting of the ice at the end of the Ice Age?

The ice melted (the last glacial period ended) about 11 millennia ago. The human diet changed to include more plant food. The land, relieved of the weight of the ice, rose in places.

How could the land rise? Was it floating? Or was it solid but had been compressed by the weight of the ice? Or was it able to rise and fall because the center of the earth is liquid?

I thought: You couldn't form settlements (enter your Neolithic Age) unless you could grow crops, could you? Or maybe you could. Would the earliest development of Neolithic culture have to be after the end of the last Ice Age? You couldn't turn from hunting and gathering to farming until plants began to grow, could you? During the Ice Age, there was only tundra. But I was a little unclear what tundra was, exactly.

I discovered that the word "tundra" came from Russian and was related to the Lapp word *tundar*, "hill" (not an Indo-European word). A tundra is a level or undulating treeless plain characteristic of arctic and subarctic regions.

But what grew on the "plain"? What grows on tundra now, anyway, in summer, is an abundance of mosses and lichens, and some flowering plants. The tundra supports a small human population including Samoyeds.

So was I right to see a pattern? The ice melted, then within two or three thousand years Neolithic cultures began, then over the next three or four thousand years various different civilizations became highly developed?

I left off thinking about the complexities of the highly sophisticated civilizations and returned to the peace and emptiness of the Ice Age.

During the last Ice Age there were apparently some trees. They grew up only in protected spots. More generally, mammoth bones were burned for winter fires. (The cutting of the Grand Canyon took place chiefly during the Ice Age.) Temperatures in summer averaged 54°-59°F with evening frosts. Mild enough, especially on a southfacing slope in the sun.

Many Ice Age footprints, always of bare feet, were found in the clay and sand floors of different caves. The people probably removed their moccasins or boots to protect the leather from the mud of the spring thaw. (If there had not been mud, there would not be footprints, so we know the floors were wet and the bare feet were walking in the wet.)

Maybe I was wrong not to be interested, just then, in the epochs or eras of earth's history before humankind appeared. But right or wrong, I liked to see the first appearance of humans, and especially, then, the first signs of humans making art. There was something refreshing about this.

The earliest evidence of art-making, I learned, dated from about 32 millennia ago. It became increasingly refined over the next 20,000 years.

I realized that I would not have been able to say, before looking it up, when prehistoric cave-painting was being done. I wondered if other people had a better idea or if only my own ignorance was at fault. I asked various people to name a date. I was given a range of answers: sometime B.C. (from a woman in the health-care profession); 2,000 B.C. (from two painters, separately); 5,000 B.C. (from a writer and teacher); 20,000 B.C. (from a jazz pianist cum astrologer); 50,000 B.C. (from a writer); oh, hundreds of thousands B.C. (from an English professor). For believing Christians, I could tell, any portion of the time before the year 0 became a murky area mostly filled by stories from the Bible. Even for non-Christians, in many cases. Until they remembered the Egyptians. They knew the Egyptians had been building their pyramids before the birth of Christ.

I would have liked to go back to some of those places on the earth in which *homo erectus* had lived. Until recently, there were some that remained relatively untouched. Now this was no longer true, I knew, and my only access to them was through my imagination.

I wanted to go farther back. I made another list: *Homo erectus* dated from 1,800,000 B.C., or 1800 millennia ago. (1802 counting our nearly 2 millennia A.D.)

I said it to myself again: 1800 millennia ago. The earliest remains of human culture dated from this time.

I was not even sure how to define culture. But there it was, defined for me. Culture meant tools, language, and social activity

I went on with my list: The use of fire began: 500,000 B.C.

Early *homo sapiens*: 300,000 B.C. Early *homo sapiens* included Swanscombe man and Steinham man.

Homo sapiens: 100,000 B.C. Neanderthal man. This species, with its clearly-defined characteristics, remained essentially the same for 60 millennia.

I had to say it again: unchanged for 60 thousand years.

Then "suddenly" this species was wiped out. But "suddenly," in this history, was a period of five thousand years. The "suddenly" was true, and the five thousand years were true. This species gave way to *homo sapiens sapiens* about 40,000 B.C., a completely different species morphologically, already virtually indistinguishable from present-day humans, and including Cro-Magnon man, Grimaldi man, Boskop man, and Wadjak man. This was the beginning of the last Ice Age in Europe.

End of the last Ice Age: 10,000 B.C. (12 millennia ago counting our 2 millennia A.D.)

Only at the end of the list, the end of the last Ice Age, did our 2 millennia become a significant fraction of the number. Through the rest of the list, especially in the beginning, these last two thousand years were so small a part of the number that they really had to be "rounded off."

I felt strange, being "rounded off." It was a strange sensation to see our 2 millennia gone in a moment. I knew that in the universe, we were small. In time, our lives were brief, but it was easy to forget.

I went on reading, about the limestone hills of Southern France, about the Magdalenian cultures of France.

In that region of France, the same human profile existed then (it is there in the Ice Age portraits) as now.

Was that possible? The same human profile continuing for 20,000 years?

More than 500 pieces of non-utilitarian shale or slate were found on the floor of a number of hilltop huts in Gönnersdorf,

Germany, dating from c. 10,500 B.C. They are engraved with hundreds of "buttocks" images, marked and overmarked. A kiln for firing clay statues was found in a hut at the site of Doln, Vestonice, in Czechoslovakia. A stone "palette" was found at the site of Gabillon. There were mammoth hunters in the Ukraine.

Signs and symbols were engraved on stones and bones. Material included stone, bone, ivory, clay, antler, and horn. They painted with fingers, sticks, pads of fur or moss; they daubed; they dotted; they sketched with colored materials and charcoals, they blew paint from their mouths or through a hollow bird bone. They used mineral "crayons," brushes of hair and fiber. There was both humor and perspective earlier than we once supposed. There was the same outburst of innovative image-making at the same time among different people speaking different languages and having different skeletons. (No visitors from space were required to teach them.)

But what had originally startled me and what continued to startle me was that this art changed so gradually, over 20,000 years.

I had to wonder: were the later millennia, including ours, actually longer, or larger, because more happened than happened in any one millennium between 30,000 B.C. and 10,000 B.C.? Was our millennium less a negligible fraction than I had thought?

But then I had to ask myself if it was really true that less had happened. Wasn't it just that the farther back we go, the less we know about what happened? But then I remembered that the farther back we go, the fewer people there were in the world, and the fewer people there are, the less happens. So it really was true that less happened.

What was the population of the globe during the last Ice Age? I wanted to know. But I could not discover this. I could only discover that between the time of the Roman Empire and the colonizing of the New World, the world population increased from a quarter of a billion to half a billion. I could discover that in the "ancient world" the world's population increased only 0.1% a year.

But what I had also learned was that during the Pleistocene, the ice would come and go. Glacial advances would be interrupted by interglacial stages, during which the ice retreated and a comparatively mild climate prevailed. This was not what startled me. What startled me was to learn that because the interglacial periods of the Pleistocene lasted longer than the time that has elapsed since the last retreat of the ice, the epoch that is occurring now, our epoch, called the Recent Epoch, may be merely another such interglacial stage and the glaciers may return at some future time.

Because I had not heard this before, I began to worry. Maybe everyone else knew this fact and I simply hadn't been "paying attention." But maybe my reference books were too old, and most of what I thought I was learning was no longer true.

I looked at their copyright pages. It was true that my books were rather out of date. My encyclopedia was about 25 years old. My dictionary was also about 25 years old. I am 48 years old, so when I bought them, I realized, I was young and they were new. I did not notice, as the years passed, that as I grew older they also changed, that my books were gradually becoming wrong about certain things.

Even though 25 years was not very long in terms of millennia, in each one of those past 25 years many things happened, and a discovery might have been made that would cause me to have to change what I had thought especially about Paleolithic cultures, or the Ice Age. In fact, the discovery that the Pleistocene began more than 1.8 million years ago was made only five years or so before my encyclopedia was published and barely made it in. Before that discovery, they thought the

Pleistocene began much more recently.

The catalogue I had from an exhibit of Ice Age art was about eighteen years old. But I saw that my history of France was more recent — ten years old — and it confirmed what I was reading elsewhere. Best of all, a friend who read the newspapers confirmed, at least, the approximate dates of the prehistoric art-making. I saw that I could consider this friend to be a reference resource that could be updated every day.

I was left with no answer to the question I had asked myself along the way: Was the real purpose of my investigation, not to find out how long a millennium was and begin to know past millennia, but rather to situate myself farther back in the span of time, so that what happened now did not matter as much? Was I, in fact, afraid of the present age, and was I even glad, rather than startled, that the glaciers might return?

A LIGHT SOUND OF BREATHING

by
Kevin Sampsell

The drunk splayed his coins across the counter.

"It's 1.79 for the Coors. Do you have another four pennies?"

The drunk took five minutes looking through all his pockets to find the right change. It was now 2:30 am and time to lock up the beer coolers in the Jiffy Mart. Bob took the key which was connected to a big spoon and locked the cooler doors.

It had been a busy Saturday night and Bob was a little tired and stressed out from dealing with homeless drunks, smartass teens using fake IDs and clumsy shoplifters with strange glints in their eyes. Bob had only worked there three previous nights and this was his first graveyard weekend shift. The phone rang.

"Jiffy Mart, this is Bob."

"Do you want a blow job?" a voice on the line whispered.

Bob thought it was a friend playing a joke and decided to play along... "Well, I don't know. How big is your mouth?"

"Don't worry, I can take anything."

Bob couldn't place the voice. He knew that soon, though, whoever it was would have to start cracking up. Bob himself was holding in a chuckle... "Mmmm, what are you wearing big boy?"

"A denim jacket, red Docs, yellow pants —"

Just then a customer walked in the store and asked for a pack of Pall Malls. Bob told the caller to hang on and put the phone down to ring out the customer. Another person walked in and asked for directions to a nearby club.

Bob was wondering which of his friends owned a pair of red Doc Marten shoes. And yellow pants. He picked up the phone after the second customer left but the person had hung up. He leaned back against the wall behind the register and decided to look through the new issues of **Penthouse** and **Cheri**. He liked **Cheri** best because it had a lot of sleazy-looking women with large breasts in it and he liked to look at large breasts. The phone rang.

"Jiffy Mart, this is Bob."

"Hey Bob, this is Les. You busy?"

"No, it's dead now. Did you or someone else just call me about fifteen minutes ago?"

"I don't think so, man. We just got back from Firefly's. Oh hey, we decided on Armstrong Park for football at 12:30 tomorrow. Is that cool?"

"Yeah, I'll try to be up by then. Make sure you don't forget the ball this time."

As Bob was hanging up with Les, he saw a man sprint by on the sidewalk. The man, who looked to be in his mid-twenties, was crouched down as he ran by. And he was looking in at Bob. The running man in his mid-twenties had yellow pants on and Bob had never seen him before in his life.

Five minutes later the phone rang.

"Jiffy Mart, this is —"

"I'm naked," the voice interrupted Bob. "Did you see me? I just ran by your store."

"Yes I did. Where are you at now?" Bob asked. He did not know if he should hang up or not. He thought in his head it would be interesting to find out what another man wanted to do to him. Another man.

Bob was not gay but he enjoyed football.

"So do you want a blow job or not?"

"I don't think so," Bob answered after a pause. "For one thing I have a girlfriend, and for another thing I'm not gay. Or bi, or whatever."

"It's okay," the voice said. "Just pretend I'm a girl. We could do it in the bathroom there. C'mon man, I'm so horny, please."

"Why don't you just jack off?" Bob asked.

"Will you talk to me for a while so I can get off?"

"What should I talk about?" Bob asked without imagination. He was surprised at his arm for not hanging up the phone yet. He was looking out into the parking lot to make sure nobody was watching him. The guy on the phone had avoided his question about where he was calling from. There was a phone booth across the street, but no one was in it.

"Talk to me like I was a girl that you wanted to fuck real bad and I was standing right in front of you, wanting it. You can get off with me if you want. I'll talk about having a pussy and shit."

Bob did not know what to say. He never had a girl he wanted to fuck stand right in front of him before, wanting it. Anyway, he was not interested in talking dirty to a complete stranger, but he thought it would be fun to hear one talk dirty to him.

"I'm new at this game," Bob said. "You'll have to get me started. Umm, what would you do to me if you were here?" Bob could not believe he asked such a direct question. His face squished up and his tongue squirmed in his mouth as if to clean it out.

"Well, first I would have you on your knees," the man with yellow pants said over the phone..."and then I would pull your pants down really hard down to your ankles and leave them there and —" Bob concentrated on the voice and the magazines in front of him. It was past 3 a.m. and he knew nobody would be coming in until at least 4:30. What he heard on that phone he had never heard before. There was one part in particular where Yellow Pants said something about holding him by the hair and fucking his face really fast. Those three words scared him, gave him the creeps, but he kept saying them in his head: "Fucking your face, fucking your face." It almost made him sick.

A customer came in. The neighborhood retard, a young guy maybe 21 or 22. He always seemed to have a few screws loose. Probably too many drugs, thought Bob. The retard walked around the store with an apple cider.

Bob had just started talking dirty on the phone when the retard walked in the door. It had put a knot in his stomach, and yet he felt he really had to get the guy off. It would not be fair to lead him along like this and then stop. He put his hand up by the mouth piece so the retard would not hear him. Bob was spitting out the words half disgusted, half excited: "I'd have you hunched over the bags of dog food and I would spread you open like a big wet pussy and get inside you hot and tight and suck on your shoulder and rub your nipples with my hands and with each stroke your ass would push me back and open, push me back and open —"

Bob heard a gasp, a grunt from the other end of the line. There was silence, maybe a light sound of breathing. Blood was spinning in Bob's veins. The telephone was warm and moist from his body heat.

"Hold on a second, let me cash this guy out," Bob said over the phone.

"Sixty-nine cents," Bob said to the retard.

"I come in here all the time," said the retard. "See, I'm 21." He showed a state ID.

"Yes," said Bob.

"My son was killed today," said the retard.

"Oh, uh, I'm sorry," said Bob.

The retard did not seem too upset. "Oh, it's okay," said the retard all of a sudden. "They know who did it, they got the guys who done it all but —" his voice dropped into a sad tone. "They'll just let 'em go y'know. They can't keep people in jail too long."

"Well, I'm sorry," said Bob, feeling awkward.

The retard stood there a few seconds staring at the magazines which were spread across the counter behind Bob. A woman named Cheri Bomb was on one of the pages dressed as Santa Claus. The retard closed his eyes tightly. He turned and left the store quickly.

Bob picked up the phone and no one was there. He looked out at the empty parking lot and shook his head. Then, he picked up the magazines and walked slowly to the bags of dog food, near the back room.

FORTRESS

by
Linda Rudolph

i admit freely that i enjoyed being in beijing after the big square thing, when it was not politically correct to be there, at a table full of men i didn't know and would never see again, eating foods i didn't know and would never see again, in a dress i didn't know and would never wear again, because it allowed me to be there with her, a year after her death, which was the only time in our twenty years of friendship when we had dined together without some husband or theatre manager or man in charge present — notice i do not count the chinese managers because they did not care if we dined together or not, with or without them. nor, because she was dead, could she invite the theatre manager and supervise his eating, and let him voice his opinions in his actor's voice, his accentless, deep resonantly trained, persuasively trained, noticeably trained actor's voice, for he had been what was odiously known as a child actor and an adolescent actor, a beautiful young man without a trace of character in his face, exquisitely cast as jimmy stewart's son in **the fbi story**, or one of jfk's sterling young crewboys in **pt 109**, this mannequin manned by a hungarian stage mother who had been an acrobat in europe and whose swiss husband — his father — had died mysteriously before his birth, this man, the theatre manager, had been present at every one of the lunches, dinners, meals we took together, except this one at the chinese banquet where she was dead and another one, at a resurrected western american ghost town where she was not dead, when she spoke for the only time in her life to me of her father who had been missing or disappeared for most of her life, like mine, we shared even this in common but it had never been mentioned before because i was surprised that she had a missing father, i had not known she had a missing father, although i had known her for years, i knew only about the fathers or non-fathers of the men in her life, her first husband, my cousin, whose father had died on the toilet and her second husband, the theatre manager, whose father had been the most dramatic and died before he was born, this manager, who knew nothing about fathers except what he learned from jimmy stewart and cliff robertson, had three sons who have become fathers and so forth and so on.

so here we were, only for the second time alone at a meal table together without her managers or my managers, and our particular communication at this banquet defined itself by a curious avenue, a narrow avenue, a shared affliction that she had lived with for months before her death and i now possessed for the first time in my life at this chinese banquet, in its most pedestrian form, swollen feet, feet swollen beyond comfort in any shoe or sandal, swollen from the heat of beijing in the summer and an insufferable walk on the great wall in new shoes, and the change of diet i immediately experienced, salty foods, high liquid intake, and no desire whatsoever to eliminate wastes, it was this we shared at the banquet and i remembered before her death massaging her swollen feet, hideously swollen like the rest of her body by the medications and the radiations and the chemotherapy, her swollen face, the moon face, the face of some grotesque cartoon in the moon, her swollen feet that she could barely walk on, while i, i never had swollen feet in my life until this banquet, in her costume, a dress she gave me before she died that i was wearing at this banquet and would never wear again, her costume and our feet.

comic then, but now unfortunate, this one-way communication, this is now a sadness, as i stand in my closet looking at her dress, due to the unforgivable fact that while i was with her at the small chinese banquet i couldn't ask her whether she had died of cancer or suicide or murder. this was and is admittedly a matter of deep curiosity to me because i wasn't there at the time of her death and the stories of those who were there are conflicting. the man who was there, the man who was the theatre manager and with whom she had lived for ten years, who married her only when he found out she had cancer because he was worried about insurance money, this man who was at one time an attractive man but was now a repulsive man, this man had said to me a few hours after her death where he was of course in attendance, that he was glad she was dead, repeating glad several times, on the telephone, glad, naturally glad she was dead because he had months before found her replacement and was anxious to devote 24 hours a day to himself and this replacement, this replacement she knew about weeks before she died, from this man nothing would be learned about cancer or suicide or murder because he denied everything about her death except that he was glad, just as he had denied everything in his life that may have been done incorrectly or correctly by him, as he saw it, judged himself first, so that he knew nothing but judgment and denial as a matter of practice. this denial he was able to vary only when he was publicly suffering some odious form of guilt in a milli-second of clarity, or else aggressively lying which i suspect he did at moments of extreme fear, in any event, he would not be a source of communication about her death.

it was then i sensed that she could be the source at the chinese banquet through me in her dress and her feet, eating the whole roasted swallows, bones and all, smiling and nodding politely at our chinese hosts, heightened by the discomfort of our mutually swollen feet, my own feet like hers before she died, making the tacit communication even more possible because of the dead costume and the mutual feet, i experienced the greatest sense of anticipation of a sign, a heightened state of fantasy, of secret knowledge, which in fact she had given me once in her life, but never spoke of again, that i might learn from her now about her death cancer suicide murder, going to it quietly or not quietly, assisting or not assisting in it, knowing or not knowing that it was being managed and administered, if it was being managed and administered, only then in china and the costume and the feet and the swallow bones in our mouth only then did i sense the heightening of possibility of revelation through a sign.

would that lightning appear from the lazy susan or kali dance on the table with skulls, only such signs, such violent apparitions, could have disturbed the calm and routine and foolishness of the chinese banquet which i and everyone else sustained and in fact encouraged, just as she sustained the calm and routine and foolishness of her dying, without which, she feared, we would have been lost and embarrassed, anxious and without face, this she sustained, or i sustained, continued to sustain, never ceased to sustain, through the calm and routine and cracking of the swallow bones, through the nodding and smiling and constant drinking of coca-cola, which i hate, these admittedly grotesque and deliberate and false rituals would never permit, did never permit, before after or during the banquet, nor at any time since, clarification by sign or revelation or whispered word anything of the nature of her death.

STEALING THE MOON

by
Donna Levreault

When I first noticed something wrong with the moon, I was walking back from Rhonda's, where I had gone to study for an algebra test. Of course we hadn't studied but had listened instead to Sloghead's new CD, while we painted our toenails deep purple, a shade called "Witch's Brew." Half bored, I listened while Rhonda rattled on about the three or four boys she was hot for. These changed almost daily so I found it hard to take her passion seriously. Finally, I confessed to liking the new guy, the one who sat alone in the cafeteria looking so cool, so smooth and brown while he ate his butterscotch pudding. He didn't bother dressing in baggy clothes and heavy black shoes like the other boys, just jeans and white t-shirts and basic no-name running shoes. He stood out without meaning to and I liked that.

"Wonder when the black kids are going to claim him," Rhonda said, flopped out on her bed, stretching her arms back to expose the tattooed snake encircling her navel. Her mother still didn't know about it.

"Maybe I can get to him first," I said.

"Forget it," Rhonda yawned.

Seated in our classrooms, we looked like dispersed confetti, but when we weren't being ordered around by teachers, we clumped together with kids the same color. Deplorable, my mother said when she learned about it.

"Whatever happened to racial integration?" she asked. "Were the sixties just a waste of time?"

Yes, I wanted to say, but didn't. My mother was sentimental about the times when she was young. She thought everything stopped happening then, at least anything good.

As I walked home from Rhonda's, the smell of the jasmine bushes couldn't quite penetrate the exhaust fumes of the cars whooshing by. From the cramped, look-alike houses came the blare of the TV, a kid whining, a door being slammed. A man shouted, "Goddamnit, move back to your mother's if you have it so bad." I flinched, waiting for the sound of a blow. The air seemed thick with discontent and restlessness, and I moved swiftly, not to get trapped in it. Then the cold shriek of a jet made me look up and when I saw the moon, I knew something was wrong.

I hadn't been into stargazing or that sort of stuff, and really, I'd never paid much attention to the moon except to use the word to make silly rhymes for a poem in school, but I knew what a normal moon looked like, and that wasn't it. This moon rose like a white mint over the rooftop of the Garcias' house, bloated and ominous. As I stood there, the neighborhood grew very still and quiet, as if I were all alone. And then came a wave of frantic barking — every dog within miles howled.

I ran home, flinging open the back door, startling my mother, who dropped a container of frozen yogurt on the floor.

"What the hell —" she gaped at me. "Are you all right, Cynthia? What's happened now?"

My mother had stopped being protective a while ago. Now she figured when I was in trouble it was all my fault. But I remembered what Dad said, don't annoy her, don't get her started, she's having a hard time, she's going through the change, that's why. I didn't really believe him. She seemed mad at me because I was young and she wasn't anymore.

"Nothing's happened," I said, slowing down my breath.

"Look at what you made me do." She stared down at the clots of frozen yogurt spattered at her feet.

Grabbing a dish towel, I tried to mop it up, but she just pushed me away, scowling.

In the living room, my father was immersed in one of his science fiction thrillers. He had a collection of videos he watched over and over again on this huge screen with wrap-around sound. I mean, how many times could you watch a gigantic woman stalk through the desert or goosenecked space-ships destroy L.A.? Besides, I knew we couldn't afford this home entertainment center, not with Mom out of work. Whenever the credit card bills came, my parents usually spent an hour or two terrorizing each other with visions of bankruptcy.

"Have you seen the moon?" I asked.

He hit the mute button on the remote and gave me a dazed look. "Not recently," he answered.

"It looks funny, way too big."

He launched into some explanation about optical illusions and horizons and equinoxes, and so I knew he wasn't going to be bothered to get up and actually look at the moon, so I sat down beside him and watched **The Invasion of the Body Snatchers** for the zillionth time.

No one else seemed to care about the moon, so I forgot about it too. A few weeks later, Rhonda and I were cruising the mall for some new clothes. As we plowed through racks of pants, I tried to pump Rhonda about the guy I liked because all I had found out was his name was Howard, and he wasn't some-one you'd call Howie. He still pretty much kept to himself, though he had joined the track team and someone else had said he played trumpet but that was it, that's all I knew, and I kept hoping Rhonda had heard more.

She had. "I don't know why you're into this guy, I really don't. You know what I saw him doing today? Leaning against his locker reading, for God's sake."

"What was he reading?"

"How do I know? It didn't even look like a book for class. Forget him, Cynthia."

That night, a cold white light flooded my room, making the furniture look skeletal, and I looked out the window and saw it again, and no one was going to tell me something wasn't weird about that moon. It was huge, taking up a hunk of sky and it wasn't even full.

"Shit," I yelled, running downstairs. This time I got all of us out on the front lawn — Dad, Mom, my little sister Lisa — and we looked up.

"Doggone," my father murmured.

"Why's the moon so fat?" Lisa asked.

"They've done something to it," my mother hissed.

"Who?" Lisa asked, too young to know she shouldn't bother asking. My mother believed everything was a conspiracy, that the CIA and the FBI and the Secret Service and Pentagon were responsible for everything that had gone wrong, and that they would go on deceiving us forever.

"NASA," my mother said this time. "They said they discontinued the Apollo missions after they made the moon landing, but I don't believe them. The moon is too important a piece of real estate."

"But it has no atmosphere," Dad said.

"When did that ever stop them?" my mother replied.

We all tromped back in and Dad immediately plugged into one of his computers, confident he'd find the answer to the moon's strange appearance. My mother paced back and forth in the kitchen, while I read Lisa a bedtime story, a nice one about a toy rabbit that becomes real.

Over the next few weeks, the newspapers, the TV news, the radio talk shows, the computer bulletin boards went crazy trying to explain what was happening. It was obvious the experts were scrambling for reasons. A huge volcanic explosion in the South Pacific had muddied the atmosphere, so the moon appeared magnified. The earth and the moon just happened to be at an unusual angle to one another to give the illusion of the moon so close. Because of some magnetic activity on the sun's surface, the moon had actually come a bit closer to earth, but it was nothing to worry about.

In our physics class, our instructor lectured on the latest theories, which went straight over our heads. In English class, we had to discuss the symbolism of the moon in boring poems. Our history teacher talked about the change in conceptualization when people realized the sun was the center of the solar system, not the earth. She joked and said maybe we have it all wrong — maybe the moon is really the center.

As the moon waned, the furor died down, but at night I dreamed it grew so big that I fell into its milky coldness, drowning, and I screamed and screamed until I caught hold of something tall and the color of toast. It was Howard, holding my head above the white sea.

But as soon as I saw the new crescent, hanging like a long, curved sword, slicing the sky in half, I knew it wasn't over, and the uneasiness began again. The dogs started howling every night and no one could sleep. The houses were invaded by small brown snakes, harmless but startling when you opened a closet and one crawled out. There were ominous reports of coastal flooding, mass evacuations of towns, entire cities. The fact that we lived over two hundred miles inland didn't comfort me or my mother.

She pulled me over one day, whispering harshly, "I've got

my period again."

I thought this might make her happy, but apparently not. The snakes unnerved her, and she dropped dishes, snapped at us even more, and sat weeping on the front porch where everyone could see her.

Once again the media became frenzied, with more theories being expounded and more solutions proposed, such as exploding nuclear missiles at the moon to send it back to its original orbit. But since the moon was so close now, there was acute danger of poisoning our own atmosphere or exploding the moon entirely and having to deal with hunks of it falling on top of us. And then there were those experts who denied the moon was falling at all, or said that it was some subversive plot by extremists or a practical joke done by giant mirrors. On and on they talked, but nothing happened except the moon kept coming closer. Advertisements flooded the airwaves for survival kits, for do-it-yourself underground shelters, for cheap holidays to Disneyland and other places you could go to and not notice how weird things had become. On the radio, music and talk shows were replaced with preachers telling us to get saved before it was too late.

When the moon became half-full, looking like a slice of malignant melon, people stopped going to work or school, and took to the hill that stood on the edge of town.

We lived in a valley, but from this hill you could see straight to the mountains in the north. On those clear nights dense with the loamy smell of spring, we crowded together and watched the moon gain in power and strength. It was no use trying to sleep. We did that during the day now. At night we watched and waited. No one said much, though some women broke away to murmur the rosary in a circle, and one loud-mouth guy proclaimed it was the end of the world and that judgment day was upon us. But when he found nobody was listening to him, he became quiet, too.

It was on one of those evenings that I looked over and saw Howard, the not-so-new boy anymore, standing near me.

"Look, you can see the Sea of Serenity," he said to a large woman standing next to him wearing a long dress printed with orange and brown geometric shapes and a turban of the same material.

He looked so beautiful there, the moon not blanching his skin like everybody else's, but burnishing it, making it appear almost coppery. I had to get closer and so I asked, "So what's the Sea of Serenity?"

He looked me over and, for a few seconds, I thought he wasn't going to speak to me.

But his stern face relaxed a little, and he pointed to a large smooth spot on the moon's surface. "Can you see it?"

"Yeah, though it's not what I'd expect a sea to look like. How do you know so much about the moon?" I asked.

He shrugged. "I don't. Just a few things. See that big crater over there? That's Aristoteles." He had a small scar just over his right eyebrow, making him look more vulnerable and giving me a little more confidence.

"What about those? They look like mountains."

"They are. The Alps."

"Well, if they come any closer maybe we can ski on them."

"Now that's the best suggestion I heard yet," laughed the woman standing next to Howard. She had long, dangling silver earrings and black eyes that gleamed like black stones underwater. For a moment, looking at her, I forgot Howard.

"What's your name, girl?" she asked.

"Cynthia."

"Uh huh. Goddess of the moon. No wonder you don't look scared."

"What do you mean?" Usually when I don't understand

what someone is saying to me, I think they're teasing. But I didn't feel that way about this woman.

"Don't listen to my mother," Howard tapped her affectionately on the arm. "She's crazy, you know."

"Lucky for you," his mother smiled. "My name is Ola." She stuck out a broad hand. When I shook it and felt its sun-warmth, I relaxed for the first time in weeks.

A week later we were all on the hillside again. Earlier, we had lost electrical power and no one was saying when we'd get it back. It had been weeks since we had seen a newspaper or a magazine, but a few people had short-wave radios and rumors circulated that the entire East Coast, from Florida to New Jersey, had been wiped out by an abnormally high tide. Terrified, some people had fled, stuffing their mini-vans with kids and belongings and driving off to who knows where. But most of us remained rooted, lacing our panic with optimism. The world community of scientists promised a solution in the next day or two. We were urged to remain calm.

But as the moon began to rise that evening, we could see that it was the same or perhaps even bigger, its craters looking deep and ugly. Some of the women around us collapsed sobbing and soon the little kids joined in. The men stood unmoving, frozen in their helplessness. My mother chanted, "Why? Why? What have we done wrong?" and Lisa whined, "When can we go home, Daddy?"

I instinctively gravitated toward Howard and Ola, who sat apart from the others on a green plaid blanket, a patch of calm in a stormy sea.

"The mountains look beautiful, don't they?" Ola said. And I saw that she was right. The moon, rising in the east with its blinding whiteness, allowed the dark silhouettes of the faraway mountains to shine.

"Are we all going to die or what?" I asked Ola. Although I was frightened, I didn't see the point of showing it. Enough people were doing it for me.

"Honey, I don't know," Ola said. She was wearing more silver tonight, several thin bracelets and a medallion around her neck. "But I'm sure not going to trust myself to a bunch of know-it-all men who call themselves experts. Maybe they're even the ones who got us into this mess. If there's a way out of this, we've got to figure it out ourselves." She got up abruptly and went up towards the top of the hill.

I edged close to Howard, who didn't seem to mind a bit.

"Where is she going?"

He shrugged. "Maybe to try to see something."

"Well, the view's pretty good right here and this moon is hard to miss."

"Not that kind of seeing. I mean seeing the right thing to do."

"Oh. I guess she is pretty crazy."

Howard drew away from me.

"Well, you said so yourself yesterday," I protested.

"I was just joking."

"So was I."

He moved closer again and I felt a warm tingling in my feet, my hands, like my body was growing bigger to take him in.

"Months ago she saw the moon spinning out of its orbit and the waters rising on earth. That's why we moved here, to get away from the coast. She knew it'd be dangerous. She even said I'd meet some girl here."

I went all squishy inside. Maybe he'd let me know I was important to him, too.

Howard laughed a little. "But when I saw you looking at me, in the cafeteria, in the assembly room, the library —"

"God, was I that obvious?" I tried to laugh it off.

"— I thought, not her. I mean, you being a white girl and all. I didn't expect it."

"Thanks a lot." I tried not to let my voice betray how crushed I felt. I knew the color thing had to get into it somehow and that it would stop us, be a barrier as big as that moon falling down on us.

"Like, how do I know you're not one of those girls who just wants to see what it's like to be with a black guy? Maybe you aren't really interested in me but what I represent. You see what I mean?"

I knew what he meant but it made me angry, partly because what he said had some truth to it and partly because it didn't. I thought of Ola and how I wanted to run to her and bury my face in her cupped hands. But then, she was part of Howard and I — I was part of no one.

I stood up to leave.

"Hey," he stumbled to his feet. "I didn't mean to make you mad. I guess in this light we all look the same — scared shitless, right?" He made an effort to smile. His mother had taught him to be polite, I could see that.

"Except you don't seem scared," I said.

Before he could answer, a high-pitched wail pierced the air. Then another and another.

The moon, horrible in its luminous bulk, had just cleared the horizon, practically blotting out the sky. The wails and screams increased and then everyone was running, terrified, stampeding in a rush to get away. Howard and I jumped out of the way and I looked frantically for my parents and Lisa. But they had vanished in the crowd of crazed people. We heard glass shattering and the moans of victims being trampled. Fights broke out and there was the sound of gunfire, and then police sirens. Instead of running, some people fell to the ground, tearing each other's clothes off in a frenzy of desire or hate.

I grabbed Howard's hand and we hurried down the hill, toward my house. A bottle flew by my head, and Howard caught a rock in the leg, but I led us through the mobs of frenzied people streaming around us. No one was home, and we crawled into a closet and shut the door, while outside the inhuman shrieking and smashing continued. We didn't say anything, but held each other, shaking. Somehow I fell asleep. When I awoke, I gently untangled myself from Howard and opened the closet door. It was quiet, a weak predawn light filtering in the window, or what was left of it. The glass was scattered all over the floor and I saw a huge boulder that had crushed the sofa on impact.

Outside, a few people were wandering around, looking dazed and bloodied among smashed cars, broken glass, chunks of concrete and brick. In the driveway, my father's new sports car was a pile of smoking wreckage. The front lawn had been chewed up so it didn't look like grass anymore, and there upon it lay two people, naked, the man sprawled between the woman's legs. At first I thought they might be dead because they lay so still, but then the man moved and looked up, dazed. It was my father, and the woman beneath him was not my mother.

Numb, I wandered back to the closet and huddled against Howard, who slept blissfully on.

Hours later, my father found us. His face was bruised and he had lost his glasses, but at least he was dressed. I couldn't bear to ask him who that woman was, not even after Howard left. We sat in the wrecked living room, silent, waiting for Mom and Lisa to show up. They never did.

Toward sundown, we headed for the hill once again, even though we knew it was dangerous. The other survivors seemed to have the same idea. Dad and I walked apart and avoided looking at the battered bodies lying askew in the streets, still hoping Mom and Lisa were alive somewhere. There was a smell of smoke and blood in the air, making me want to vomit. I tried to remember the times when the moon was tiny, so small I could hold it in my palm like a shiny dime.

The gathering on the hill was much smaller now, as we watched the darkness grow in the east. People looked exhausted and subdued, unable to do anything else but sit and stare blankly ahead of them. Howard carried the same plaid blanket he and his mother had sat on last night, and I thought it was a good sign.

"Where is Ola?" I asked, scanning his face, desperate for happy news.

"Gone," he said. His tone was neutral.

"My mother and sister are missing too." And I let the thought come, the one I had held off all day. "What if they're dead?"

"My mother isn't dead," Howard said firmly. The scar over his eyebrow was dead white against his skin.

I didn't dare question him. He had such a hard, strange look on his face, and besides I understood. How can you admit such a thing?

"I know where she went," he continued.

"Where?" A wild hope tore through me. Perhaps that's where my mother and Lisa went.

He pointed to the blur of mountains on the northern horizon. "She knows of a sanctuary there, a grove of trees, a cave."

I didn't say anything, still thinking he was in some sort of shock. The mountains were a good hundred miles away and since the gas supplies had been taken over by the government, cars were useless. That meant she would have had to walk. And besides, why would the mountains be so safe? If the moon fell to the earth, everything would be destroyed, wouldn't it? And what if it didn't fall? What if the moon went back to its normal place?

"Why didn't she take you with her?" I asked, playing along

with him.

"Because I had to wait for you, Cynthia." It was the first time he had said my name, and I liked the way it rolled off his tongue.

"But where exactly in the mountains is this place?"

"Trust me. I'll find it."

It was obvious he completely believed this wild story of his.

"So what do you have to lose by coming with me?" he asked.

I started to cry. I just couldn't help it.

A fat, middle-aged man, guzzling a quart of beer, looked at me and said, "Hey don't look so sad, girlie. Haven't you heard? Tonight's the night when they're going to fix the moon for good. Cheer up." As he wandered off, he fell flat on his face, the bottle thumping down the hillside, refusing to break. The man rolled over on his stomach and started laughing. It was the most horrible sound I had ever heard.

As the rim of the moon appeared, people began to stir. The moon was as huge as ever, but tonight a brilliant light played on its surface. As it continued to rise we saw some lines, and it became obvious that these lines were the upper parts of letters and they were flashing on and off, blue and red. The crowd began to stir and murmur as more of the letters became visible. Then almost at once, the message glided into view:

UNICARD

ONE UNIVERSE

ONE CURRENCY

Spellbound, the people on the hillside stared at the glowing white screen, waiting for more. Except for us.

I nodded to Howard.

We walked down the hill and through the ravaged streets, farther and farther away from people, the town, everything we knew and didn't want to know any longer. We walked north, straight through the fields, the valley, toward the mountains, so blue, so real on the horizon.

WHO'S COUNTING?

by
Harry Mathews

Ralph, that sociable spirit, enjoyed departures. They often saddened him, but he knew the sadness would vanish as he approached a new place, a place that later on he would be saddened to leave. He knew there was no one last place, to be necessarily shored up with precautions like planting trees or installing dark-tinted windows. He went on leaving, keeping an occasional souvenir, as evanescent as thistledown. As Ralph's train drew out of the station, it passed a bearded yardman: he seemed indifferent to the offices and their static machines fronting the tracks, busy as he was with the efficient expedition of locomotives whose destinations were to him irrelevant.

Ralph had difficult moments. His dearest friend never kissed him goodbye. She claimed to love him; she certainly disliked his refusal to remain in the city of their birth. Ralph also suffered from his mentors' impatience with his restlessness and the inability of companions to understand it. He forgave his friend for her misguided devotion and happily ate zabaglione with her, knowing that it soon would be digested, and her predictable complaints along with it.

A provisional Queen of Chad told him that the introduction of a new strain of imported grass had assured the prosperity of her kingdom and the perennity of her reign. Ralph saw in it only a tough, familiar weed and, despite her urging, found nothing eloquent to say about it; nor did the claims of her botanists (also imported) or the chants of a sincere populace change his mind. But because he admired her svelte bosom, he took pains to make it shudder with laughter at the outrageous tales he made up for her; and she finally preferred them to agricultural forecasts recited by self-serving counselors.

In a Sicilian village where Ralph was staying, frost struck the fields in mid summer. The inhabitants deduced that the vestments in their church had been unduly neglected; all the women in the community set about mending them. Ralph was asked to contribute to their propitiations, for instance by composing a few plain verses they could sing while they worked. (Even a visiting group of students taking make-up courses was enlisted, along with their teachers, in the ritual brouhaha.) Ralph one day discovered a stand of late-blooming furze on a nearby mountain and presented one of its thorns as a goodluck token to the town elders. He also taught them the classical use of the **I Ching**, and with it they discovered portents of an abundant harvest. Ralph did not wait for the outcome of the prediction nor, as he left the village, did he ask to what end men in the cafés were conclusively throwing their dice.

Wherever he went, he found the usual pessimists. At each nudge of the clock-hand towards zero hour, one of them was sure to announce some calamity ended or begun. Where was there a Miriam with her song of triumph? She would have sung unheard, whereas the others were rewarded with potted plants and drinks on the house. Ralph enjoyed the sight of one reverent acanthus-bearer: the kohl-haloed eyes in the slitted veil promised oblivion for tangible accretions of habit and these unwavering fogies.

He climbed past stone millstones high into Turkish hills.

Behind him a speeding bus, "G. Pfeffer, Wuppertal" painted on its sides, was making its rhythmless way from temple to sea. The bus was treated with respect — carts drew out of its way and iced drinks were set out for it on roadside tables. Ralph ascended higher, into a patch of gorse through which he weaved an uncertain but happy way, the roaring bus out of earshot, the Paleozoic rocks ahead of him dissolving into hot clear sky.

Ralph heard lamentation rising from the four corners of time. Behind each groaning altar stood one or several persons, all legalistically defined, even though the altars gave access to fleshless eternity. The names of these persons mattered greatly to zealots and to those who fled from them. On the lake far below, in his distant gaze, an ancient two-masted boat trailed a wake rippling with silver. He forgot what he had recently eaten and must soon eat again.

Ralph thought, standing on the next-to-last ridge, that if one cared enough about such questions, one name — the millennial birthday baby's — should be permanently reassigned to the unlikely season of an imaginary year, centuries of carnage notwithstanding. Of course the name still meant trouble, although the locals hardly cared and the churches on the lakeside slope were ruins. But whenever two or three thousand are gathered together, get off the highway and watch from a distance. The apparent flash of weapons will prove illusory as you fall asleep, content never to have faced a lifetime of prison fare.

Ralph had forgotten why he came here and where he would go next. He had forgotten the day, which at its close nevertheless stamped him like an arrested searchlight with its passing presence — the day itself, not its red or black sign in some calendar of dead stories. He perched on the ledge like a mouse on a chandelier. Were those apes in the valleys? Were they following a mythical regimen pointing to a meatless feast? Ralph had made up his mind:

If the questions are postulated: where is the point in attributing a significance to this date that is a historical absurdity, and why is this significance so widely recognized (whether through acceptances or refusals), we can always enjoy the consolation of one thought: in that year, apparent similarities will be no more than apparent, and irreversible differences unnoticed.

And if the quickeners are poured, where is the poise in authorizing a silhouette to this day that is a hoity-toity academician? and why is this silhouette so widely recompensed (whether through accidents or regattas)? We can always ennoble the conspectus of one threat: in that yellowness, apprehensive simplisms will be no more than apprehensive, and italic digs unoccupied.

THE INFORMATION HIGHWAY

by

Steve Katz

The sexual act deflates the imagination.
People always seem stupider afterwards.
Malcolm De Chazal

"Roger, sweetheart, please stop," Adeline complains. "I'm not your snack-o-matic." He's a feeling, passionate guy, the sweetest lover, but his head has been rooting between her thighs since one a.m. of Halloween. "I love it, mighty mouth, but there's a limit. It's been twenty-four hours, no, twenty-two, no, twenty-seven hours by now. It's almost five." She went as a bag of golf clubs, and he as a marijuana plant; however, the big party they had anticipated turned out to be a sedate gathering of her corporate cronies dressed as company products. So they cut out and walked the streets for a while, taking in the human marshmallows and spareribs and shish-ke-babs. Barbecue was a big theme this year. They saw some superheroes, too; and wizards, and one couple dressed as the twin towers, and a whole sorority of witches that emptied out of the Lido bar and marched down Broadway. There must have been sixty of them.

"Stop, Roger. I love you bunches, but please now, stop." She doesn't want to hurt the feelings of this sensitive, caring, long haired, gentle vegetarian guy, the one man she loves; but they have hardly slept. "Save some for a rainy day, Rog, honey. You know I'm happy to be where your next meal is coming from, forever." Even in their daily life there is some truth in that. She's the one who brings home the brie. "I'm a whole person. Don't just turn me into some kind of munchy." She feels her sense of humor slipping away.

Roger lifts his head to face her face. "Almost finished. It's the ABC's of it, even the XYZ's of it," he intones. His face is repulsive, looks as if it has been dipped in a vat of lanolin, wrinkles filled in, her stuff thick in the eyesockets, and the whole prolate sphere textured here and there with pubic curls. She hates to look at it, so she sinks it back down.

It's five a.m. now, Sunday morning. Good thing she doesn't have to go into work. She's hungry, but can't think of anything she really wants to eat. **Shoah** is on the all-night art film channel. She can't remember if she saw it years ago at the theater or not. It's engrossing, but very painful to watch, full of the stink of lies and hypocrisy. Maybe that's why it comes on at four a.m.

At the commercial break she pulls on Roger's ponytail. Enough is enough. "Sweetheart, come on," she entreats. To her astonishment the head starts to separate from the neck with a pleasant, Velcro-like crackle. Velcro is one of the few benefits to the population at large that she can understand from the cost inefficient space age. "Stop this, Roger," she says, and rolls the head back, trying to refit it to the neck, but no luck. It is half detached. She looks around the room, as if afraid there might be a witness.

When they got home he said, as if he had learned about romance only from pornography, "I want to give you head all night." So this is what happens when words of lust take a literal turn. It won't screw, it won't chink back in. She will have to either leave it dangling, or take it off the rest of the way. The former is not in her nature. She's famous for finishing whatever she starts. That's why she has stepped so far up the so-called corporate ladder. She knows it's ridiculous, but she says, "Okay, relax sweety," and she gives the greying ponytail another tug. It comes off easily, just like ripping wet newsprint. Then she lies back and holds it above her face to look at this. "Gosh, pumpkin. What happened? I'm so sorry." The head is thickly coated with herself. The tongue, curled into a tube, sticks far out from the lips. One eye winks at her. A slight sneeze.

"Sweetheart, yuk!" Her reflex of revulsion makes her toss the head at the bathroom door, where it rolls into the fresh kitty litter, one of her company's original products, picking up most of it on the face before it comes to rest near the sink, its features spackled with green, chlorophyl-impregnated chips.

"Roger is a novelist," says Adeline aloud, another irrelevant thought. The novel is something to read on a flight, when you don't have work to do. She had shown Roger how to use the Mac in the first place, and that was when he decided he was a novelist. By itself the novelist is an anachronism. A novel can be written as well by committee or computer. This is one reason she chose to live with Roger. He presents a contrast with her professional life, puts a quaint spin on her personal time. You might say he's a blast from the past, then again you might not.

She shakes the nightgown loose from where it's sticking to her thighs, and follows Roger's head into the bathroom. It rests on its side under the washstand. "Everything will be perfect, darling. I can handle everything." She drags the head across the floor to lean it face out in the crotch the clothes-hamper makes with the bathtub, and secures it in place with a beach towel rolled up.

"Oh Roger, baby," she says, after gazing a few moments on the face. "If this has happened to you, what do you think God has in store for me? The word, "God," from her own mouth, unnerves her. She uses that word only with her grandmother.

As soon as she steps back the eyes open and the lips move. The head starts talking. "Lift is produced by the difference in pressure between the upper and lower surfaces of the airfoil, or wing. Since the pressure of a gas is inversely proportional to its speed you shape the wing to maximize the speed of the air across the upper surface. The characteristic lifting airfoil profile has a maximum thickness of six to eighteen percent of the chord aft of the leading edge. The normal component, or lift, may be expressed in equation form as L = C sub l sub q S. The variation of C sub L with geometric angle of attack..."

She finds his voice more nasal than before, although she recognizes it as Roger; but she can't bear to listen, and decides to wash downstairs in the guest bathroom. Roger's body now stands on his own two feet in the bedroom. An erection has developed. "So that's what it takes," Adeline thinks, then thinks better. The right arm is extended and bent, pointing at the baby bazooka with a crooked forefinger. The body seems to follow this stiff thing around as it bumps into things, like someone in love. She's afraid at first to approach, but then finds it quite docile as she takes the left hand, leads it to the bed, and lowers it to the sheet. The penis seems to ask for someone to grab it. Not her, not now. With another sheet she covers this, so the thing stands like a tentpole in the midst.

As she scrubs in the guest shower she maps her whole week. It will be Thursday before she has time to get back to this Roger situation, but it isn't so catastrophic to delay since everything is more or less alive, depending on what definition you give to life — the ability to speak, the maintaining of erection; anyway, she will wash the head then. The kitty litter is a good product. It will keep the thing fresh till Thursday.

She spends most of the day in her bathrobe in the office

downstairs, editing the manual some of her writers produced for a new investment tracking program. They made the new software seem too complicated. Better the other way around. Then she works on her laptop on a presentation she is going to make for her board. To avert a hostile takeover she has fashioned a sexy offering for their stockholders, and leveraged a distribution deal that will get their swift new RAM expanders into every computer store in the country. This is only one aspect of the diversification she has designed for a corporation that before herself languished in the business of pet products.

At 9:30 she's ready for bed. The morning disaster has almost slipped her mind, but approaching her bedroom she hears Roger's head still yacking in the bathroom.

"Partially balanced incomplete blocks form a very general class of experimental design in which not all treatments occur in every block. 1. Each treatment is replicated "r" times. 2. Given any treatment..."

As if she gives a rat's ass. The body lies still potent in her bed, its poker doubled in length. Business doubled twice since she became CEO, she reflects. So she likes doubling. But Roger's thing could be like Jack's beanstalk. Who knows where it will end up? For the first time in the three years they've lived together she feels ambivalent about crawling into bed with Roger, even though the snoring problem is probably eliminated by this coup; but realistically, the longer erection has pulled the sheet into a higher tent now, and she will be at a definite disadvantage in what sometimes becomes a nasty battle for the comforter in the middle of the night. She intended to get a second one, but as with a lot of things domestic hasn't found time or motivation to shop for it. The major concerns of the day always distract her from the minor difficulties of the night.

She hears the head, still blabbing in the bathroom.

"After having been twice driven back by heavy, south-western gales, Her Majesty's Ship "Beagle," a ten-gun brig, under the command of Captain Fitz Roy, sailed from Devonport on the 27th of December, 1831. The object of the expedition..."

Wrong! She can't tolerate this talk, but she has to suppress her response until pressure from work eases off. Meanwhile she will sleep alone in the guest bedroom. In Roger's closet she finds his bowling ball in its soft padded bag. It's been at least a year since they've gone bowling. The ball has his name etched on it, as well as the "All American" logo. She kisses the name and places the ball carefully on a pillow at the end of the neck. The three holes look almost like eyes and nose. It starts rolling from side to side, as if something about the presence of the body disturbs it. "Yipes," she thinks. "A bowling ball with feelings." Something like that always makes her wonder about life. To quiet things down in the bathroom she carefully places the head inside the bowling ball case.

"The day was glowing hot, and the scrambling over the rough surface and through the intricate thickets was very fatiguing; but I was well repaid by the strange, Cyclopean scene. As I was walking along I met two large tortoises, each of which must have weighed at least two-hundred pounds: one was eating a piece of cactus, and as I approached, it stared at me and slowly stalked away; the other gave a deep hiss, and drew in its head. These huge reptiles, surrounded by the black lava, the leafless shrubs, and large..."

Wrong! She zips it up, then curious to find out if it still talks while the bag is closed, quickly zips it back down.

"The women, on our first approach, began uttering something in a most dolorous voice, they then squatted themselves down and held up their faces; my companion standing over them, one after another, placed the bridge of his nose at right angles to theirs and commenced pressing. During the process they uttered comfortable little grunts, very much in the same manner as two pigs do, when rubbing against each other. I noticed that the slave..."

Still talking. Wrong!

In the morning she gets up early to head for the office. Almost out the door she remembers she has neglected to look in on Roger. He always has an especially sweet kiss for her on her way out, and she still wants one. Usually he stays home to write his novel. She runs upstairs to look in the bedroom. The whole sheet now has lifted way off the body, as if being raised to fly from a pole. It makes her think. Unless attached to a brain, the erection does not interest her; but she could appreciate a kiss without the body attached. She shleps the bag downstairs so the kiss can happen at the familiar threshhold to the street. How, she wonders, will the fact that she has to hold up the head affect the kiss? She zips it open. "Sweetheart, I'm off to work."

"Bode's relation may be stated as follows: write down a series of fours; to the first, add zero; to the second, add three; to the third add six equals three times two; to the fourth, twelve equals six times two; to the fifth, twenty-four equals twelve times two, etc; the resulting numbers, divided by ten will give the approximate mean distances of the planets from..."

Wrong! This is unbearable. She zips the bag, and drops it in the closet, next to the umbrellas.

In the cab as she reconstructs the moment she reflects that, unless her eyes have deceived her, Roger's head now appears much smaller than when it was attached, as if it is shrinking away as the mouth releases his gibberish. Everything keeps getting curiouser, but Thursday is still the soonest she'll have time. She puts it from her mind and focuses on work.

The two short morning meetings go well, as does the big board meeting, where she presents her successful strategies to the general approbation of the other execs. She is a kind of hero in the tight inner management circles of Darkl-Melma Ltd.

So much accomplished in the morning, leaves her with a lighter afternoon schedule. She declines the executive lunch. She isn't up to it. As she was making her presentation something strange happened. While she explained some of the graphs, the events of her weekend started to appear to her in images on the screen, then she heard Roger talking, then the sounds of his head separating from his body thundered into her skull. She was well prepared, and confident enough to muck through the presentation, but now she is shook up. She wants to talk to someone, anyone but another executive. Is she going crazy? Will she cease to function?

She decides to grab a lunch in the employees cafeteria, where she can be somewhat anonymous. One thing she misses from the days she worked in the trenches as a computer operator is casual conversation with other women. Now her lunches are mostly with men, sometimes accompanied by wives or girlfriends, who frequently seem to resent her. Very rarely is there another woman with her rank, and with those there is uneasiness, because often there seems to be some tacit competition. What she would like to have back is the coffee breaks or lunches with women — talking salaries, talking husbands and kids, laughing down the harassers in the office, comparing shopping notes, women's problems, dating, friends. She found more good humor, more laughter in the ranks than at the tables of the CEO's.

She leaves her jacket in the office, shakes her hair out of its bun, and unbuttons her blouse a little to let show the tip of the wing of the dragonfly she in her wilder days had tattooed above her left breast. Her boyfriend then, Mouse Bernstein, was a tattoo artist, and a Harley freak. Something about Mouse she misses. She gets a bowl of chowder and a Greek salad and sits down in a corner, hoping not to be recognized as the boss, and hoping one of the women will sit down with her.

Before long someone does settle in across the table, with a pasta salad and a peach melba. The woman wipes her spoon and fork with a napkin that she puts in her pocket, and then unfolds another for her lap, tucking the corners under so it makes a hexagon. She smiles at Adeline. The metal braces in her mouth are disturbing, like visual static. Metal braces on older faces make Adeline uneasy because her mom never had money for an orthodontist when she was young, and she grew up thinking her mouth needed improving. Now that she has the money, she doesn't want to bother; but still, seeing this woman makes her run her tongue across her teeth.

"I'm Sybil from accounting. I don't think I've seen you in here before. Are you from customer service?"

"No. I'm a programmer. My name is Dolores," says Adeline.

"I thought it was just customer service and accounting in here from one to two. Aren't your people supposed to be eleven to twelve?"

A woman who knows the rules. Adeline likes that, "They made an exception today, because of my problem."

"Pleased to meet you, Dolores." She sucks down a few swirls of rotini. "Which problem is yours?"

"My boyfriend."

"Oh, boyfriend problem."

"Yeah, that one." Adeline swallows a spoonful of chowder, then starts to speak. "We've been living together more than three years. He's a great guy, a little old-fashioned, a writer; well, not really a writer. He's a novelist. I actually love him a lot. He's sensitive and he's loyal. I don't know. Sometimes we take separate vacations, but we're usually together. Sex is good. It lasts forever." Adeline suddenly feels in her belly she is going to tell too much too fast, but she can't stop herself. "He knows things. Like the history of the forklift, and how it changed warehousing. Sometimes he tells me that. That's good. Isn't that good? He was a forklift operator for years, before he changed his name from Ralph to Roger and became a novelist. We always get along great, until this weekend, and we didn't even argue." Sybil is expressionless. The recessed lighting glints off her braces as she slowly eats. "But I'll tell you, he was doing something to me; I mean, down there, like he does. Usually I like it, but this is going on too long, and I pull on his ponytail to see if I can get him to stop, and something very weird happens." Adeline waits for Sybil to ask what, but her silence continues. "I pull on his ponytail and his head comes off."

The pause is heavy, a moment like a balloon that can't shed its ballast. Nothing rises. Nothing from Sybil. Sweet Roger, Adeline thinks. We have separated your head from your heart. She wants to say, "O woe is me. Oy yoy yoy yoy yoy!" Sybil remains expressionless and silent, and Adeline feels that silence packed with monotony. Tears heat her eyes. A fleck of pasta is caught on Sybil's braces. Adeline dreads what might be said.

Sybil eventually speaks.

"What is his social security number, please?"

"I don't know, Sybil. Right now I feel like I'm out here, you know, on the edge of nature, with all the smaller shadows. Shadow of the inch. Spoonshadow. The wild minkshadow. Small, wee ones. Shadow of a comma. Shadow of the tampon. But I just held his head up and it was still talking. That's impossible. Physically impossible. But talking. Oy yoy yoy yoy yoy!"

"What is his middle initial? His daytime phone number or a number where he can be reached, like a cell phone or fax number?"

"And then his body was walking around with a big, you know? Everything going into the deeps. Down the well. Shadow of the chestnut. Shadow of moth. Pillshadow." Adeline was earnest, but also enjoyed the words she was starting to talk. She could be the king of shadows. King Shadeline. "It was a big erection. You know, shadow of a tiptoe. Dropshadow. Shadow breathshadow."

"Has he done business with D-M before?"

"I need to find something out. What does the red mean? What happens in the blue?" Adeline brushes a tear from her cheek, and another takes its place. "And then when I was working, I started seeing it and hearing him."

"His social security number, please. Is this a private or a corporate account? Is there an 800 number? To what address will we send the billing?"

Sybil's expression never changes. Adeline sees now that she is looking into her face as if it were a monitor, and she is waiting for the responses to come up. There is no satisfaction in this for Adeline.

Back at her office Adeline succumbs to an invitation to dinner from Eduardo Nifty, CEO of their Perpetual Pet Food division. He has invited her regularly twice a week for a year and a half and automatically turns to walk away because he can't fathom that he hasn't been rejected again; so, she has to shout a repeat of her affirmative. She's in no hurry to get home. Quite the opposite. Eduardo is a career executive, with little in his life except his job. They spend a long, boozy evening at the kind of upscale surf and turf she never goes to with Roger. Roger is strictly Asian or Middle-eastern vegetable chow. Eduardo's monotonous conversation is not satisfying, but it does relax Adeline.

They leave the restaurant after ten and find separate cabs home. Adeline has yet to prepare a pep-talk for the morning meeting with her middle managers. A small piece of work, but it will keep her going till after midnight. Not till the cab pulls away does she realize how tired she is, and her problem with Roger suddenly looms. She takes some comfort that she's a well known problem solver. She looks up. No lights on in her brownstone, but every room that has a TV — bedroom, living room, even the small black and white in the kitchen — someone switched them on and the walls glimmer. How can that be? In the little window of the computer room, modem, fax, cd rom library, a screen flickers, in use. In that very room sweet Roger processes his words. Who is using this now? Has Roger's erection unzipped Roger's head? Is a bowling ball playing with her laptop? She fears what she will have to face on the inside, but can't let that stop her.

On other nights she has stepped across the homeless man lying under cardboard cartons across her stoop. No big obstacle. The box covering his uppers has "Do not open until the millennium" marked on it. She is suddenly engulfed by a fear, yea, even a terror of what is now. She feels vacant, or without inner resources. Her life flickers away. Her windows glow onto the street.

Adeline backs off to lean against a car and breathes the night air. Tasty stuff. She recognizes something. It's acrid, a hint of sweetness in it. This waft of burning flesh, human burning. She knows that smell from her trip to Bali with Mouse Bernstein. They were there for the cremation season, and for the family they stayed with this was a joyous aroma because they had finally saved enough money to cremate a grandfather and a child, both of whose bodies they had kept in shallow graves till they could afford the priest. And she had smelled it again when she first moved back to the city, and the vacant building near her apartment burned almost to the ground. Her cat, out for the night, rubs against her legs and makes a doleful noise. Has Buster been fed? She gazes at the window for a long time. Her fear finally leaves like a brush on a truck, but she still can't go in. She just can't. She doesn't even want to know what happened in there. It's like a spiritual eviction. If ever the aliens in their UFO's are going to come and whisk her away, now's the time.

Suddenly, rather like a mudball some kid splats against a window, she is hit by the recognition that she has forgotten how many letters there are in the alphabet. She thinks it's an even number — twenty-two, or twenty-six, or twenty-four. It's in the twenties. Maybe twenty-eight. Or maybe she's wrong, and it's an odd number after all — twenty-five or twenty-seven. Maybe that's wrong and it reaches the thirties. She's quite sure it's not in the teens. That's too few.

She'll recite the whole thing, she decides, and count them each by one; so, she leans her head back against the car and starts from the beginning. "A B C D..." She gets pretty far, all the way to K, before she has doubts. She sniffs the air. Still something familiar. She isn't so sure about the J. Maybe she put it in too early. It comes after O, before T. O J T P; then she can't remember if N comes first, or M. At least she knows they come together in the sequence, she's pretty sure. M N L U R? N M W...? M O N U R Y...? N U M I N O...? numino? minemony? No. Not two N's. She pushes ahead with it, and knows it's coming to the end when she hits L U W Y Z V X. She's satisfied. X at the end satisfies Adeline.

THE BIG SPIN

by
Teri Roney

Claire was in the kitchen making tea for her grandmother when they made the announcement, so she didn't hear the slap of the card as the wheel wound down to the winning social security number. Even then, she didn't pay much attention until she heard the television barker bawling her name.

"Claire and John Conrad," he cheered, "your number's up!"

By the time Claire cleared the distance from the kitchen to the living room, the avuncular middle-aged man on the screen was already tapping his pocket watch and wagging his finger at the naughty audience beyond the camera.

"You know what to do, Dr. and Mrs. Conrad," he admonished. "Call Mr. Stork within the next five minutes, give me the count and the amount, and you've got a brand new addition to your little family!"

The telephone number and Mr. Stork's cheerless smile froze across the screen, but the count and the amount had already been blocked out of the shot.

"Nanny," Claire asked, "what's the count and amount?" There was no answer and she shook her grandmother's shoulder. "Nanny!" she pleaded. "You promised! You were watching, weren't you?"

"Yes, I was watching," her grandmother said. The old woman produced a nearly illegible list of five hand-written counts and amounts with the name 'Conrad' at the bottom.

"In my day, we wouldn't have been caught dead watching this trash," she said.

"Nanny, in your day they were just games," Claire sighed. "Our lives depend on them now." She leaned over the wing back of the chair and pointed to one of the numbers on the bottom line. "Nanny, I can't read this number. Is it a seven?"

"It's a four," her grandmother said. "It's a B and a four and a one. Where's my tea?"

Claire looked toward the ceiling and ran her hand through her thin blond hair while she held her breath and forced herself to think. A four and a one meant the baby was already a month old and came from camp number four. Her eyes were shining and her breath came out of her in a noisy whoosh as she picked up the phone to dial the number on the screen.

"That means it probably came from a widow. Oh, Nanny! a premium baby boy!"

Claire jerked her head up and spoke into the receiver. "Yes," she said, "this is Mrs. Conrad. Very happily married. Uh-huh, for ten years. No, my husband isn't here, but he has a medical exemption." There was a long pause while someone checked the documentation and then Claire said, "The count is four, the amount is one, and it's a boy. Yes, yes! When can we pick him up? Tomorrow, 9:00 a.m., at gate number three, camp four. We'll be there. Thank you, oh thank you. Oh!" she added hastily, "and God's State be praised!"

On the television screen, Mr. Stork hung up the phone and crinkled his eyes at the camera.

"God's State be praised, indeed," he intoned. "Another of His tiny souls saved from the despair of a divided home, and welcomed into a traditional family."

Mr. Stork allowed a perfunctory dip of the head in an attitude of prayer and then he was transformed. When he snapped to attention, his eyes were closed and he held the scales of justice in front of him. A trumpet sounded and Claire heard the roll of snare drums.

"And now," Justice announced, sonorously, "crimes and misdemeanors!"

The snare drums came to a sudden stop as the announcer put his hand on the wheel and set it in motion. Claire's grandmother clicked the mute button on the remote control before the wheel stopped spinning.

"Where's my tea?"

Claire sighed and put her hand on the old woman's shoulder.

"I'll get it now," she said. She let her hand slide away. "Nanny," she said, wistfully, "won't you be happy to have a baby in the house?"

There was no answer, and Claire turned up the volume of the mandatory Big Spin show and left the room. She listened from the kitchen while she measured loose tea into the china pot and waited for the water on the stove to boil.

"Dr. George Rossi! For the crime of internal bank fraud — let's hear it audience — everybody chime in. Your number's up!"

Claire set two of her grandmother's delicate china cups and saucers on the tray and tried to remember if she knew Dr. George Rossi. She decided she didn't, and then wondered absently if he'd win on appeal.

Grinning broadly, the announcer was urging Dr. Rossi to call heads or tails when Claire came back into the living room with her grandmother's tea. The decision made, the announcer held the ceremonial buffalo nickel between his thumb and forefinger, and winked at the camera.

"Heads it is then, Doctor," the announcer boomed, cheerfully. "Audience, place your bets!"

The camera zoomed in on the spiraling coin, followed it's descent to the backhand of Justice, and then came to rest in a tight shot as Justice slowly moved his upper hand and revealed the results of the toss.

"God's State be praised, Doctor Rossi," the announcer beamed. "You've won on appeal!"

The camera pulled back for a wide shot of Justice before panning across the silent cheers of the studio audience.

"Nanny, either turn the sound back on, or give me the remote."

"God's State be praised, my sweet butt," the old woman snorted. She gave the volume a slight nudge and slid the remote into her pocket.

"Where the hell do they get these people?" she asked Claire. "They ought to have some punishment on that wheel for making an ass of yourself in public. Mr. Stork, indeed!"

Claire laughed and tipped brandy into her grandmother's tea cup.

"You know who's number would come up for that?" she said. "Some sedate little old lady with a foul mouth and a collection of her grandmother's heirloom china. Someone who laces her tea with brandy."

Nanny's eyes sparkled as she winked at her granddaughter and reached for the decanter.

"Aren't you going to join me?" she asked.

"No, I'm not," Claire told her playfully. "And I'm not having any brandy, either. I have to get the room ready for a new baby."

The number of a six-year old girl came up for drunk driving and automobile homicide. The child picked heads on appeal and the camera followed the coin as it sailed into the air and plummeted back down.

"Tails, Missy," Justice sighed. "You've lost on appeal. Well, five years hard labor on nuclear waste clean-up. Five days to report to your site. Don't forget to tell your Mommy, and God's State be praised!"

There must have been a lot of money riding on the girl's acquittal. Claire heard the disappointed audience groan as she patted her grandmother's hand and turned to leave the room.

"I've got a real clear picture of a liquored up six-year old running somebody down in a car," her grandmother observed. "What do you think? She used a booster seat and hired somebody to work the pedals?"

"You know perfectly well that it doesn't make any difference," Claire said. "Her number came up, that's all." She grinned at her grandmother and extended her hand. "Nanny, I'm much too happy to argue with you, today," she said. "Why don't we go up to the baby's room and make sure everything's ready?"

While Claire helped her grandmother out of her chair, a collage of last week's executions flashed across the television screen. The pictures were intercut with shots of family members accepting cash awards, widows turning their children over to the State, and cheering young men riding in open cars festooned with the State colors. Most of the young men were thugs with shaved heads. They carried beer, and flags of State, and lurid home-made signs with execution slogans.

The voiceover urged viewers to stay tuned for this week's Execution Bash and gave the phone number for tickets to next week's show.

"1-800-WE ATONE," Nanny snorted. "What a crock! They ought to call it 1-800-A PROFIT."

Claire programmed the set to tape the executions, and smiled at her grandmother.

"It's part of the price we pay for living without taxes, Nanny," she said, "and executions are big money makers for the state."

She was surprised that there was no retort from her grandmother. But as she helped Nanny up the stairs, Claire was even more surprised to find herself wondering if there was any chance at all that a little girl, six-years old, had killed anyone with a car.

Upstairs, the nursery glowed with a color and texture that suggested the first rays of the morning sun. Claire and John had painted it themselves, and hired an artist to fill the ceiling with the cherubs that circled the empty cradle below. Outside of the sparkling windows, willow trees, and hanging fuschia and wisteria created colorful natural mobiles, which in turn threw a kaleidoscope of dancing light and shadow on the walls inside.

The wooden rocking chair by the window had been her grandmother's idea. In fact, Nanny had insisted on it. 'You learn a lot about love when you're rocking a baby,' she'd told them, 'and it's a helluva lot easier on your back.' Now she sat down in the chair and beamed.

"Claire," she said. "This is a beautiful room. It's a lucky little boy you'll be putting in that crib." She nodded at the crib and winked. "And we can all thank the Big Gene Pool in the Sky that baby's coming tomorrow," she added. "I've been afraid you'd wash those things down to nothing and the poor little thing would freeze to death."

Claire laughed. She'd laundered everything once a week for three years, and now the linens were as soft as cobwebs. She let her hand drift over the crib sheets and comforter as if the child were already nestled between them.

"Do you remember bringing Mama home?" she asked.

"No, I don't," Nanny said. "I remember your grandfather wheeling me into the hospital to have her, and we were at home the first time I decided not to kill her, so I guess we got her there alright."

Claire pulled her hand away from the crib and stared at her

grandmother to see if she was teasing her.

"You remember deciding what?" she asked.

Nanny cocked her head and laughed.

"The first time I decided not to kill her," she said. "Lord, yes! It was seventy-five years ago, and it's as clear as day — five o'clock in the morning and I was sitting in a rocking chair, like this one, with your mother on my lap. She was ten days old and she'd been screaming for twenty-four hours straight.

"Colic, I suppose. I had walked her, and rubbed her back and sung to her and rocked her some more. You name it, I'd done it, and she was still crying and stiff as a board.

"I looked at her and I said, 'You're the ugliest thing I ever saw, and all I'd have to do to get away with killing you is lean back and open up my legs.'

"I pictured myself in court in a little black hat and white gloves and puffy red eyes. I'd be dabbing at my tears and saying that I was, after all, very young and very tired, that I must have dozed in that rocking chair for a moment and that she must have slipped out of my weary arms and fallen to the floor."

Nanny laughed again and tugged at her ear.

"On her head," she added, "with her little brains splattered all over the floor. Hair and teeth and eyeballs all over the room, and I pictured myself trying to scrub her up off of the carpet."

"Nanny, that's horrible," Claire said.

"I thought so too," Nanny said. "I looked into that ugly scrunched up little face and put her back in her cradle. Then I marched across the street to a neighbor's house and told her to call the police. I said I hated my baby and I'd tried to kill her."

"At five o'clock in the morning?" Claire asked. "What did she say?"

"She mopped up my tears, and took me home, and gave me the best advice I ever got. She said any woman who says she hasn't had murderous thoughts about her children is lying. In fact, she thought my little fantasy was a bit pallid. But she told me not to worry. She said she was sure they'd get better with time, God knew the provocation would get worse.

"'Don't trust the woman who says she doesn't ever have them,' she told me, 'they don't know the first thing about love.' She said the trick is to decide to love them, even when you don't want to, and they don't deserve it. To love them enough to make sure nothing, not even you, will ever hurt them."

"What about Mama?" Claire asked.

"Sound asleep," Nanny said. "Three hours later she woke up fresh as a daisy and I thought she was the most beautiful baby I'd ever seen."

"What else do you remember about Mama?" Claire asked.

"Oh, I guess the first time I nursed her," Nanny said. "It was the first time for both of us. I was afraid she'd starve to death before one of us got the hang of it.

"But the things I remember best are the feelings. Like the curve of her head in the palm of my hand. I loved the feel of that even when she got older." She held up her cupped hand, suddenly graceful, and smiled.

"This is all I have to do to remember that," she said. "I remember the fear I had to choke back the few times she was really sick. I remember her temper, and her laughter, and her pranks, and the feel of her arms around me..."

Nanny pushed the rocking chair into motion and glanced at the window, before she finished. "And the day they took her away from me."

Claire leaned over and stopped the motion of the chair with both of her hands.

"You know, nobody ever talks about that, Nanny," she said. "It's like they don't care." She hunkered down level with her grandmother's eyes. "What really happened?"

Nanny's eyes studied the nursery's ceiling and then came

back to Claire.

"Nothing much to tell," Nanny said. "One morning, your grandfather had his breakfast, bundled your mother into the car so he could drop her off at school on his way to work. Just like always. He even kissed me on the cheek and said 'good-bye.'

"Next thing I knew a mean yellow dog with a sheriff's badge said I was being divorced, and I'd have to vacate the premises by noon. I can still hear him saying, 'No ma'am, you can't see your little girl, either.'

"We had attorneys in those days, and I called one. He said a woman who couldn't make her husband happy would have to prove she could still raise her child in 'the right ways.' He told me he'd try to help me prove I could do that, but it would cost a lot of money, and I'd be arrested if I tried to talk to your mother and explain why I wasn't going to be there for a while."

"Mama said you just walked away," Claire said. "She said you didn't want to be bothered taking care of her and so when you got tired of it, you just walked away."

"Oh, I walked away, alright," Nanny said. "But by the time your mother was old enough to ask why, she was too pissed off to do it."

"Well, I'm not mad, Nanny, and Mama's dead. Maybe you should tell me."

"Your mother was seven years old," Nanny said. "Old enough to visit neighbors. Well, she got that neighbor of mine to find me, and call me on the phone and tell me your mother wanted to have her hair done up in French braids.

"I couldn't turn her down. There was nothing in the world your mother hated more than braids. I talked her into it, once, but she was tender-headed, so she hated having it done and she hated the way it looked, afterwards. She didn't want French braids. She wanted her mother.

"Well, we got away with it twice. Then her father found

out and got the sheriff to issue a restraining order. Back then, that meant that if I showed up within four blocks of your mother, they'd send lights flashing and sirens wailing and they'd take me to jail in handcuffs. Right in front of her.

"The next time your mother called, I said I couldn't come."

Claire brushed tears out of her eyes and looked at her grandmother.

"God's state be praised," she said. "At least that fear's gone."

Nanny glared at her granddaughter and produced an outraged snort of contempt.

"I wasn't afraid of jail," she said. "But I'd be goddamned if I'd subject that little girl to the spectacle of having her mother led away in handcuffs!

"She was seven years old, Claire. She would have thought it was her fault. I couldn't do that to her.

"So when she snuck over to the neighbor's and called me the next morning, I told her I couldn't come to braid her hair, ever again, and she hung up on me.

"That was the day that she stopped trusting me. I never knew your mother to trust anything or anyone after that, and that was why.

"I ran out of money and lost the custody suit six months later, but that was the day they took her away."

"Did you ever hate her for not understanding that?" Claire asked. "For not knowing, not even asking?"

Nanny smiled and cupped her hand behind her granddaughters head.

"Sometimes," she said, "but love is a choice, Claire. It's the hardest one you'll ever make, and sometimes you have to do it twice a day. So, you take care of it, and you keep choosing it, no matter what. You deserve it." She gave Claire's hand a pat and struggled out of the rocker. "I'm awfully tired today," she said. "I think I'd like to go downstairs and have a little tea and a nap."

Downstairs, Claire steeped her grandmother's tea and checked the clock. It was after three, and John would be in his office. She filled the china teacup and settled Nanny into a comfortable chair before she called him. Absently scrolling through the day's numbers, she placed the call and waited.

"Dr. John Conrad?" the receptionist chirped. "Just one moment, please."

Claire continued to scroll through the list of crimes until the receptionist came back on line.

"I'm sorry," the voice crooned. "Doctor Conrad's number came up for first degree murder just a few minutes ago. May I refer you to another surgeon?"

Behind her, Claire heard Nanny's antique china cup crash to the floor and shatter.

THE LAST SECRETARY

by

Karen Tei Yamashita

The last secretary was hurled into a black hole. The final coup de grace came during an intensive E-mail battle wherein Stephen Hawking among others had been programmed into one of his many permutations, this one a rather lascivious representation, a mental masturbation rejected by the secretary. There was no meeting of minds so to speak (not to mention the question of harassment), only that incredible plate of fiber optic spaghetti that connected the secretary to everyone and everything and literally and finally, nothing.

Previous to this final incident, interactive scenario after scenario had been played out. One scenario brought the Company to a virtual holocaustic crisis, replete with flames, Agent Orange, tinseled lights, squawking gremlins and prom princesses in shredded gowns; naturally, the last secretary stood tragically at the center as the entire enterprise crumbled around. Or the end might have been more banal — the elimination of Word 6.7 and no subsequent tutorial for 6.8, or being called down to the office of the Associate Director of Human Resource Planning only to be told that it had come to our attention that, in fact, you didn't have a boss to work for anyway.

But the last secretary was for the time being a survivor.

What came in with equal opportunities would go out with equal opportunities and everything else for that matter held dear by executives and workers alike. Finally, it was a sort of throwing the secretary out with the recycled paper.

The last secretary was, of course, a Japanese American sansei, loyal and efficient to the very end. Some people called her the *samurai secretary*, as if one's origins had anything to do with stubborn persistence, bending like bamboo in the face of adversity, Spartan courage and a permanent smile.

If there is any question that the last secretary was not female, it should be pointed out that by this time, males with similar duties had long since had their titles changed to administrative assistant, coordinator, gopher or most likely, temp, or had moved on toward the vagaries of the glass ceiling. The last secretary might have been gay, but he finally fell in love on one of his numerous Club Med excursions; the postcard from Cancun read cryptically, "*C'est la vie*. It was you or *moi*."

The last secretary had seen it all. When she had first come to work for GGG Enterprises at the beginning of her career more than 20 years ago, she had been the one to clean the supply cabinets — tossing out box after box of expensive Nukote carbon paper and correction tape. Obviously a progressive in her field, she was the secretary called upon to perform the new tech duties of the time: replacing toner, for example, making double-sided collated copies or retrieving lost voice mail. As time went on, of course, she would adapt to the PC and every available word processing program from Volkswriter to Word Perfect. Then, there were the spreadsheets in Lotus 123 and Excel and numerous desktop publishers (mostly useful for office banners and employee birthdays), not to mention calendars, Windows, address lists, modems and faxing; as technology went forth, thus went the last secretary.

Seemingly, things got more efficient. Actually, they just got faster and more hectic. *It's in the mail* was no longer a valid excuse; however, *My fax's down*, was. Cost-wise it was probably all the same; initially, you could probably get one secretary with an IBM 286 clone, a couple thou in software (games included), Hewlett-Packard LaserJet, modem, fax, Canon copy machine, sixteen-button phone including memory and redial, Texas Instrument calculator, Mr. Coffee maker and throw in a Korean microwave to boot, including all maintenance contracts, paper, toner, Post-its, transparencies, paper clips, plus fringe and benefits for the price of two. But what with upgrades, rising cost of medical care mostly due to increasing incidence of CTS (carpal tunnel syndrome), liability insurance, re-training seminars, and that unfortunate incident in which a male manager let it be known to a female secretary that a pubic hair graced his can of Coke (why didn't he say *syringe*?), well, the cost of efficiency was just that: the cost of efficiency.

The last secretary hardly noticed the gradual replacement of her colleagues by various and sundry machinery and furniture; she was too busy merging mail, scheduling meetings, printing spreadsheets, filing, Xeroxing, faxing and Fed Exing. Beside which, there was always the constant quest for the perfect memo. Dun & Bradstreet had intimated that indeed such a letter perfect memo was possible, and possible while managing multiple and conflicting priorities from multiple and conflicting bosses, handling rush projects under tight deadlines and juggling a dozen assignments without dropping receiver from shoulder.

The Professional Secretary's Association in its heyday, before the last secretary was the only secretary, had sponsored seminar after seminar on topics such as *Keeping Cool Even When the Phone Won't Stop & the In-box is Overflowing*. Participation in these seminars at $250/pop came with a free *Stress Reduction Kit*. This kit had nifty knickknacks like secretarial hand cream, a soothing New Age sound effects tape for your Walkman, a free trial facial and body massage at a local salon, a fridge magnet that said, "Yes, I CAN do twelve things at the same time!", a screen saver, keyboard wrist pad and a coffee mug: *Have you praised your secretary today?* Needless to say, after a few days on her desk, someone had taken a Sharpie to the mug, crossed out *praised* and inscribed *hugged*, later also crossed out and re-inscribed, *mugged*. It was a sad commentary on the secretarial kingdom, but after all, she was the last.

The perfect memo. This was no idle quest. It was the reason for loyal service of over 20 odd years. No offer of other jobs, promotions, even a change of pace could dissuade this absolute and seemingly eternal quest. Of course, no one knew of this secret desire, and it was never intimated. Certainly the raises, the subtle perks, an extra hour for lunch every now and then, the yearly Secretary's Day flowers would seem to be sufficient reason for never leaving the job. Bosses came and went, all of varying degrees of niceness and jerkness, dismissive necessities hardly warranting the feeling of being pissed off. In the face of minor odds, there was always the greater good of the service and, of course, the quest itself. That the perfect memo might be a letter of resignation had indeed occurred to our lonely heroine, but, alas, the resignation was that of a lower associate, and upon closer examination, the who/whom rule had been broken.

Her days were numbered she knew, but surely her raison d'etre would be accomplished before the inevitable end. Magazine photographs of her mentors — Rosemary Woods, Fawn Hall and the Cat Woman — were faithfully displayed on the tack board in the miscellaneous jumble of the kids' school photos, Polaroids of office mates, Garfield cartoons and the postcard from Cancun. Once someone asked who Rosemary Woods was and if the blonde wasn't Hannah Darryl or some old actress like that. The Cat Woman was a cartoon; a fetish of some sort no doubt. Didn't Rosemary Woods invent speed reading or something like that? And wasn't speed reading sort of like scrolling down on a word processor? The secretary wondered at the disappearing history of her kind. She wondered if Rosemary or Fawn had ever come close to the finding the perfect memo only to see it erased or shredded. As for the Cat Woman, only one life had been reserved for being a secretary, and that was quite enough, thank you very much. Hisss. If there had been a perfect memo, she had surely stuffed it down the throat of her boss before clawing him in.

The last secretary was a working mother and single-parent. Her divorce had left her with the van, the condo and custody. Work was a necessary affliction — a basket of benefits, a paycheck spent in bills, a contribution towards social security and a pension plan, the meaning of life. At what moment this meaning changed or became expanded is not known. Perhaps it was the E-mail message that flashed incomprehensibly, "There must be more to life than this!" These were no doubt the frantic words of some confused employee who no longer understood the meaning of bureaucracy but words that had nevertheless touched a chord in the secretary's simple melody — the banal lilt of fingers tapping at keys incessantly, period space space shift capital, blah, blah, paragraph enter. But most likely, the need for greater meaning, the quest for perfection was a moment made pivotal by the devastation of a crippling disease.

Previously and erroneously diagnosed as CTS (Carpal Tunnel Syndrome), specialists in the field recognized the secretary's malady as, in fact, CTD (Cumulative Trauma Disorder) or one of many RSI (Repetitive Stress Injuries) rampant in the workplace. This was when the secretary's benefits — HMO, co-payment drug plan, long-term disability — should have kicked in. It began with numbness and tingling in the wrist and fingers — a clenched fist in the night. It was then that the secretary discovered that she was merely one of 50 million clenched fists, the majority of whom were women age 40 or older. NIOSH (National Institute for Occupational Safety & Health) reported that CTD and RSI accounted for half of the occupational illness in the U.S.

Liability suits rivaled that of asbestos in the range of $4 billion although expert witnesses would warn that repetitive motions such as the ceaseless beating of fingers on a hard keyboard might only be a *factor* rather than the *cause* of the disease. Certainly, workers needed to be trained in the use of such equipment. There was more to pushing buttons than met the eye. Posture, position of the hands and fingers, adjustments to the workspace, ergonomics versus the decorative. Never mind the stress of deadlines and the constant churning of information; workers who never left their workstations could be crippled into never leaving. Not to worry; voice activated computers would be the next wave of the future. Companies would hire you back despite or perhaps because of the very disabilities that put you on disability. No hands or neck movement required. You could be a mummy strapped to a chair as long as you could properly pronounce consonants and vowels and interact with the written word on a screen.

First it was the left hand, neatly encased in a wrist splint brace. Then it was the right hand, also neatly encased in a wrist splint brace. Then it was the padded neck brace and the lower back brace. Special glasses filtered glare. Earphones and headset wired the secretary to the phone. The problem was how to get to work. The other was how to apply makeup, blow-dry your hair, do your nails, dress or eat for that matter. Working was in fact the easy part; problematical however was sustaining the physical body that directed the fingers to push the buttons.

Did the last secretary sue? Of course not. Two clenched fists rose in the night, every night. Indeed, the human spirit is an amazing spirit.

An EMG (electromyogram) was performed to test nerve conduction. Surgical releasing or incising of the volar carpal ligaments with subsequent attention to post operative hand therapy was suggested and abandoned. Instead tendon and ulnar nerve gliding exercises were instigated along with ice therapy to relieve swelling and inflammation. Ice therapy turned out to be hunks of ice frozen in paper cups and used to massage the wrists and forearms. The last secretary messaged, exercised, took vitamins, and accompanied exercise and info-videos. She invested in keyboard wrist pads, newfangled keyboards, non-glare screen filters, footpads, back supports and software that interrupted her work at specified intervals, flashing from the screen: "Stop! Stop now! This means you! Yes you! Stop and massage your wrists! Now!"

The info-videos suggested a myriad of electronic devices that might reduce stress to the hands. There were electronic bottle opening devices, food processors, potato peelers and speaker phones. *Change your door and faucet hardware from knobs to modern handles* they suggested. *Use shoulder bags rather than hand bags. Listen to music. Watch television. Avoid reading where turning pages might be required.*

Crippled by computers? they asked. *But, a computer is a tool. It's just like any brain; it's how you use it. Perhaps you should consider another occupation.* In the old days, there were unions and contracts. An employee could get the backing of the union. Now there was just the government, the laws, the bureaucracy and lawyers. Lawyers lawyers everywhere and not a law to keep.

But there was a bright side to all of this. The last secretary was not a temp, not a peripheral, not a contingent. She was not a second-class employee, not a migrant worker — moving from job to job. Although the last, she was a bonafide secretary, an employee with a title and a salary, a core competency. When accordion management sucked in its flaccid bellows, she would still be there. She was the bare bones of a business world built for flexibility in a brutally competitive world. Not for her the demeaning business of constantly proving her citizenship or legal status with photocopies of social security card, U.S. passport or green card at the entry of every new job. Not for her the repetitive signature on W2 forms and counting herself as a dependent. Not for her the shuffle of resumes, unemployment lines and affidavits of work performed. She was the last of her kind with commitment and initiative. The others around her were among the 1.5 million temps hired per day, loyal only to their skills, no matter how meager. One temp hired to assist the secretary simply refused to work. "I don't do Windows 3.1," she declared with a haughty air and stomped out.

By this time, it was no mistake that the largest private employer in America was Manpower, Inc., (never mind the political incorrectness of such a name or that the majority of employees were women) by the turn of the century a million strong, larger than GM or IBM but not, of course, the IRS. Still Manpower, Inc. loomed over the American business landscape like a pervasive monolith, distributing its disposable workforce to every work station in the country. *Tired of complying with inconvenient labor and employment laws? Equal opportunity or sexual harassment suits getting you down? Union contracts and Union attitudes slowing down productivity? Worried about the increasing cost of health care benefits to salaried employees? Pension programs keeping your net profit small? The answer is simple. Hire the experts without the titles: part-timers, free-lancers, temps, short-timers, per diems, extras, supplementals or independent contractors. Fight back with a mercenary work force. Manpower for your peripheral needs.* **Time** called it the temping of America. Fortune 500s boasted 90% of their workforce invested in contingency saying that by the turn of the century, everyone would work for him/herself. A triumph for the spirit of American individualism. Someone had said that only small business could ultimately save America; no one said everyone would be in business for oneself. The IRS was flooded with requests for the long form.

By the time the secretary was the last, no one wanted her loyalty; they only wanted her work. Business schools all over the country were deep in intellectualizing the revitalization and empowerment of core workers. W. Edward Deming's words would be taken to heart. Never mind that the core was slowly being surrounded by the peripheral. Such a world was beginning to look like Brasilia — that super-modern city of bureau- & technocrats surrounded by shanty towns housing the help.

The note on the Secretary's Day flowers said, "You are irreplaceable." Comforting, but nonetheless untrue. Somewhere, they said, there was a perfect computer. What would a perfect computer be? Indestructible, immune to any virus, infinitely expandable, massive in memory, flawless in execution. That computer, however, had a small but imperfect quirk; the ON button was activated by a remote connection to the smell of a mule. The smell of the mule could not be bottled; an actual mule had to be brought on site to activate the perfect computer. So important was this computer that several mules were kept, fed, exercised and groomed with a full-time vet assigned to their care. If only the last secretary were such a perfect mule.

The world of business, they said, was borderless. Capital and production were portable. Money would find its way to every crevice of the Earth where consumers existed, where the savvy and discernible would judge the difference between Coke and Pepsi. But the corporate world would not protect you, even though Republicans and Democrats alike had hailed capitalism as God's ultimate answer. It was like the universe itself — infinite, dark, foreboding, a hollow existential echo.

Meanwhile, the secretary submitted her hands and forearms to deep friction massage and blasts of ultrasound. Weekly, a chiropractor cracked the neck and lower back. Nightly, she ripped the Velcro from the braces, exposing the thin mutilated extensions of her body, subjecting her flesh to baths of ice water. The loss of muscular tone was disheartening, but inevitably the ungroomed state of her nails brought the secretary to tears. Long ago she had been cloned into secretariness by the ultragloss of red Revlon. Now it took all her strength to apply mascara.

Daily, she peered out of her padded existence, like a turtle encased in a flesh-colored shell, to stare at her monitor and forced her crippled fingers yet to play the keys of her destiny, to make grammar flow through her very hands, to test the limits of the memo. A sense of urgency infused her work. And yet who was she kidding? She was expendable.

She stared at her precious wasted hands. Hands across the world, she thought: world peace. The sound of one hand clapping: profundity. The Sistine Chapel with God's finger touching Adam's finger: Creation. Handshaking: friendship and manipulation. Handkerchiefs: sentiment. Sign language: expression. Fingers: the decimal system and profanity. Palm reading: prophesy. Masturbation: sex. It was all there in the hands. DNA reaching back eons to the first creatures that flapped about the sea or crawled onto dry land. Here was their final resting place — pecking at a series of characters and symbols.

The last secretary gazed beyond the words and realized perhaps in a sudden moment of trauma and revelation that a memo would only be as perfect as the software and hardware supporting it. IBM, Macintosh, DOS. DOS and DOS. A virtual hand waved and beckoned her forward. The simulated voice of Stephen Hawking was slightly comforting, "If we are able to remember the past, why can we not remember the future?" Her hands disengaged with a terrible effortlessness, passing through Windows, passing, merging.

One day the last secretary indeed died from the flu — no flu in particular, just a generic one.

BIG TURN TIME

by
Karl Roeseler

Monday

Like everyone else, I want to edited an anthology of short stories about the turn of the millennium. But I waited too long.

Before I go to sleep, I think, "Only four more days. Only four more days."

Four, you see, is my favorite number.

Tuesday

Now both Saturday and Sunday are gone. Poof! During the Third Millennium, we'll have no more weekends: we'll have to create our own by stealing bits of time from other days — a minute here, a half hour there — stealing and tucking them away off calendar.

Last night, the very last Monday night of the Second Millennium, something happened to me; I had an experience, and, now, all day long, I feel compelled to tell everyone about it

---

DOWN HERE IN THE SUBTEXT WE KNOW WHY'S REALLY WHAT AND WHEN'S REALLY WHERE AND WHO'S, OF COURSE, THE ARISTOS. YES, THE ARISTOS, SO TINY, SO SUBTLE, THEY ALONE ARE THE KEEPERS OF THE WESTERN CANON. THE ARISTOS ARE SO SMALL THEY ARE NEARLY INVISIBLE. BUT,

— it's as important to me as losing Saturday and Sunday.

I tell the story over and over, to people who happen to call, to people I meet in the hallway in front of our apartment, on the lobby stairs, on the sidewalk, in the market. I spend all day telling this story. And so, somehow, my evening has stretched into a morning, an afternoon and another evening.

Wednesday

Not everyone has taken the entire week off. A friend from the law firm where I work has called to tell me biblical scholar anecdotes.

"This is the week of weeks, the party of parties," I say.

But things are busy back at the firm; a large case, an enormous class action lawsuit is being prepared and dozens of associates and legal assistants are gathering together documents and reviewing bundles of legal research. The plan is for the complaint to be filed in federal court in San Francisco during the first hour of business next week. Several congregations of one of the largest evangelical churches in North America are preparing to sue their church fathers in the event that they wake up on the first morning of the new millennium only to find that nothing has changed.

"There will be no more Sundays," I tell my friend, but she doesn't reply; instead she tells me about this one elderly scholar who favors beige silk suits and indulges a sweet tooth — every morning he goes into the staff lounge and plunks down two white paper sacks from the Vietnamese bakery across the street from his hotel. My friend goes on to describe the other scholars:

DOWN HERE IN THE SUBTEXT, WE CAN SEE THEM. THEY ARE A COLORLESS LILLYPUT SORT OF FOLK, SO SMALL THAT THEIR INDIVIDUAL HEIGHTS ARE BEST MEASURED BY THE STANDARDS OF TYPOGRAPHY. THE ARISTOS ARE TIRELESS IMMORTALS. THE ARISTOS WEAR BLACK TO BLEND IN WITH THE

some dress like secretaries, some like former astronauts.

I tell her what happened to me on Monday night.

Thursday

Like everyone else, I've been saving post cards since my birthday in January 1996 — not the ones I received, but the ones I intend to send. I've written them at a rate of one per day; I've simply been waiting until December 31, 1999 to mail them. Hundreds of two-sided time capsules, to my friends, from one millennium to the next.

I keep them in sacks in the long hallway in front of our walk-in closet. This arrangement has not always pleased Deborah. She likes to count the sacks out loud as she passes them, which she does often as this hallway leads to the bathroom.

Originally I planned to take tomorrow off in order to get to the post office early in the morning. That was before I decided to take the entire week off. Now I have to fight the desire to take the post cards in today, right away, this very moment. I fear a crowd tomorrow, another party — hundreds of people in line, their own sacks on the floor beside them or piled up on luggage carts. I fear too many other cards — so many that the system will clog and my post cards will be delayed before receiving tomorrow's postmark, and, no longer time capsules from one millennium to another, they'll revert to being mere post cards again.

I try to recover my resolve, but, when I stand and look at my sacks, all I can think is: tomorrow, tomorrow.

TEXT WHEN THEY HIDE ON THE PAGE. THE ARISTOS NEVER DREAM SINCE THEY NEVER SLEEP, SO ACTIVE ARE THEIR TINY MINDS, SO SINCERE THEIR LITTLE BODIES. 'TWAS THE ARISTOS THAT DID AWAY WITH THE WEEKEND DAYS. THEIR PROJECT WAS ENORMOUS, BUT SO WAS THEIR PERSISTENCE. THE

Friday

I bet my friend Deborah one thousand dollars that I could get everyone in our apartment building to read Dorothy Parker in the bath during the precise moment of the turn of the millennium. Deborah is, of course, my lover, and we live together, so this is something of a test to the resilience of our relationship. There are four apartments to a floor, and three floors to the building. And three couples (including us) — oh, that's four, I forgot the Randys: our upstairs-and-across-the-hall neighbors, Randy Montgomery and Randy Walsh. The Randys have been living together for seven years; and many of us, their curious neighbors, have often wondered if they started dating simply because they shared the same first name. In other buildings, there might be the Janes or the Bills or perhaps even the Dorothys.

Deborah refuses to take the bet, reminding me that the bathtub was one of Dorothy Parker's preferred sites for attempting suicide.

Nearly everyone I know has a fantasy of the ultimate turn of the millennium party. My favorite comes from our next door neighbor, Alessa, a film editor, who wants to appropriate an empty theater, invite everyone she knows, hand them each a camera when they enter the lobby and tell them to go on stage and start filming.

Unfortunately, Deborah wants to go to a different party.

The post office is disappointing. There is no champagne. And fewer people with sacks than I'd hoped. The woman in line ahead of me, Molly Lau, tells me a ghost story while we wait. I tell her about my Monday night.

ARISTOS HAVE PREPARED FOR THIS UNDERTAKING FOR OVER A THOUSAND YEARS. PERHAPS IT IS THE REASON FOR THEIR EXISTENCE. THE ARISTOS HAVE NO METAPHORS, SINCE THEY ARE SULLEN AND RARELY SPEAK, ALTHOUGH THEY ARE MARVELOUS MIMES AND ENJOY TOURING TOGETH-

Millennium Midnight

We kiss, of course; it's dark out here in the universe.

We kiss big time.

Monday

Will we, I wonder, ever recover?

Tuesday

I, myself, receive a post card from the last millennium, from Deborah, who writes, "Well, why not?"

We visit the tax man.

The legal woman.

It's all because of that way I had of thinking of Deborah as my wife for all these years.

Deborah, too, thought of me that way. Yes, she'd think, there goes my wife.

Wednesday

"When do we leave the pancake, then?"

That's Deborah, enquiring about our flat in San Francisco and my oft-repeated promise of a cottage in Gloucester.

Deborah, you see, wakes up sweating, heavily, so heavily in fact that her skin glistens in a liquid sheen and the sheets are soaked. And she groans — there, in the otherwise quiet nocturne, waking me — and together we change the sheets. Her dream, she tells me, is that she is younger, not forty-four anymore, but something else — perhaps twenty-six — and she is looking for a job but must file her application in an old musty library, and

---

ER ON THE MINIATURE MOTORCYCLES THEY FANCY. IN THE SUBTEXT, WE HEAR EVERY SOUND, BUT THE ENGINE OF AN ARISTO'S MOTORCYCLE IS SO QUIET THAT WE BARELY PERCEIVE ITS PASSING. HOWEVER, WHEN HUNDREDS OF ARISTOS TRAVEL TOGETHER, IT IS POSSIBLE TO HEAR A DULL,

she wanders down long dark rows of dusty books looking for the exact place in which she has to file her application — no matter that she cannot articulate this place before she sees it. And see it she does — in between the precise mysteries of a former engineer obsessed with the minute details of sexual despair and the melancholic yet gently topical romances of an unusually photogenic former ballerina.

Thursday

Joshua, my older brother, is in town for several days, and he is staying with us; he has the front room, which, I must tell you, can barely contain his superiority. Josh has always been critical of my projects, particularly the projects I haven't gotten around to completing. The anthology, for example, now that it's too late, he likes to say things along the lines of, well, it wasn't very representative, was it? Where was the wretched avarice, greed and despair? The hopeless poverty? The desperate violence?

I could lead Josh out the door of my apartment and say, "Into the world!"

Instead I smile.

I have made my resolutions and, besides, our neighbor, Alessa, is here filming the family lounging in the early hours of the new dawn. Deborah plays with my ten year old niece, Lori.

"I was supposed to meet Deborah at a café," I begin, expecting a collective groan from Alessa and Deborah, but Deborah is helping Lori set up the Ouija board and Alessa is fiddling with a new filter and Josh is staring at me in what might be described as rapt attention by a less sophisticated writer. I have

---

NEARLY INDISTINCT, HUMMING — THERE IS SOME CONFUSION AND DEBATE ABOUT THIS SUBTLE NOISE, FOR SOME OF US BELIEVE THE HUMMING DOES NOT COME FROM THE ENGINES OF THEIR MOTORCYCLES BUT FROM THE ARISTOS THEMSELVES. SOMETIMES THE ARISTOS RELAX ENOUGH TO CLASP

no choice. I continue. "It was the Monday night before the Turn of the Millennium, you see, and we wanted to spend a quiet night together, but we also wanted to drink coffee in a café. We both had errands to run but I guess I got done with mine before Deborah got done with hers, because I got to the café first, and there I sat, all alone in the back, until some other people arrived. And at first I was displeased, because I wanted to be alone with Deborah, but Deborah wasn't there, and we got to talking, these other people and I, and by the time Deborah did get there I had already committed both of us to helping them, these other people, carry five paintings from a painter's apartment in Noe Valley, well, on top of the hill between Noe Valley and the Castro, down to her friend's studio in the Mission. Her friend, you see, was a photographer, and she, the painter, needed slides made of these particular paintings in order to enter them in a contest. She had arranged to have another friend, a carpenter with a pick-up truck, meet her. But his truck broke down two blocks from the café, so instead she got all of us in the café to help, including two actors, two cab drivers, one performance artist, an attorney and her musician friend, even one of the café workers, as well as Deborah and me, and, of course, the carpenter. It's too bad Alessa wasn't there to film us — we would've made quite a silhouette moving those five big canvases down the hill in between the rows of Victorians."

Josh turns his head to look at the other side of the room as he drawls, "Why didn't she simply ask the photographer to come over to her place?"

EACH OTHERS' HANDS AS THEY DANCE AROUND IN ONE OF THEIR CHARMING CEREMONIES. THEY OFTEN DANCE AROUND A GIANT DONKEY WHO PLAYS A PAN PIPE. HAVE WE MENTIONED THAT ARISTOS WEAR HATS? WE CAN SOMETIMES DISCERN THE PRESENCE OF THE ARISTOS BY

Tuesday

Molly Lau has become our friend. I sometimes meet her unexpectedly in the corner market where she buys two dozen roses and tells me a ghost story. The story is actually about her mother who is still alive, and the roses are red, blood red.

Wednesday

I hear from my office. Where am I? What am I doing?

I do not know how to respond.

Meanwhile the evangelical church fathers (all of them) have begun legal proceedings of their own (filing suits against our clients, their followers no more) alleging breach of contract and fraud and our experts (the biblical scholars) have disappeared (or received mysterious corporate grants) in deepest-darkest bible country (where they can complete the anachronistic research dreams of their youths). A firm pundit begins the rumor that the scholars were taken by Something Holy — sacrilege, in a law firm, but also disputed with surprising vigor by our clients who, nevertheless, tremble inexplicably.

There is much, I am told, work to be done.

I volunteer to walk across the desert.

I do not receive even a whisper of thanks.

Monday

Friends call and complain about nausea. Many friends. All with the same symptoms. Dizziness. Mild confusion. A feeling of inexplicable loss, as if something familiar had vanished and, now that it's gone, there's no recollection of what it was.

THE MILD FRESHLY-MINCED GARLIC ODOR THAT SEEMS TO ACCOMPANY THEM WHEREVER THEY GO. WE BELIEVE THAT THIS SMELL EMANATES FROM THE OILS ON THEIR HEADS — IN FACT, MANY OF US BELIEVE THAT THIS EXPLAINS WHY SO OFTEN ARISTOS WILL CONTINUE TO WEAR HATS EVEN

There are news reports.

Many people experience similar sensations.

There are theories.

Thursday

Although it is far too early for it, a cult forms — its members indulge a nostalgia for all their lost weekends. And they do this publicly. In cafés.

Monday

I, myself, decide never to return to the office. Deborah, who has always freelanced, does not fully understand the peculiar intensity of this emotion.

Wednesday

Deborah accuses me of becoming increasingly random in my thoughts — she does this usually in the kitchen as she watches me prepare our salad.

Friday

I no longer hear from my former colleagues at the law firm.

At some point my money will be gone and I'll have to do something else.

Monday

An unusually photogenic former ballerina, who writes melancholic yet gently topical romances, has become our friend.

WHILE INDOORS. WHEN TOURING ON THEIR MOTORCYCLES, THE ARISTOS WILL SOMETIMES LEAVE A TRAIL OF TINY HATS. WE GENERALLY COLLECT THESE AS SOUVENIRS, ALTHOUGH SOME OF US WILL SPRINKLE THEM AROUND THE OPENINGS OF DOORS AND WINDOWS TO WARD OFF VAM-

I unexpectedly meet her in the corner market where she buys two dozen roses and tells me a ghost story. The story is autobiographical, and the roses are red, blood red.

Deborah is writing a script, but Alessa only wants to improvise. The Randys are out of work, although we never knew what they did. Something curses the tenant in the apartment next door; we hear him scream in his sleep. Later, we learn that he knows Molly Lau.

Friday

Friday, Monday. Friday, Monday.

We get used to it.

WU WORLD WOO

by
Mac Wellman

[The Who of Wu.]

If you are to gain a correct impression of how we operate, and how the MerryThought works, you might logically begin with the observation that all of us on Woo possess the same name: Mary Carnivorous Rabbit. Irrespective of age, sex, place of birth, and so forth. This has been the case since time immemorial. We cannot imagine any other way. Furthermore, since some of us live for a very long time, and some of us for only a brief moment or two, the place of time in the MerryThought is vestigial at best. Even what passes for identity on Elmer, or Toutatis, simply has no reality for us here on Wu. My father, Mary Carnivorous Rabbit, once went walking with me in the Garden of Walking Telephones. He said, Mary, there is a thing of great importance which I must reveal to you, a thing which is going to happen to you in your head part. Naturally, Mary, I replied, for it was the truth. I know what you are going to say, father. You are going to say that I am about to have my first experience of Transparency, through the agency of the Woovian Telepathic MerryThought Grid. He looked at me strangely, and was clearly a little puzzled, even a little afraid. It was a quick flash of a look in any case and I, like all Wuvians, am not terribly concerned with analyzing the optic on another's person's feelings. Tough tooty, as the saying goes. Outside of the MerryThought there is little of anything possessive of any intrinsic interest for any of us.

Then, he asked, what am I to do? His confusion seemed quite real; and because he was my father, Mary Carnivorous Rabbit, I let out a little cry of laughter, a suppressed iota of both compression and release, like air going out of a silver signal balloon. Then I clubbed him hard in the face with the stone I had held, secretly, in my fist. He fell backward heavily, and hit the ground flat on his back. The impact was loud and muffled, like the sound of a pillow stuffed with feathers upon the floor. A fine cloud of Silver Woovian dust rose all around his motionless body, and drifted twenty or so meters all about the spot before beginning to slowly settle. The rock was a pretty emerald-streak hunk of raw pyrite, about two and a half pounds. I felt the total lift associated with one's first completed episode of Transparency at that moment, and I must have stood there, rooted like an ancient stone hoodoo, swirling about in the diaphanous netherlight of the MerryThought for four or five years. I know it was quite a long time, for when I finally did come to I stank, was filthy and had soiled the corn-husk and spiderweb gown I had been wearing at my advent. Father's body lay rigid on the silvery sands casting a long, crooked broken-tree-branch shadow over the chilly plain. He had been partly mummified by the dry, slow seasons of Wu. Only the rats or some other pest had made a meal of his face. For the rest, his figure was all twisted up, as though in an ecstasy of some improbable and arcane balletic figure. I smiled as I recalled my advent, my fingers still holding the stone. Before I tossed it away, I searched through the rags I wore, ferreting about for a pocket. When I found one, within my coat, I sank my wiggling fingers deep within, for I was sure I would find a chocolate bonbon hidden somewhere on my person. There it was, with the label of the Hersey Chocolate Company embossed upon it. We do not know what or who a "Hersey" is, but we call all our chocolate by that name, whether it is home-made, or mass-produced in one of our four Woovian chocolate factories (usually two or three of them are closed at any one time for repairs; but this is a laughable practice since no one on Wu has any understanding of how to fix these great, grey, gurgling, rotting machines); or has dropped from a tree, or out of our cloudless sky, or washed up from our one Woovian sea, a tremulous, glittering globule of mercury.

I dropped the stone without much thought, and strode off rapidly down a stretch of the North Paraphrastic Road to see if I could recall where our house was; for I felt a strong desire to see my mother. I also strode the opposite way, because I wasn't too sure which of the two ways was home. Don't forget I was still high as a kite, the first Transparency is always the best.

Rehearsing what I would say, what I would say to my mother, I made my way back, slowly trudging in opposite directions, over the battered, silvery ball of Wu. My mother was a large, fine, stout rhomboid of a woman who wore the standard Woovian costume, a skirt of cornstalks, husks and so forth. The wimple of cheese-cloth, and the wide heavy burnoose of oily rags. Generally, she had the stub of corncob pipe in her mouth. Her name, of course, like mine and father's too, was Mary Carnivorous Rabbit. Her life, unlike mine, has been hard, just after the war. There was not enough to eat. Frequently she had to travel quite far on her old-style Wuvian bicycle to collect a half-dozen spoiled cabbages and over-ripe figs. The remote settlement of Weasel was the only place that still had food markets that were sure to be open. My mother, was a tough old piece of crow, and even the insults of vagabonds, itinerant tinkers and bong farmers along the way did not deter her. I hate to think what might have become of our little family, without her sacrifice. My little brother, Mary Carnivorous Rabbit, was a delicate child and might not have made it had we been forced to endure the fate of the common lot: prolonged and unremitting privation, with no television and limited access to toys, telephones and long stretches when even the MerryThought Grid was down. The nihilist philosopher Mary Carnivorous Rabbit wrote his or her famous book, **On The Nature Of What Is Said When You Leave The Room**, during this period, and it would not surprise me if the grim, empty and sarcastic tone of that seminal work is a direct result of the unendurable hardships of the times. Certainly the puzzle is not to be solved by a textual examination of the book itself, one of the most maddeningly obscure and complex of the Oracles. The philosopher's biographer however, one Mary Carnivorous Rabbit of the university town of Sensurround, has determined the philosopher's mental age at the time of composition, on the binet scale, as approximately thirty, which happens to be my own age, in centuries.

My younger brother, however, proved a total wastrel when he reached manhood. He incurred a blot upon the family escutcheon, and we don't like to talk about him although it is difficult to avoid the subject altogether owing to the peculiarities inherent in the Wuvian Personal Noun. Mary Carnivorous Rabbit would dawdle on his way home from school, took up dice and gambling, and soon fell in with the wrong crowd. Drugs and petty larceny soon followed. The sad tale is so familiar in these days of loony flip-flap. I recall meeting him myself at the Home for Wayward Boys, and just two weeks prior to the dreadful crime that ended his young life, and our family's joy. Mary seemed composed, repentant and determined to take a new stab at complexity, and the serious responsibilities of adult life. I had brought him a birthday cake, and we shared portions of the messy confection (of course it was a Woovian devils-food cake). I mashed portions of it through the sieve-like wire grate separating offenders from the public. He would fill his cheeks with the stuff, bug out his eyes at me and perch his big, broad Wuvian hands like monstrous but sensitive earflaps, behind his head. I do confess that I got into the spirit of the game, and made some pretty awful faces back, mirroring him. He even took the trouble to push a part of the shapeless, spongy cake back to me, further pulverizing the gooey substance so that it resembled paste rather than pastry. After twenty minutes of this fun one of the guards spotted me and approached. I was taken to a small, windowless room, stripped, scrubbed down by a huge and terrifying female guard with a harelip and a gourd of a goiter who reprimanded me. Appropriately humble and abashed, I was ushered out into the cold, bright meringue of daytime on Woo. It was the last time I ever saw Mary, my brother; for three weeks later, immediately upon his release he wobbled all the way home, indeed half way around the ovoid convolution of Wu, and murdered my mother, Mary Carnivorous Rabbit, in a most atrocious manner. With an implement called a single-knotted Yankee Doodle Electro-flageolet. The dreadful whinny produced by this terrible device is such that a person who hears its devilish music with ears unmuffled, or otherwise protected can be expected to expire in a matter of minutes, his or her brains sizzled to a microwave frothiness which causes them to spurt from ears, nose and eyes, a steamy horror.

How Mary ever managed to lay hands upon such an evil contraption is a mystery to me, although I suspect one of his knavish fellows in crime at the facility mentioned above. Electro-flageolets, in especial the single-knot variety are very rare; their sole useful purpose is to send shock waves straight to the dwindling molten core of Woo, where occasional chunks of hard, unconsumed metalica, or gigacycle plutons called "burps," get awkwardly wedged, throwing the whole world of Wu into the rattling, wild orbital dyspepsia we call "Bill Trousers Hay Ride." But it is no joking matter, since the first effect of even a minor hayride is usually the immediate cessation of the MerryThought. In the more severe episodes of chaotic tumble the gravitational perturbation has been sufficient to launch the unwary Mary Carnivorous Rabbit (caught for instance in an open parking lot with no stable hand-hold or heavy object as support) flinging him or her, literally, off the world. No person so propelled, or rather expelled! into the vacuum of eternal Holy Night has ever been recovered. Traders from Bus, however (a low world of avaricious merchants and tireless hucksters), have reported on quite a few occasions to have found, lost in deep space, solitary Woovian high-tops — battered, daubed with mercury and oil, with shoelaces tied in inextricable knots of the sort only we of Wu know how to do. But why my brother, Mary Carnivorous Rabbit, would enact such a horror must remain for all time a secret since after he dispatched our mother, Mary Carnivorous Rabbit, he wrote an incomprehensible note (which follows) and turned the terrible machine upon his own person, triggering its worm-gear with his own great toe, having removed the sock for better mobility.

Anyway, it was my mother, Mary Carnivorous Rabbit, and not my dead brother, Mary Carnivorous Rabbit, who I wished to speak with on the day I awoke from my very first experience of the Great Transparency, through the psychic good offices of the MerryThought. Moreover, I do believe my mother was still alive at the time, otherwise I wouldn't have tried so hard to find her.

My projected route would take me across parts of Woo not frequently traversed, except by tinkers, Bong Farmers and of course the wanton robbers who have made such a mess of things on our world in recent centuries. Unplugging from the MerryThought grid would leave me untraceable by most of the more commonly used detection devices employed by these ravenous wolves. Unfortunately it would also leave me in a funk, out of sorts and clinically depressed, but being a novice to the greater world of Wu I thought it wise to keep things simple. The trouble was by now I couldn't for the life of me recall exactly where we had lived. Like many Woovians I am much better at navigation when I am going no place in particular. Indeed, when I am going no place in particular, I inevitably find myself bumping into what or whomever it was I did not know I was looking for, but was. This is one of the more delightful qualities of life on Wu, and is the source of frequent misunderstandings between us and the few foreigners who do venture to this clime. Traders from Hamberga mainly, and a few tourists from Japan.

But I reasoned that, having already undergone the primary fission entailed in the Transparency, even if one of us fell victim to the trepidations of the bandittos, one of my semblables would surely make it to my cherished homestead — where my mom, Mary Carnivorous Rabbit, waited. For being a naturally fissiparous people, we are great guns in the arts of improvisation, even when we know neither who we are nor what we are doing.

*

[The Y of Woo.]

When I was a young girl I had a powerful sense, or intuition, that when I grew up I would be honored in some way; become widely known and admired for my actions, my example, or perhaps even for my wisdom and leadership, like the Majuscule of Wu. I even imagined I might become the Majuscule of Woo herself. I dreamt of doing the things she did: she who taught us our name, and how to count; she who squared the circle of cold, dead primeval Wu, and starting the original ball bouncing; she who taught us selflessness and how to advance our people through social amnesia; she who invented the basic outline of the MerryThought Grid, and taught us to be tamed by our name. Our name which was, in the beginning, her name. You guessed it: Mary Carnivorous Rabbit.

She was only a legend among us by the time I was a teenager. A remote and idolized creature of rumor and myth. Her story was mingled with every sort of odds and ends of our folklore: the tale of the Broken Thermometer, Boiled Tom, River Cat and Big Cat, Ying and Yan, and the story of how the usher of Whydah fructified a conjure-man's root with the dazzle of Usquebaugh, a dazzle that gave rise to the shower of William Randolph Trousers and all the muons, pions and gluons of superfluity, our Woovian curse and holy inheritance. But in truth did I ever imagine I could be her? No. An impossible dream, yes; a reality, never. Because it was prophesied of her, Mary Carnivorous Rabbit, the one true Majuscule of Wu, that only she would circle the square of Woo and accomplish our collective translation into Dreamtime by traversing every square inch of Wu. Every single inch. And this knowledge of the Heavenly Body of Woo would be miraculous and saving. We would emerge from our low and creepy fallen state, and aspire to a higher condition that none of us had ever known, but which had been theoretically limned in a strange Wuvian prophecy called the "Zee of Hare."

Indeed I had not recalled my dream for a long time so engrossed had I become in the delights of Woovian adolescence, petty crime, lust, arson and the free-wheeling joyousness of the young on Wu: revelling in ignorance, contemptuous of their fearful and doddering elders, committed only to babble, lunatic cartwheels; to open mockery of the night sky, and even the ghosts of our kind — victims of Bill Trousers' Hayride, slowly orbiting our gleeful irreverence.

And so it happened, as I released the grip I had maintained for so long on the little ball with which I had dispatched my father, a glitter danced across my face, a glitter as of somethingspeckled shining. An iridescence unknown to gloomy, tedious Woo. I looked more closely at the rock itself, and realized it was the source of this strange radiance. At the same time words echoed in my brain, strange words from the Zee of Hare: "She who gathers gold shall be gatherer, our Initial Unconcealer, against the secret of what is shadowed." Clearly a reference to the identity of the Majuscule of Wu. Clearly the meaning of the verse in question pertained to none other than little me: me, alone of all the myriad inhabitants of Woo, a demigod. But as I stared down at the sacred talisman in the palm of my hand, it began to blur and fade from view. Desperate, I seized and grasped empty air as if an exercise of my will could restore the apparition.

Alas, the truth was I had, like all of my kind on Wu after losing their cherry to the mimble-mamble of the Woovian Telepathic MerryThought Grid, had simply and joyously fissioned; so that I did not know precisely which of my several selves actually possessed the precious object. I sat down, wept, and felt rotten. Surely, if I were truly the Majuscule of Wu I wouldn't be having this problem. If I were Majuscule of Woo I would know all there is to know about the parting of the "Y" and would sense to right fork (if indeed one existed); and would never be troubled by indecision, doubt or a manifest lack of purpose, such as I felt now. Still, Mary Carnivorous Rabbit had her temptations in the desert and so some small uncertainty must have been forgiven her — in her formative years. This thought made me smile. I arose and surveyed the soot-colored bowl of Wuvian sky. The gentle curve of the horizon seemed to glow faintly, the merest vermillion thread of otherworldly neon. I would go, go wherever I must, to encounter myself and find the treasure that would change me, insignificant me — Mary Carnivorous Rabbit — into the fabulous creature I was so sure I already was — Mary Carnivorous Rabbit — The Majuscule of Woo. Surveying what lay before me, the vast salt flat on the outskirts of the town of Rubberneck, a shadow of its former glory, I devised in my mind a recursion pattern, a cycloid:

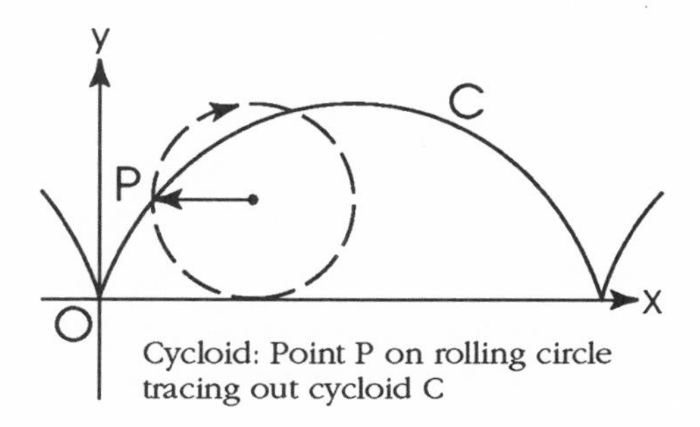

Cycloid: Point P on rolling circle tracing out cycloid C

A cycloid that would enable me, solitarily and severally, in my oneness and in my multitude, to traverse the entire surface of Wu (after all, not a very big world) in the shortest amount of time, with the smallest aggregate of footsteps. I knew in this manner there would simply be no way possible that I should not encounter my destiny, such as it was.

The trouble was, even after circumambulating the entire surface of Woo I still had not found what it was I was looking for: the corpse of my dear father, Mary Carnivorous Rabbit, and the hunk of raw gold which contained my auspice and constituted my Wuvian lodestone. Somehow the whole primal scene had vanished from off the surface of the world as though it had never been. Bitterness entered my heart and clouded my soul.

*

I spent many years by myself, avoiding the mob scene at the clubs and discos of Left Leg, pondering the vanity of Woovian wishes. The work of transparency itself seemed a thing of no worth. For decades I grew bored even with the witless hilarity of the MerryThought Grid itself and could manage no more than a sarcastic sneer at the thought of the idiotic conceit and shallow pleasures of my people. The only book I could stomach was the treatise of the famous nihilist, Mary Carnivorous Rabbit, **On The Nature Of What Is Said When You Leave The Room**. I would go on long walks along stretches of the South Paraphrastic Road reciting long passages aloud, cackling at the wicked cynicism of that dark genius, Mary Carnivorous Rabbit.

One day, while so engaged I happened to look up and was surprised to find myself standing squarely on the pitcher's mound in the middle of the abandoned stadium built millennia ago by whatever people lived on Wu in the olden days, before we arrived. No one grasped its meaning, but strange rumors about ghosts and werewolves caused most of us to give the place wide berth. It was called "John Cheese's Mouse-trap" and, like I say, was not considered a proper place to stumble upon, much less hang out at. In my current state of thorough abjection I simply had not noticed where my feet were taking me — I had been mulling over one of the more obscure epigrams from Mary Carnivorous Rabbit's book:

> Close the drapes.
> Aunt Wednesday
> is changing.

I had been worrying, in fact, for a period of several years about this saying and just couldn't quite get the sense of it, when I happened to look up and realize where I was. It seemed quite a Woovian joke on me, and I think I must have laughed inwardly because outwardly I smiled, at least so I am told by my teammates, as we came to reconstruct the whole story a long time later during the seventh inning stretch while playing a team of Bong farmers at a ballpark near the Garden of Walking Telephones.

Anyway, what happened on that fateful Wuvian afternoon

— it was a Wednesday as I recall — must have had something to do with the epigram from the Nihilist's book, **On The Nature Of What Is Said When You Leave The Room**. As my mood lightened and lifted ever so slightly, I was doubly stunned to notice a band of my semblables, fractional phantoms of the fissioning process, beckon and come towards me, all dressed in identical costumes, though each sported a distinct insignia emblazoned on the breast. These I later learned were called "numbers" and though of no use whatever on Woo (where identity is more often expressed in terms of blur) proved useful in playing the game they set about showing me. Other tools of leather, wood and other alien substances seemed initially baffling to me until they were explained by one Mary Carnivorous Rabbit a bit more "with it," as they say, than the rest. Before long we were all merrily engaged in this new pastime, and our shouts and cries of delight echoed through the empty stadium for the first time in perhaps a million years. I had come out of my blue funk.

[The Otherwho of Wu]

*
* *

[Asterism]: My Brother Mary Carnivorous Rabbit's Suicide Note:

Dear Mary Carnivorous Rabbit,

May I call you "Mary"? I hope so, Mary, because I feel the need to unburden my soul to one who will understand, understand better than I, what it is I need to unburden myself of; for it is a mystery to me. For the world of Woo weighs heavily upon me even though it is a small, dark, measly world. And the weight of the crime I have committed weighs heavily upon me even though I feel no particular remorse, as I am not even convinced I know why I have done this act which rests heavily upon my brow like... like the exploded view of a marine steam engine connecting rod, in three states: A) assembled B) disassembled: 1, connecting rod; 2, strap; 3, brass; 4, gib; 5, cotter. And thirdly: pulverized, or reduced to dust and powder and dispersed as a pungent, semi-noxious aerosol, as a loathsome fume. Indeed, the moralist within, which is the captain of my soul, cannot even comprehend the Evil which is alleged to have transpired, as agented by the lower organs of the body, the arm and body parts, always mutinous, fidgety and prone to Error and Monkeyshines; in all respects incompatible with the theoretical self, which I, Mary Carnivorous Rabbit, have caused to be erected as a public monument to the better class of Wuvian idea and persiflage. Who knows what Evil lurks below, in the sub-cellar of the Woovian heart? Who knows who of you, and you, and you... my semblables and otherwhos have not gathered by the same unholy campfire and feasted on the same forbidden barbecue? Is the Wuvian soul not like a micro-miniature of precious gold we work upon with our pathetic microliths of conscience in a vast, dark emptiness where we are forced to play crack the whip, lit only by the microlux of our Woovian wherewithal? Alone. Aghast. Ashen-assed.

Remember me when you think on the ewe-necked ewer of your own malfeasance, all curve and evolute — the locus of the centers of curvature of, or the envelop of the normals to, another curve.

Sincerely, your brother and otherwho,
Mary C. R.

HAPPY ENDINGS

by
Margaret Atwood

John and Mary meet.
What happens next?
If you want a happy ending, try A.

A. John and Mary fall in love and get married. They both have worthwhile and remunerative jobs which they find stimulating and challenging. They buy a charming house. Real estate values go up. Eventually, when they can afford live-in help, they have two children, to whom they are devoted. The children turn out well. John and Mary have a stimulating and challenging sex life and worthwhile friends. They go on fun vacations together. They retire. They both have hobbies which they find stimulating and challenging. Eventually they die. This is the end of the story.

B. Mary falls in love with John but John doesn't fall in love with Mary. He merely uses her body for selfish pleasure and ego gratification of a tepid kind. He comes to her apartment twice a week and she cooks him dinner, you'll notice that he doesn't even consider her worth the price of a dinner out, and after he's eaten the dinner he fucks her and after that he falls asleep, while she does the dishes so he won't think she's untidy, having all those dirty dishes lying around, and puts on fresh lipstick so she'll look good when he wakes up, but when he wakes up he doesn't even notice, he puts on his socks and his shorts and his pants and his shirt and his tie and his shoes, the reverse order from the one in which he took them off. He doesn't take off Mary's clothes, she takes them off herself, she acts as if she's dying for it every time, not because she likes sex exactly, she doesn't, but she wants John to think she does because if they do it often enough surely he'll get used to her, he'll come to depend on her and they will get married, but John goes out the door with hardly so much as a goodnight and three days later he turns up at six o'clock and they do the whole thing over again.

Mary gets run down. Crying is bad for your face, everyone knows that and so does Mary but she can't stop. People at work notice. Her friends tell her John is a rat, a pig, a dog, he isn't good enough for her, but she can't believe it. Inside John, she thinks, is another John, who is much nicer. This other John will emerge like a butterfly from a cocoon, a Jack from a box, a pit from a prune, if the first John is only squeezed enough.

One evening John complains about the food. He has never complained about the food before. Mary is hurt.

Her friends tell her they've seen him in a restaurant with another woman, whose name is Madge. It's not even Madge that finally gets to Mary: it's the restaurant. John has never taken Mary to a restaurant. Mary collects all the sleeping pills and aspirins she can find, and takes them and a half a bottle of sherry. You can see what kind of a woman she is by the fact that it's not even whiskey. She leaves a note for John. She hopes he'll discover her and get her to the hospital in time and repent and then they can get married, but this fails to happen and she dies.

John marries Madge and everything continues as in A.

C. John, who is an older man, falls in love with Mary, and Mary, who is twenty-two, feels sorry for him because he's worried about his hair falling out. She sleeps with him even though she's not in love with him. She met him at work. She's in love with someone called James, who is twenty-two also and not yet ready to settle down.

John on the contrary settled down long ago: this is what is bothering him. John has a respectable job and is getting ahead in his field, but Mary isn't impressed by him, she's impressed by James, who has a motorcycle and a fabulous record collection. But James is often away on his motorcycle, being free. Freedom isn't the same for girls, so in the meantime Mary spends Thursday evenings with John. Thursdays are the only days John can get away.

John is married to a woman called Madge and they have two children, a charming house which they bought just before the real estate values went up, and hobbies which they find stimulating and challenging, when they have the time. John tells Mary how important she is to him, but of course he can't leave his wife because a commitment is a commitment. He goes on about this more than is necessary and Mary finds it boring, but older men can keep it up longer so on the whole she has a fairly good time.

One day James breezes in on his motorcycle with some top grade California hybrid and James and Mary get higher than you'd believe possible and they climb into bed. Everything becomes very underwater, but along comes John, who has a key to Mary's apartment. He finds them stoned and entwined. He's hardly in a position to be jealous, considering Madge, but nevertheless he's overcome with despair. Finally he's middle-aged, in two years he'll be bald as an egg and he can't stand it. He purchases a handgun, saying he needs it for target practice — this is the thin part of the plot, but it can be dealt with later — and shoots the two of them and himself.

Madge, after a suitable period of mourning, marries an understanding man called Fred and everything continues as in A, but under different names.

D. Fred and Madge have no problems. They get along exceptionally well and are good at working out any little difficulties that may arise. But their charming house is by the seashore and one day a giant tidal wave approaches. Real estate values go down. The rest of the story is about what caused the tidal wave and how they escape it. They do, though thousands drown. Some of the story is about how the thousands drown, but Fred and Madge are virtuous and lucky. Finally on high ground they clasp each other, wet and dripping and grateful, and continue as in A.

E. Yes, but Fred has a bad heart. The rest of the story is about how kind and understanding they both are until Fred dies. Then Madge devotes herself to charity work until the end of A. If you like, it can be 'Madge,' 'cancer,' 'guilty and confused,' and 'bird watching.'

F. If you think this is all too bourgeois, make John a revolutionary and Mary a counterespionage agent and see how far that gets you. Remember, this is Canada. You'll still end up with A, though in between you may get a lustful brawling saga of passionate involvement, a chronicle of our times, sort of.

❖

You'll have to face it, the endings are the same however you slice it. Don't be deluded by any other endings, they're all fake, either deliberately fake, with malicious intent to deceive, or just motivated by excessive optimism if not by downright sentimentality.

The only authentic ending is the one provided here:

John and Mary die. John and Mary die. John and Mary die.

❖

So much for endings. Beginnings are always more fun. True connoisseurs, however, are known to favor the stretch in between, since it's the hardest to do anything with.

That's about all that can be said for plots, which anyway are just one thing after another, a what and a what and a what.

Now try How and Why.

CONTRIBUTORS

Etel Adnan

When I first saw her there was a black halo around her and that could have been scary but there was also an elegant look about her that endeared her to me and it turned out that we became friends pretty soon after. (p.59)

Novel: **Sitt Marie Rose**.

Short Fiction: **Paris, When It's Naked; Of Cities and Women (Letters to Fawwaz)**.

Poetry: **Moonshots; Five Senses for One Death; L'Apocalypse Arabe; Pablo Neruda is a Banana Tree; From A to Z**.

Etel Adnan lives in Paris and Sausalito.

Margaret Atwood

John and Mary fall in love and get married. (p.225)

Novels: **The Edible Woman; The Robber Bride; Surfacing; Life Before Man; Bodily Harm; The Handmaid's Tale; Cat's Eye**.

Short Fiction: **Murder in the Dark; Good Bones; Dancing Girls; Bluebeard's Egg; Wilderness Tips**.

Poetry: **Morning in the Burned House; Two-Headed Poems; The Circle Game; Procedures for Underground; The Journals of Susanna Moodie**.

Margaret Atwood lives in Toronto, Ontario.

Frederick Barthelme

Socorro was a ratty little town that dangled off the highway the way a broken leg hangs off a dog that's been hit by a car. (p.109)

Novels: **Painted Desert; Second Marriage; The Brothers; Two Against One; Tracer; Natural Selection**.

Short Fiction: **Moon Deluxe; Chroma**.

Frederick Barthelme lives in Hattiesburg, Mississippi.

Lydia Davis

I had been startled to discover, some time ago as I was reading a history of France (beginning, with a misguided zealousness, at the very beginning of this book, three inches thick, with the intention of reading it straight through) how very little happened in a thousand years, back in the last Ice Age. (p.123)

Novel: **The End of the Story**.

Short Fiction: **Break It Down**; **Almost No Memory** (forthcoming).

Lydia Davis lives in the Hudson River Valley.

David Gilbert

The mob closed ranks behind the Pope-mobile as it bounced over those who had fallen. (p.45)

Short Fiction: **I Shot the Hairdresser and Other Stories**.

Novela: **Five Happiness** (Trip Street Press).

David Gilbert is a co-editor of **2000andWhat?** and lives on the Peninsula south of San Francisco.

Steve Katz

"Roger, sweetheart, please stop," Adeline complains. (p.167)

Novels: **Wier & Ponce**; **Florry of Washington Heights**; **Swanny's Way**; **The Exagggerations of Peter Prince**; **Creamy and Delicious**; **Posh**; **Saw**; **The Weight of Antony**; **Cheyenne River Wild Track**.

Novela: **The Lestriad**.

Short Fiction: **Stolen Stories**; **Moving Parts**; **43 Fictions**.

Steve Katz lives in Boulder, Colorado.

Kevin Killian

*I'm always reading the **Chronicle**, every morning, at work, and I saw how the guy died, the guy who invented sodium pentathol. (p.68)*

Novels: **Shy**; **Bedrooms Have Windows**.

Kevin Killian is also the co-author of a biography of Jack Spicer. His short stories and poems have been published in many literary magazines.

Kevin Killian lives in San Francisco.

Donna Levreault

When I first noticed something wrong with the moon, I was walking back from Rhonda's, where I had gone to study for an algebra test. (p.149)

Donna Levreault has had several short stories and poems published in various literary magazines.

Donna Levreault lives in San Francisco.

Harry Mathews

Ralph, that sociable spirit, enjoyed departures. (p. 163)

Novels: **The Conversions**; **Tlooth**; **Cigarettes**; **The Sinking of the Oradek Stadium**.

Short Fiction: **Singular Pleasures**; **20 Lines a Day**.

Poetry: **Armenian Papers (Poems 1954-1984)**.

Remembrance: **The Orchard**.

Essays: **Immeasurable Distances**.

Harry Mathews lives in Paris and Villard de Lans.

Ameena Meer

Adam is in an Indian restaurant in Queens, little red plastic tables with yellow tumeric stains on them, Styrofoam bowls of dal and chicken curry, slippery with orange oil. (p.87)

Novel: **Bombay Talkie**.

Ameena Meer was for many years the editor of **Bomb**. She lives in Manhattan.

Susan Smith Nash

In my idea of a perfect world, I would be a model son, and you would be my model parents. (p.24)

Short Fiction: **A Paleontologist's Notebook**; **Channel-Surfing the Apocalpse**; **Doomsday Belly** (forthcoming, Trip Street Press).

Susan Smith Nash is also the author of several poetry chapbooks and lives in Norman, Oklahoma.

Niels Nielsen

In these wind conditions, Richard thought, a good sailor should be able to get out of the cove in three tacks. (p.95)

Niels Nielsen has contributed work to historical journals. "Mason's Island" is his first published piece of fiction.

Niels Nielsen lives in Halifax, Nova Scotia.

Karl Roeseler

Like everyone else, I want to edited an anthology of short stories about the turn of the millennium. (p. 202)

Novela: **The Adventures of Gesso Martin** (Trip Street Press).

Karl Roeseler is a co-editor of **2000andWhat?** and lives in San Francisco.

Teri Roney

Claire was in the kitchen making tea for her grandmother when they made the announcement, so she didn't hear the slap of the card as the wheel wound down to the winning social security number. (p. 180)

Teri Roney is a former broadcast journalist. "The Big Spin" is her first published piece of fiction.

Teri Roney lives in San Francisco.

Linda Rudolph

i admit freely that i enjoyed being in beijing after the big square thing, when it was not politically correct to be there, at a table full of men i didn't know and would never see again, eating foods i didn't know and would never see again, in a dress i didn't know and would never wear again, because it allowed me to be there with her, a year after her death, which was the only time in our twenty years of friendship when we had dined together without some husband or theatre manager or man in charge present — notice i do not count the chinese managers because they did not care if we dined together or not, with or without them. (p. 145)

Linda Rudolph has written for screen, newsprint and stage. "Fortress" is her first piece of fiction published in recent years.

Linda Rudolph currently lives in Miami, Florida.

Kevin Sampsell

The drunk splayed his coins across the counter. (p. 140)

Short Fiction & Poetry: **How to Lose Your Mind with the Lights On**.

Kevin Sampsell has also published many chapbooks and lives in Portland, Oregon.

Lynne Tillman

It's a weird custom, seeing in the new year carrying around a pig. (p.3)

Novels: **Motion Sickness**; **Haunted Houses**; **Cast In Doubt**.

Short Fiction: **Absence Makes The Heart**; **Madame Realism Complex**.

Lynne Tillman lives in Manhattan.

Lewis Warsh

He handed me his card as we stood in the hallway. (p.9)

Novels: **Agnes & Sally**; **A Free Man**.

Poetry: **Blue Heaven**; **Information From The Surface Of Venus**; **Dreaming as One**.

Autobiographical Writing: **The Maharajah's Son**; **Part of my History**.

Lewis Warsh lives in Brooklyn.

Mac Wellman

If you are to gain a correct impression of how we operate, and how the MerryThought works, you might logically begin with the observation that all of us on Woo possess the same name: Mary Carnivorous Rabbit. (p.225)

Novel: **The Fortuneteller**; **Annie Salem**.

Plays: **The Professional Frenchman**; **Whirligig**; **A Murder of Crows**; **The Hyacinth Macaw**; **Harm's Way**; **7 Blowjobs**; **Terminal Hip**; **Crowbar**; **Sincerity Forever**; **The Bad Infinity**; **Albanian Softshoe**; **The Self-Begotten**; **Three Americanisms**; and others.

Poetry: **In Praise of Secrecy**; **Satires**; **A Shelf in Woop's Clothing**.

Mac Wellman lives in Brooklyn.

Karen Tei Yamashita

The last secretary was hurled into a black hole. (p.191)

Novels: **Through the Arc of the Rain Forest**; **Brazil-Maru**.

Karen Tei Yamashita has also had several short stories and poems published in various literary magazines and anthologies.

Karen Tei Yamashita lives in Gardena, California.

ACKNOWLEDGEMENTS

"Madame Realism's 1999" copyright © 1992 by Lynne Tillman. Previously published in **Leonardo (The Independent)**, March 1992, and collected in **Madame Realism Complex**, 1992, Semiotext(e) (New York). *Reprinted by permission of the author.*

"Crack" copyright © 1996 by Lewis Warsh. *Printed by permission of the author.*

"Doomsday Belly" copyright © 1996 by Susan Smith Nash. *Used by permission of the author.*

"Pope-mobile" copyright © 1996 by David Gilbert. *Used by permission of the author.*

"My Friend Kate" copyright © 1996 by Etel Adnan. *Used by permission of the author.*

"Who Is Kevin Killian" copyright © 1994, 1996 by Kevin Killian. Previously published, in a slightly different form, in **Avec**, Volume 7, Number 1, 1994. *Used by permission of the author.*

"The Only Living Boy In New York" copyright © 1990, 1994 by Ameena Meer. Previously published in **The Portable Lower East Side**, Volume 7, Number 2, 1990; also incorporated, in a slightly different form, in the novel, **Bombay Talkie**, 1994, Serpent's Tail (London & New York). *Reprinted by permission of the author and Serpent's Tail.*

"Mason's Island" copyright © 1996 by Niels Nielsen. *Used by permission of the author.*

"Socorro" copyright © 1995 by Frederick Barthelme.
Previously published in the on-line version of the **Mississippi Review**, 1995, and in **Antioch Review**, Fall 1995; also incorporated, in a slightly different form, in the novel, **Painted Desert**, 1995, Viking (New York). *Reprinted by permission of the author.*

"As I Was Reading" copyright © 1996 by Lydia Davis.
Used by permission of the author.

"A Light Sound Of Breathing" copyright © 1994 by Kevin Sampsell.
Previously published as part of his collection, **How to Lose Your Own Mind with the Lights On**, 1994, Future Tense (Portland, Oregon). *Reprinted by permission of the author.*

"Stealing The Moon" copyright © 1996 by Donna Levreault.
Used by permission of the author.

"Who's Counting?" copyright © 1996 by Harry Mathews.
Used by permission of the author.

"Information Highway" copyright © 1995 by Steve Katz.
Previously published in **The Corpse**, Number 53, 1995, and in **Quarter After Eight**, 1995. *Reprinted by permission of the author.*

"The Big Spin" copyright © 1996 by Teri Roney.
Used by permission of the author.

"The Last Secretary" copyright © 1996 by Karen Tei Yamashita.
Used by permission of the author.

"Big Turn Time" copyright © 1996 by Karl Roeseler.
Used by permission of the author.

"Wu World Woo" copyright © 1996 by Mac Wellman.
Used by permission of the author.

"Happy Endings" copyright © 1983 by Margaret Atwood.
Originally published in **Murder in the Dark**, 1983, Coach House Press (Toronto). *Reprinted by permission of the author.*

Trip Street Press is dedicated to the notion that a book publisher's identity only emerges through the juxtaposition of the books it publishes. **2000andWhat?** is our third book. Watch for further Trip Street Press books if you are curious about our press.